Remembering Louise

Remembering Louise

ANNA GILBERT

HODDER AND STOUGHTON
LONDON SYDNEY AUCKLAND TORONTO

267847

Trans. Norfolk
13.4.78 fen

(J.F.R)

1

I SAT, JUST as I am sitting now, at the parlour window of
the old house in Silvergate, one evening in early spring.
It was neither the time nor the place for ghosts. The fire
burned bright; the kettle sang; daylight had scarcely begun to fade. The shops, including our own, would not put
up their shutters for another three hours at least. My
mind, I believe, was on the muffin man. He should be
passing at any minute.

And yet, especially when there is a hint of rain in the
air, as there is now, I have only to push open the side
casement above the narrow street to remember, with a
thrill of something more than fear, the moment when the
haunting began.

Except for the firelight the room behind me was dark,
as it is now; as it always was. My occupation — I was
plaiting hair for a mourning bracelet — might have
seemed a melancholy one. It had no such effect on me.
Mourning jewellery was one of our specialities. I had
worked at the bracelet all afternoon, weaving and twisting
the hair in a double coil round fine gold wire. Only when
it was ready for Thomas, my father's apprentice, to fit
the gold clasps, only then did I sit upright, push open the
window and look down into the street.

The air was fresh with the promise of rain. The pave-
ments were empty: not a passer-by on either side. Half-
blinded by the close work, I saw the cobbles lift and sink
like bubbles. The black timbers of the gabled houses
wavered and grew rigid again. Then my vision cleared
and further up the street on the opposite side by the
print-seller's shop, I saw a figure: the tall, slender figure
of a man.

It was when he moved, perhaps that I noticed him.
Even then, for a second or two it seemed as if one of the
long oak timbers had moved because he was long too

5

and dressed in black and there was a wooden stiffness about him as if he had been there for a long time. It was difficult to account for the feeling that although this was the first time I had noticed him, it was not the first time I had seen him; that he had been part of the scene for some time, like the pillar-box down by the bridge or the statue of Sir Robert Peel in the market place.

With a little shock — yes, I remember my sudden intake of breath though there was nothing, just then, to fear — I realised that he was looking straight at our window, which overhung the pavement by several feet. He had not turned his head suddenly when I opened the casement. My impression was that his eyes had been fixed on the window already. If he had moved, it was to get a better view. He had been waiting then, and watching.

Nothing in the world could be less remarkable than his presence. Wickborough was full of soberly dressed gentlemen, most of them clergymen, who liked to loiter outside the book and print-shops in Silvergate on their way to and from the Abbey. The stranger was not a clergyman. As to whether or not he was a gentleman ... Oddly enough, for we were sensitive on such points in those days, the question did not arise. I gave no thought to it. I simply saw him at once as a human being, pale-faced, intent; — and — this was the remarkable thing that placed the experience in a category quite its own — a human being with something to *impart*.

I felt on my face the full impact of his gaze. Had we been nearer, we might have been looking into each other's eyes. But even across the forty yards or so that separated us, I was aware of the peculiar quality in him that has haunted me ever since. I felt it in the long droop of his unbelted ulster; in the wedge of pale face between dark side-whiskers under his narrow-brimmed hat; and in his black cotton gloves: an utter sadness.

I must be careful not to exaggerate or prolong an experience so fleeting nor to give it the colouring which, naturally enough in view of all that followed, it has for me now. But the sight of the man was unwelcome. It shook me out of my untroubled mood. I closed the window, shutting him out, and with quite an effort thought of other things.

It was reassuring to see in the chimney-glass that my eyes were neither red-rimmed nor bloodshot: I did so want to look my best the next day. Suppose it should rain! Praying for fine weather, I resigned myself to an umbrella. But the tall thin man must still have been in my mind when Thomas shouted urgently upstairs:

"He's coming, Miss Hester. He's coming."

I swung round to face the door, my heart thumping.

"Just coming out of the bakehouse now."

The usual scramble to find the right coins was tinged with relief. Muffins were fourpence a dozen in those days. I rushed to the blue teapot in the corner cupboard for the money and put it into Thomas's hand as he rose like a porpoise from the dark twist of the stairs. By the time I had set out the tea-things and unlocked the caddy, he was back.

"It's starting to rain."

In despair I counted out the spoonfuls: one each for Mrs Wragge, Thomas and me and one for the pot.

"Do you think it will be much?"

"There's no telling. It'll keep customers away." Thomas was genuinely sorry. "There's not a soul about."

We shared out the muffins: three for Mrs Wragge, three for me, the rest for Thomas. We each toasted our own and ate them in our own domain: I in the upstairs parlour, Thomas in the little room behind the shop, Mrs Wragge in the kitchen. One pot of tea served us all.

Thomas carried a cup of tea to the kitchen and retired to his own quarters, leaving me to enjoy my favourite hour of the day. I sat on the rug, toasted my muffins and ate them slowly, thinking as usual of Julian, until Thomas came back with his washed cup and plate.

I showed him the bracelet. He took the gauzy coils in his big, sensitive hands — perfect hands, my father said, for a craftsman — and examined my work carefully. His approving nod and smile were gratifying. He was not easily satisfied.

"You've got the right touch, I will say, Miss Hester.

I'll finish this right away. It was expressly ordered for tomorrow. Funny, isn't it, that people should need a thing like this to remind them?"

"Or to show that they remember," I suggested.

A souvenir of the dead, made with the hair of the departed! I had made dozens of them, as light-heartedly as if they were kettle-holders. But now, as if that part of me responsive to sadness had become more tender, the bracelet took on a new solemnity. It lingered while we discussed the final touches. The buckle was to be in the shape of a serpent's head with a small stone for the eye.

"Garnet or turquoise?" Thomas asked. "They didn't say."

"Turquoise," I said quickly. Red eyes were abhorrent to me.

Thomas waited, an ear cocked for the sound of the bell below. Father was out of town for three days, this being the time of the year when he cleaned and regulated all the church clocks in the diocese.

"I brought this up to show you, Miss Hester. What do you think of it? Master said I could have a try."

Thomas's work was his passion. Like my father he thought of little else.

"They're all the rage they say."

Insect brooches were indeed all the rage just then: caterpillars, bees, spiders, immobile-looking flies of gold and silver and set with semi-precious stones.

"It's a butterfly, supposed to be."

A butterfly it certainly was, with enamelled wings of saffron and azure and gold antennae of wire so fine that they quivered at a touch: a creature more than life-like: a butterfly intensified. Thomas laid it on the red plush arm of the chair by the fire, where the light coaxed it to the verge of movement. A stirring, a flutter of yellow and blue and it would dash itself headlong into the flames.

"It's pretty," I said, half disliking the thing. It was almost too alluring. "There's no doubt it will sell."

"Oh yes. It'll sell all right. Some women are silly enough for anything. Mice, bats — they'll sew any mortal thing on their hats and gowns these days. It should fetch fifteen shillings or a pound. Master'll give me a commission on anything I make in my own time. It's a frivolous sort of thing but cheerful." He picked it up affectionately. "It makes a change from the jet brooches."

At the door he paused and looked round. In its worn, informal way the room was comfortable, as it still is: crowded with the haphazard collection of objects that settle down together in a house of great age; and there were modern touches: a pianoforte with rose-coloured candle-shades: antimacassars on the balloon-backed chairs: a Derby china bell-pull.

"By the way, I've found out who those two are." Thomas was referring to the two figures in Parian ware on the mantel-shelf. "They're Roman goddesses. The one with the sheaf of corn is Ceres and the other one, in the helmet, is called Minerva."

I listened with respect. Father had always said that Thomas would go far.

"They add a stately touch," he said, "and yet it's homelike too up here. But you're quiet on your own, Miss Hester. What will you do? Read a book maybe.?"

"I have the new Young Ladies' Treasury."

My work was done. The evening was my own. When Thomas had gone, I got out my sewing basket and sewed fresh net frills into the wrists of my striped saxony dress ready for the next day; then, feeling disinclined to strain my eyes over close print, went again to the window and peeped out.

Fergus the lamplighter was going up the street. At his magic touch the jets grew, one by one, into yellow lanterns. Over the shining cobbles moved an occasional umbrella, propelled by an invisible owner. I watched Fergus until he came to the lamp outside the print-seller's. Did he glance curiously into the shade under the projecting upper storey? The lamp flickered and settled to a steady glow. There was no one there.

With a sudden joyful sense of freedom I leaned out. Into the wet evening air came the crash of the Abbey bells as the ringers practised a change. In the narrow strip of sky between the roofs I caught a glimpse of stars, the dazzle and sparkle of life beyond Silvergate. There was no one to talk to, so much to tell. I must write to Louise, my almost forgotten sister.

With my writing desk on the table by the fire I sharpened my pen, began "My dear Louise" and at once, as usual came to a halt. Presently it would be easier but always, at first, the name posed a problem. A name should summon up the identity of its owner. For me Louise had none. In a moment the trifling difficulty would be overcome. This letter like all the others would be written to myself and merely directed and posted to Louise.

Still, I felt obliged to think of her. Stretching memory, I could just take her in. I had been eleven and she sixteen when after our mother's death she had gone to Blair-gouroch Castle on the west coast of Scotland to be placed in the care of the housekeeper, Mrs Maple, a distant connection on mother's side of the family. There she would learn the higher skills of service and house-keeping from the lady's maid, the stillroom maid and from Mrs Maple herself. There presumably she would remain. I remembered my mother's death but not Louise's departure. The greater loss had overshadowed the lesser. Besides, having Julian, I had not missed Louise.

For me she was no more than an excuse to put pen to paper. Since there was no one else to write to, I wrote to her, quite often and at length: effusions to which her own letters could scarcely be called answers. Dutifully trying to establish some sort of contact with Louise, I skimmed the half dozen letters it had taken her seven years to write.

"In summer there are a great many flies ... Mrs Maple is well pleased with the currant jelly this year, especially the red. I have made labels for thirty-two jars, fifteen black and seventeen red ... Mrs Maple has suffered from rheumatism these two months past."

A handful of facts recorded with exquisite neatness of penmanship, about jam, the laundering of lace and Mrs Maple's health. The absence of any reference to any living person other than Mrs Maple gave to the letters a kind of exclusive refinement: a slender point on which I could establish a relationship as ethereal as a will-o'-the-wisp.

It served. All that was needed was the shadowy notion of an ear into which the tumultuous current of my own inner life could be pitilessly directed. What did I write? Goodness knows. Whether the stars, the bells and the fire-lit room were lavishly described, I have mercifully forgotten. I fear they were. But they were not uppermost in my mind.

"Julian has been highly complimented on his dissertation. It is entitled" — I paused to prepare myself for the impressive syllables — " 'Dissertation wherein a challenge to the doctrine of Everlasting Punishment contained in 'Essays and Reviews' is examined and refuted'." There could be no mistake. I had given my whole mind to learning it. But having written it, I read the title again several times, feeling almost numb with pride. "Dr Thorkeld, the Principal of St Aidan's, has brought it to the attention of the Bishop. This is an important event in our" — the last word was blushingly and heavily crossed out — "in Julian's life. As you know, he has always hoped some day to be in orders. I find the study of theology most interesting, especially when Julian explains it to me. He has read most of Law's "Serious Call" aloud to Mrs Windross and me. Next Wednesday we are to begin on Butler's "Analogy of Religion" but tomorrow is Mrs Windross's day for collecting her rents at St Mary-on-Audley. Julian and I will go with her as usual. The weather is uncertain. I intend to wear my striped saxony with my ivory medallion on a black ribbon but it will be necessary to wear a mantle at this time of the year.

"Thomas Griff has taken to making insect jewellery. I shall not wear any. I am sure Julian would dislike it."

Stopping at the end of half an hour to ease my fingers, though not for inspiration, I glanced again at Louise's letters, re-read a paragraph and caught in it the first faint throb of a living pulse; nothing directly stated but a hint, a clue, emerging from the list of trivial facts as the essen-

11

tial fruit might be said to glow from behind the labels on the pots of currant jelly.

"There has been a great storm. The sea was more frightening than ever. It was dark all day. All the candles were lit at luncheon." Louise yielded once more to her preoccupation with numbers. "There are eighteen candles in each of the candelabra. Without Mrs Maple, I would have been afraid."

My own impetuous flow of ideas was arrested. Blairgouroch rose stormbound upon a cliff above a tumult of waters, braving the darkness with its frail host of candles. (How many candelabra, Louise had, surprisingly, not said.) The picture faded. I was left with a brief but disturbing curiosity as to Louise's place in it: an impression of Louise as distinct from her surroundings. It was gone. All that remained was a suspicion that the world might be dangerous: a delicious, thrilling conviction that with Julian one was safe.

My eyes itched. The dread of red lids sent me anxiously to the glass again before finishing the letter with a scrawl, "Your affectionate sister, Hester," and rummaging for wax and taper to seal it. I don't think it occurred to me as I wrote the direction that there must be other people at Blairgouroch Castle besides Mrs Maple and Louise; nor did I spare a thought for what Louise might have found there when at the age of sixteen she had gone — or been sent — away.

2

FATHER CAME HOME at noon the next day. I was just setting off on my visit to Mrs Windross when he got down from the cab. He looked tired. The care of the church clocks was becoming a trial to him. It involved tedious waits in country stations and long walks from one village to another. He never slept well away from home. But in another year Thomas would take his share of the work, which was well paid at a guinea for each clock.

"You'll give my compliments to Mrs Windross," father said when he had paid off the cabman.

"Yes, father."

We stood for a minute on the sunny pavement under the wrought-iron bracket with the sign: "Oscar Mallow: Clock and Watchmaker: Silversmith: Jeweller." The smell of bread rose from the bakehouse on the bridge. Outside his shop Mr Jacobson, the print-seller, was taking the air.

"You've been writing a letter."

"Yes, father." I held it ready to post. "To Louise."

He said nothing. It occurred to me — the idea was quite new — that he ought to have said something.

"You'll be off to St Mary-on-Audley this afternoon?"

"Yes, father."

In so far as his expression changed, it expressed approval.

"Julian will bring you home? No later than nine."

"Yes, father."

In the shop a medley of clocks struck twelve. From the pavement it seemed a living chorus; a score of voices brought into harmony by a common need. To father they were indeed living things, more demanding and certainly more interesting than the members of his household. Involuntarily he took out his gold repeater to check the time.

"Very well then. You'd best be off."

Leaving him, I was myself again. The first step away from the door was a step into freedom.

"Hester!" I turned. He was frowning. "You're not going by way of the Chare?"

"Oh, no, father."

I hesitated, waiting for him to go indoors. The pillar-box was at the bottom of the street, just short of South-well Bridge. Behind it a flight of steps dropped steeply to the disused wharves, where in the old days before the railway came to Wickborough, barges had put in to unload coal and timber. Beyond, a labyrinth of dark and filthy alleys led to the forbidden area of Sparrow Chare;

13

and as I looked down, across the bright triangle of pavement at the top of the steps, it seemed as if a tall, thin shadow moved. But the mid-day shadows were short. There was no wind to stir them. Whatever it was, if it had substance, I just missed seeing it or noticing it, perhaps, until it was nearly gone. A sudden urge to confide in father made me almost blurt out:

"I've seen a man, watching our house."

The impulse was momentary. I never confided in father. The fear of seeing his eyebrows rise impatiently and the devastating sense of distance between us, kept me as usual silent. Besides what was there to tell?

He nodded, dismissing me.

Having posted my letter, I glanced down the steps, greasy still from yesterday's rain, and heard the slow footsteps of someone walking along the wharf towards Sparrow Chare, some one bolder than I, or more indifferent. Even without father's warning I would not have dared to go alone through the warren of run-down dwellings and ill-famed pot-houses in the oldest part of the town. The Chare was not absolutely unknown territory. As children Julian and I had raced through it once or twice, heads down, hand in hand, dodging piles of rotting refuse and emerging at the bridge, unharmed, with a delicious sense of sin. Occasionally in daylight I had used Nidgate, a street roughly parallel with Silvergate, as a shortcut to the west end of the town; but even Nidgate was too near to the Chare to be considered respectable.

I went up Silvergate again at a good pace and through our own shop window saw father already seated in the little wooden compartment where he spent most of his working hours. He had not even taken off his great-coat; but he had put on the green-tinted spectacles with side-pieces like blinkers that cut him off from the world.

"You're having a day out?"

Our neighbour over the way had pushed open her window.

"Yes, Mrs Setterwort. With Mrs Windross."

"She'll be collecting her rents. You'll have a pleasant walk by the river."

14

Mrs Setterwort's upstairs parlour window was no more than twelve feet from our own. Had the panes been less thick and clouded, we could have kept each other under close scrutiny. We usually tended our window-boxes at the same time and could almost have watered each other's geraniums. Though we never met, so far as I can recall, under any other circumstances, the similarity of occupation had brought us to quite an intimate friendship. I endured her advice as I endured her chimney smoke when the wind was from the west.

"You're looking very nice, dear." She leaned forward like the figure-head of a ship. "Saxony, isn't it? It should wear well. Yes, it's a wonderful thing to be young."

I smiled suitably, anxious to go.

"But take my advice, dear. Don't be in too much of a hurry. It's as well to look about you when it's a question of your whole life."

As if in contradiction, Mr Setterwort dropped the blind of his shop door. It was dinner time. Had Mrs Setterwort looked about her with sufficient care before committing her future into the hands of Mr Setterwort — thick-necked, silent, ruddy as one of his own copper-kettles? He shot home the bolt with the effect of a snarl.

"Other things need to wear well besides your gowns." The role of soothsayer came easily to Mrs Setterwort. "There's good lasting material in people as well as cloth. I always say," she finished cryptically, "it's better to be looked up to than down on."

I left her to the tedium of her homespun husband. How could she bear it? And to be still wearing a cap with floating ribbons in the year 1876! Of course the poor woman must be forty at least. Coming out into the market place, I forgot her.

Sparrow Chare was less easily forgotten. By a rare turn of events, it was to put out one of its tentacles that very afternoon and draw me into its unwholesome atmosphere. Physically it was never far away even from the leafy eighteenth century streets whose gardens stretched down to the Audley on the outskirts of the town. It was in the last of these, Buckingham Street, that Mrs Windross lived and Julian when he was not in residence at St Aidan's College.

Every Thursday I could begin to dream of Sunday, when I walked home from church with them and ate my dinner at their house. On Sunday night the week already began to shape itself towards Wednesday, when we spent the afternoon and evening together, as close-knit a trio as if we were already related. Julian's father and mine had been partners, our mothers closely attached. Julian could have succeeded to his father's partnership in Mallow and Windross, the principal clock and watch-makers in Wickborough. But he had chosen a different career with the support and, I now see, persuasion of his mother. Since her husband's death Mrs Windross had exerted on Julian a loving but relentless pressure to enter the Church. It was the only way in which he could raise himself into the sphere of gentlefolk where, she was convinced and so was I, he rightly belonged. My father had bought them out of the business and a considerable part of the generous sum had been spent on Julian's education.

It was of his studies that we were talking as we came down the front steps that afternoon. Mrs Windross was already waiting in the street, still debating, as she had been for the last hour, on whether to take a sunshade or an umbrella. A passing cloud clinched the matter. On reflection, it did much more. It gently set in motion a sequence of events less gentle.

"Here, Julian." She handed him the sunshade. "Take this back and bring me the green umbrella. It isn't summer yet. And tell Janet to keep an eye on those towels and fetch them in if it rains."

I walked with her to the end of the street where a narrow alley led to the field path. A tall garden hedge cut off our view to the right. On our left rose the ramshackle back-yard walls of the seedy dwellings on the outskirts of Sparrow Chare. It was a place to avoid after dark. In daylight with Julian in the offing it seemed safe enough. I had relieved him of the picnic basket when he went in-doors and Mrs Windross was carrying the leather bag

16

with a brass ring that she always took for her rents. It was empty as yet, but as we sauntered down the path and waited there, deep in town gossip, a passer-by would not have known whether we were setting out or returning.

We were both startled when a man stepped over one of the tumbledown walls: a tattered ruffian like a hundred others in the Chare. In his corduroys with a muffler round his chin and a moleskin cap pulled down to his ears, he could have been a waterman to a horsekeeper, but he had the desperate look of a man living on the edge of starvation; and we were more than startled when he came close enough for us to smell his foul breath and unwashed clothing.

"Come on, missus." He thrust himself between us. "Hand over your money."

He had grabbed the leather bag and given Mrs Windross a push that sent her reeling against the garden hedge when — oh, the relief of it! — Julian appeared. He positively leapt along the alley, seized the man by the scruff of the neck, held him for an instant like a frightened scarecrow and then with a powerful jab of his left fist, knocked him down. It was splendid; or so it seemed at first. What's more, as the man lay struggling to get up, Julian still white with fury, hauled him up again by his ragged shirt front, shook him violently and knocked him down again.

This time the man did not move. Would he ever move again? Mrs Windross and I clung to each other, sharing, I have no doubt, a vision of magistrates, Assize Courts, condemned cell, the final, fatal dawn.

"Oh Julian! You may have killed him."

"Yes." He looked at me in alarm. "You don't think . . .? He was whiter than ever. "But what else could I have done? What about mother? One can't allow that sort of thing."

I stole a sickening look at the inert body. His moleskin cap had fallen off, uncovering the thatch of red hair he had probably hoped to hide.

"He's a skimpy-looking sort of fellow." Julian sounded miserable. "There's not much credit in knocking out a

17

specimen like that. The worst of it is —" at any other time his consternation would have amused me — "I enjoyed it."

"Don't stand there talking." Mrs Windross's voice quavered hysterically. "Do something. Someone may come — and see."

"Look! He's breathing."

I knelt down, laid my hand on the man's forehead and spoke to him while Julian rushed off with the same impetuous haste he had shown in knocking him down. He was soon back with cordial, a basin of water and a wet towel, snatched no doubt from the clothes-line. We bathed the fellow's face, and when his grey skin had taken on a healthier tinge, propped him against the wall. He began to recover his wits.

"I wasn't going to . . ."

It was not in any sense an apology. He glowered at us and particularly at Julian with such a black spirit of ill-will that I longed to be rid of him.

"That's all very well." Julian clapped a wet cloth on his victim's forehead. "But you thought you could set on two unprotected women, didn't you?" There was no anger in his tone. There could be no triumph either, in so unequal a victory.

"Drink this. Look here, I know you. You're Josh Blakey. I should have recognised that red mop."

By this time Janet had joined us.

"Shall I run for the policeman, sir?" she whispered.

"No. That won't be necessary. Besides, he has a wife and children. It wouldn't do them any good to put him in prison."

I would never have dreamed of questioning Julian's decision. He must know what was best. The students of St Aidan's were well known for their rescue work in the poorer districts of the town. All the same I felt privately that Mrs Blakey and the children would be very much better off on their own.

"You'd best come home, ma'am," Janet said, "and sit down for a while."

"No, no. We're late as it is. Give me your arm, Julian,

18

until we get to the seat by the mill."

As Julian lingered, I offered mine. We went on slowly. Looking back a minute later, I saw Julian take a coin from his pocket and give it to Blakey.

"Let that be a lesson to you," he said firmly.

There seemed to me to be some doubt as to what the lesson was; nor did Blakey show any sign of having learned it. If anything about him had changed, it was the degree of his resentment. He showed his black and broken teeth in a grimace of furious contempt as he took the money, got unsteadily to his feet and tried to put his battered cap over the vinegar plaister we had bound to his forehead.

When we turned into the field path, he was leaning against the wall, watching us out of sight.

"He looked half-starved," Julian said apologetically.

"Let us hope," I said piously, "that the Bishop never hears of *this*."

"Which bit of it do you mean?" Julian laughed. "My physical violence or the financial reward of his?"

We discussed the moral aspects of the affair as we followed the path upstream, through the woods.

"What ought I to have done, Hester, instead of knocking him down? Appealed to his better nature, I suppose, if he has one. Then he'd have gone off and robbed somebody else, committed murder even. Blakey's the sort of bully to take advantage of the weak and helpless and respect a show of strength. He won't attempt anything of that sort again in a hurry. I've saved him, quite likely, from hanging. Nothing happens by accident. All things work together for good."

I felt that his judgment was somehow at fault; that in some inexplicable way the incident had placed him at risk. The danger was surely past but its shadow remained. It was my first experience of violence. If Julian had killed Josh Blakey! How that would have darkened the world! Until then I had never thought of him as needing to be protected; and even then my uneasiness was as undefined as a foreboding. All that I was sure of was that he was dearer to me than ever.

As for Mrs Windross, she seemed none the worse and soon walked ahead as usual, her grey skirt swaying placidly between her sensible boots and serviceable bonnet. It was a day of singing birds and dangling hazel catkins, of pink and white wood anemones in the shade and new lambs in the open pastures. But the sun had gone when we came to St Mary-on-Audley and we were glad to take our refreshment in one of the cottages instead of out of doors.

One of Mrs Windross's elderly tenants had taken to her bed in an illness that might well be her last. Our visit coincided with that of the doctor. By the time we were ready to leave for home the rain had come on in earnest. Julian and I persuaded his mother to accept Dr Sidlow's offer of a ride home and she went off under his gig umbrella, leaving the green one to us.

"You must hurry home, Hester," she said as they drove away. "I shall never face your father if you go down with congestion again. But if you walk quickly you'll take no harm."

To walk quickly was out of the question. In ten minutes my fringed mantle was sodden wet and weighed so heavily on my shoulders that to walk at all was a triumph. Yet I had the sensation of floating between the muddy road and the dripping branches. We kept close together, arm-in-arm of necessity so as to make the most of the umbrella. Beyond its intimate circle the rain bounced from radiant puddles and slid down shining tree-trunks and the sunless day seemed full of light.

At the bridge where we had once seen a kingfisher, we stopped, squeezed into one of the embrasures, to look down at the little parsonage of St Mary on the right bank : a seventeenth-century house of stone with a green garden descending by wide steps to the river's edge. Some happy combination of details — a window half open : a stone nymph gracefully drowning in the rain : daffodils bending round the bole of a birch tree : a glimpse of the tree-girt church beyond — suggested a way of life so permanent, so firmly rooted in time, that it was hard to pass it by.

"A country parsonage."

Julian spoke with the subdued exuberance I had learned to recognise as a sign of deep earnestness.

"There you have it, Hester, to perfection. No other life has so much to offer. Where else would you find such simplicity and natural charm? Look at that little side window opening on to the path. Imagine, day after day, week after week, opening that gate and taking that path to church . . ."

Like many of our generation in those days, we felt a romantic enthusiasm for the Church, finding in the ritual of its festivals and the beauty of its language a drama that others find in the theatre.

"To add one's daily mite," Julian swept on, "to the centuries of worship that have hallowed this place . . . and then, to come home to such a house . . . the tranquillity of hearth and home . . . the blessing of domestic affection . . . the sanctity of its underlying godly purpose . . ."

Julian's lips trembled with the fervour of his own oratory. They were rather full lips, not those of an ascetic. But what magnificent sermons they would preach! He might be planning one of them now, I thought, listening to the rapid flow of abstractions. For years he had practised them on me and never failed to fire an enthusiastic response, so that now, shivering in my wet clothes, I had no difficulty in re-furnishing the parsonage from attic to cellar; with piles of fragrant linen in mahogany chests; my work table in the lamp-lit window; docile maids in the well-scrubbed kitchen: and Julian — I saw him resplendent in vestments, inspired, eloquent, and behind him the full glory of the east window in the Abbey.

Some little adjustment of the imagination was needed to reduce him to the status of a country parson picking his way between the wet nettles of St Mary's churchyard but the effort was not beyond me. I had been well drilled. In childhood our games had been of the adventurous, free ranging kind. They had made me adaptable. As a dragon I had died a dozen deaths at the hands of St George, springing to life in time to fall prisoner, a subdued Cromwell, to King Charles himself, personified by Julian, characteristically, as both martyred and victorious. And always there had been the sermons, packed with large, vague prophecies, every sentence beginning: "It shall be ... It shall come to pass that ..."

"Julian," I said suddenly, having earned the right to interrupt him occasionally, "when we were little, playing churches and battles and so on, what was Louise doing?"

"Louise?" With an effort he re-directed his thoughts towards a subject he clearly found less interesting. "Louise! What did she do? She must have been there, I suppose, but honestly, I don't remember. How is she?" he asked politely and did not wait for an answer. "This place seems empty. Isn't the incumbent an old man in his eighties? Suppose he should die — after all at his age what could be more natural? — in about," he calculated, "five years' time, just when we" — I was sure he said 'we' — "are wanting to settle down. As it happens, this living is in the gift of St Aidan's. The college is the only patron I'm ever likely to find ..."

We had been over it all before, the difficulty of advancing in the Church without influence. Mrs Windross's answer to the problem took the shape of pounds, shillings and pence in the leather bag. The family property would be just enough to secure Julian from the grinding poverty that beset so many curates, and would even enable him to marry while still a young man.

Julian's solution was to work hard and attract notice by the sheer brilliance of his qualifications. In another two months he would take the second part of his examination for Bachelor of Divinity and in the following year seek ordination.

We stood dripping on the bridge in a rare moment of silence. From his expression I guessed that Julian was scaling the steep ecclesiastical ladder step by step, by way of a rural deanery and a canonry to very reverend heights indeed. My own vision of the future took the more definite form of a small stone house, a garden with birchtrees and the occasional glimpse of a kingfisher.

We tore ourselves away at last with a sigh, on my part at least, for the drowning nymph and the rain-bent daffodils.

"You're dreadfully wet, Hester."

He dragged me off at a fine pace and left me glowing at our own door.

"I won't come in. Until Sunday then — goodbye.' '

He bent his head, smiling. I looked up. Our clasped hands parted. Thinking only of our next meeting, I spared no backward glance over the long untroubled years we had shared, growing so close together that nothing surely could come between us, ever.

3

FATHER HAD TAKEN off his great-coat but he was still in his wooden cell, intent on his work under the green-shaded lamp. As I went slowly upstairs, the motley ticking of lantern clocks, of mantel, carriage, turret and bracket clocks, yielded to the slow tick-tock of our own long-case clock on the landing. When I had changed into a house dress and dry stockings, I took my bundle of wet clothes into the parlour. The fire was out. My things would have to be dried in the kitchen.

On an impulse I went to the window. It was at about this time that I had looked out the day before, or a little later. The muffin man was coming down the street with his empty tray on his head but Fergus had not yet lit the lamps. The rain, having cut short my outing, had stopped. A yellow sky over Sparrow Chare made our own shadowed street seem dark. Mrs Setterwort moved obscurely behind her window-panes like a vertical fish in a sea of cloudy green.

Cautiously, I looked up towards the print-seller's. Two or three grammar-school boys were chatting at the door, one of them leaning against the oak post supporting the gable. Down by the bridge a nursemaid was dropping a letter into the pillar-box. She stood for a moment, smiling, with the sun turning her cap and streamers to gold, then waved and blew a kiss to someone down on the wharf, someone I could not see. It was a free, happy gesture that impressed me. I have often wondered if she appeared to her unseen friend as she did to me: a sunlit figure, spontaneously loving; and I have hoped with all my heart, as I hope still, that she did.

Our house is situated almost exactly halfway down the steep incline from the market place to the river: a tall narrow house with five storeys and several mezzanine rooms. It has been altered in recent years and I have actually forgotten how many rooms there were when I was a girl, before walls were removed and doors sealed up. One of the peculiarities of a house with five floors at the front and two at the back is that the shop at street level has only a basement below, whereas the kitchen has only attics above. It opens on to a courtyard with a door to the back lane and another to the apprentices' room, designed for four apprentices and occupied at that time by Thomas, in solitary comfort.

It must have been an impossible house to clean in those days. Unlit staircases dropped abruptly into unexpected rooms with windows in unlikely places and cupboards leading to other rooms. Dusty it must have been. Dark it certainly was, with ancient smells of stone and damp and newer ones of beeswax, turpentine and roasting meat: a house to remember with exasperation — and love.

Mrs Wragge had been making pastry. The kitchen was hot enough to dry a laundryful of clothes; but she had started on the evening meal and was already cramped for space.

"I'll hang them outside for a while," I said and went down one half-flight of stairs and up another, the quickest way to the yard being by way of Louise's old room.

No sooner had I set foot inside than I remembered Louise and this time not just the name. A little whiff of memory brought back an idea of her. It may have been because this room was brighter than the others. Light from the muslin-curtained windows gave a moment of

24

illumination. The sound of Mrs Wragge slamming down heavy saucepans came clearly through whatever partitions the mysterious architecture of the house provided. I remembered that Louise had liked having a room near the kitchen. But why?

The window overlooked the courtyard with its small rockery and herb-garden. In a few weeks pink daisies, thrift and saxifrage would be in bloom. Parsley grew in a drainpipe standing on end. Squinting to the left, one saw the twin towers of the Abbey. From the right came the smell of the river.

Nothing belonging to Louise remained. A spare chair needing to be re-caned had been dumped on its side by the bed. The drawers were full of old clothing and unused linen. I had rushed in here once long ago to hide and finding nowhere, had rushed out again. In those tremendous games there had been three of us: Julian and I and Louise. We must have played together. But not here in this pale, inviolate place.

Had she been here, my sister, when Julian and I stormed impregnable fortresses at the top of any one of half a dozen unlit staircases? Gazing down on the leafless lilac bush, I thought of Louise, who must have looked down on it too. No picture of her came, nor the memory of anything she had ever said. Instead I remembered Julian and myself, breathless and hot, absorbed, impassioned. It was I who had been burned at the stake as St Joan, not Louise. When Julian went up into the pulpit with dignified, measured tread and thumped the banisters as he made his large, magnificent prophecies, "It shall come about that . . . I say unto you . . . " I had been the choir on the stairs below and the organist too. It was I who had made, in every sense, the responses. What part had fallen to Louise?

For no good reason except that a vacuum must be filled, the tantalising notion came to me that there had been in Louise some quality especially her own: some aura quite lost to me. It was certainly not there in her letters. Purged of every vulgar human aspiration, purged of almost everything except Mrs Maple, the letters had the

25

bloodless purity of the cloister. Now that Mrs Wragge had stopped clattering saucepans, no sound came from the kitchen. Louise's room enclosed a white, unworldly silence.

I left it by a slatted door on the far side; crossed a green wainscoted landing; went down a few stairs and came out in the yard. It lay in deep shadow. The door in the outer wall stood open. With a pang of fear I saw that he was there: the man: a tall, slender man in black: on our own steps; coming in. He was stooping in the doorway with his hand on the latch and yet his head almost touched the lintel.

At the sight of me his expression changed but he made no move, spoke no word. This time I saw him at close quarters, a man of seedy gentility. He was very pale, at least his dark side-whiskers made him seem so. Otherwise he was clean-shaven. His eyes were dark with that depth of darkness that gives a melancholy hue to the whole face.

Again it was the mournful cast of his face and figure that overshadowed the details of his appearance, except — my eyes came to rest upon his hands, one on the latch, the other by his side — except for the black cotton gloves. In fact although I have described him as dressed in black, it was only the gloves I was sure of. They gave him the look of an undertaker's mute.

Mute he was. For a long minute we faced each other, speechless. The bag of clothes-pegs had fallen from my hand. He moistened his lips as if trying to speak but at the same time he drew himself upright and thinking he was coming nearer, I burst out:

"What do you want? What are you doing here?"

I spoke low as if we were alone in a secret world; but fear made me brusque. There was hostility in my voice — I knew it — as if I were shooing away a stray dog. Having seen Josh Blakey, I should have recognised this man as different: indeed I did; but the violent incident of the afternoon had un-nerved me. The shock of it made me unreasonable. Yet I never for a moment thought of him as dangerous. His manner was gentle. Afterwards it

26

was the gentleness I remembered and had all the more reason to be ashamed of the way I behaved.

Why didn't he speak?

"You have no right to come here. This is a private place."

Once again I had spoken just as he seemed about to do so, and whatever the words were to have been they faded away, discouraged. Then he murmured something so tentative that it must have been my excited imagination that made me think I heard "Miss Hester". He couldn't have known my name. He had given a humble sort of smile. At least afterwards I thought of it as humble. Oh, afterwards I thought of him until my head ached and always with the conviction that the incident had actually been quite different from what it had seemed at the time. But face to face with him, I couldn't think at all, only feel. He had, whoever he was, the most extraordinary power of making me feel.

"Do you want to speak to my father? The shop door is in Silvergate."

He shook his head with a faint look of agitation. At some point he had taken off his hat. He was not young — or old. I felt in him the strange isolation of a homeless creature and he frightened me, not only by being there unexpectedly in our own yard but by the intensity of feeling he carried about with him like a stigma setting him apart.

"Miss Hester! Are you there?"

It was Thomas. I heard his feet on one of the lower staircases like earthly feet climbing into a place of phantoms.

"Thomas, come here," I called; and all at once felt nothing but pity for the man. But it was too late. He had lifted his gloved hand in a gesture of defeat and stepped back on to the top step. I saw behind him, above the wall, the pale golden towers of the Abbey, august and steadfast. With his head bent and slightly askew so that he could still look at me, he might have been a gargoyle; and like a gargoyle he served a purpose. That was it. That was the thing that gave him his disturbing power: the

27

suggestion of meaning in his appearance, as if he didn't exist in his own right but for some other reason. Why then had he not told me what he wanted?

With a despairing shrug he went away up the lane. He had closed the door behind him, I believe, just as Thomas stepped out into the yard.

"Whatever ails you, Miss Hester?"

I had sunk down helplessly on the rockery wall, still clutching my bundle of wet clothes.

"There was a man. He did so frighten me. Here in the yard. He actually came in. I've seen him before, in the street, watching." It seemed now that I had seen him in a dozen places. "Do you remember that time when the shop-bell rang and no one came in?"

"That's happened many a time." Thomas was looking at me with a puzzled frown. "What did he do to frighten you?"

"Nothing. Oh, nothing wrong. It was only by being there."

"What did he say?"

"Nothing. He didn't say anything. That was what made it so strange."

Some of the strangeness, Thomas clearly felt, was in me.

"I wish I'd got here sooner," he said thoughtfully. "You look really upset. At any rate" — I fancied he was humouring me — "let me know if you see him again."

"Yes, but you must promise not to do anything — violent. You're so strong and much younger than he is. I couldn't bear it if you knocked him down — or any such thing."

"What need would there be for that?" Thomas spoke so calmly that I felt ashamed. "A man can be sent about his business without being set upon, I should hope."

He went to the door and looked up the lane.

"There's no one there."

"I've been silly, to be frightened, I mean."

"Ten to one he's wanting to sell some jewellery. Down on his luck. Was he a respectable-looking sort of chap?"

"Yes, of course, you must be right. That just describes him. Down on his luck."

It was as inadequate a description of him as it would have been of a stricken tree or the sinister croak of a raven. Not that the man had been sinister; but he had conveyed an idea of catastrophe, either past or to come.

"Some of them can't bring themselves to go to a pawnshop when they want to raise money on an article although there are three of them in Nidgate . . ."

Down on his luck, if ever a man was; so far down that no hand reaching out to help him could save him from the abyss. With a remorse quite painful I wished, not that he would come back so that I could behave differently: I never wanted to see him again; but I wished with a strength of feeling beyond anything I had known before, that I had treated him more kindly.

I went indoors and a minute later from Louise's window saw Thomas carefully and deftly pinning my dress and mantle on the line.

4

"YOU DIDN'T SEE the bracelet," Thomas said when I was dusting and arranging the shop-window next morning. "I was bringing it up to show you but . . ." He was too tactful to refer to the incident which had distracted his attention from the bracelet. "At any rate, I parcelled it up and took it round last night."

He spoke quietly for fear of disturbing father, who had already been at work for an hour in his cubicle. However noisy the street, the shop was always quiet, not only from the influence of father's personality but because the goods we sold were not to be bought without reverent attention. It was quiet, that is, except for the clocks forever ticking, striking and wagging their pendulums as if acting out a drama of their own.

The centre of the window was kept exclusively for

watches and small clocks and behind them, the most expensive ornaments. To the right the more frivolous items of jewellery were displayed.

"You've put out the butterfly," I whispered. "It does look nice."

When I had taken out the other pieces, leaving the shimmering thing alone on the green velvet, it looked better still: at least, more attractive: almost fatefully so. Once again I felt that Thomas had been too successful. In his zeal he had somehow gone beyond the limits of good craftsmanship and produced an exotic creature with an unpredictable life of its own.

"I believe we shall have a customer, Thomas."

A young couple had stopped to look. I drew back discreetly and watched them from behind the glass partition. They were surreptitiously holding hands. I wondered how they came to be free so early on a Thursday morning and guessed that the meeting had been contrived. The young man's face was familiar. He was a messenger at one of the counting houses in the market place. I had never seen the girl before. She was plainly dressed and might have been in good service, but her face was not quite in harmony with her clothes. She had bright, roving eyes and a bold, free manner and would have seemed in her element in a gipsy shawl at a fairground. Anxious as I was to sell Thomas's brooch, I felt a slight misgiving, fearing the young man had got into dangerous company. They went on up the street but almost at once he came back and into the shop, alone.

"The brooch in the window . . ."

I never served behind the counter of course. It was Thomas who made the sale. The young man took the fifteen shillings from a leather purse with trembling hands, as well he might. It was a sum he could probably ill afford. Thomas put the brooch in a box and enclosed one of the quaint, old-fashioned watch papers father still liked to use as the firm had done for several generations: a violet paper with a border of leaves and flowers framing a Father Time with scythe and hourglass and the legend: "Oscar Mallow, Watchmaker, Silversmith and Jeweller,

respectfully solicits your patronage and recommendation."
We were proud of our watch papers.

"It's a stroke of luck for me," Thomas said, "but I'm not sure about him. He's a bit too ready to throw his money away on a bauble."

He retreated to his bench at the other end of the shop. It took me a few minutes to finish the window. In the left corner, artistically arranged on white velvet, were the pieces of hair jewellery: slides, buckles, miniatures under crystal, tiny pictures of weeping women and harps with broken strings; and above them on a series of little platforms, the rings, chains, crosses and brooches of jet. I dusted them absently, still not quite free of a troublesome depression. It occurred to me that the stranger might have wanted to buy a piece of mourning jewellery as a memento. There had been an air of bereavement about him. No one would wear black cotton gloves except in mourning. But why should he hesitate to make such a simple purchase?

A small side window was set aside for the display of second-hand jewellery: rings, tie-pins, watch-chains and châtelaines: items ranging in quality from gold to pinchbeck. It was not a branch of the trade that father liked. The pathetic transactions made him uncomfortable. One knew the type of customer at once: apologetic people, explaining that they had come to sell, not buy.

"I'm told it's valuable," they always said, reluctantly bringing out some treasure. Thomas must be right. The stranger had all the recognisable signs: poverty, respectability, shyness. He had been nerving himself, afraid of a hard bargain or worse still a rebuff. He had certainly suffered that. In these normal circumstances, I could hardly believe that it was I who had discouraged him with such brutal directness.

He had gone. At least he was not out there in the street. I felt sure that he had gone for good, in the sense that he would not bother me again. But in what sense had he bothered me? The answer was difficult to find. Absent from view he might be, but he occupied my mind as pervasively as if he had been there at the counter.

For several days I thought of him as I peeped from the parlour window; and I avoided the courtyard altogether.

Thomas never mentioned him; nor did I. By Sunday, which I spent as usual at Buckingham Street, I had contrived almost to forget him. When by the following Wednesday there was no sign of him, it was reasonable to suppose that he had left Wickborough.

Wednesday proved disappointing. The thrill of beginning on Butler's *Analogy of Religion* was denied me. From that disappointment it was possible to recover quickly. But I didn't see Julian at all. He was kept all day at St Aidan's to help to entertain an important party of visiting clergy. There was just a chance that he might call at his mother's between eight and nine in the evening to tell us about it.

The day passed pleasantly enough. We took our work into the conservatory at the back of the house and watched the rowing boats on the river below; then drank tea by the long window overlooking the garden. But I felt dissatisfied and restless and fell to watching the clock as the evening passed and Julian did not come.

I stayed as long as I dared. It was after half past eight when at last, unwillingly, I put on my hat, bravely facing the desert of time to be crossed before Sunday. A ring at the door-bell revived my hopes. Perhaps Julian had forgotten his key again. We heard Janet's voice in the hall. Presently she came to tell her mistress that Mr Julian had sent one of the maids from St Aidan's to say that he would not be coming. Mrs Windross went out to speak to her.

"I should have been here before, mum." Through the half open door I heard a rambling account of accidental delays, spoken in an accent that was not of our locality. "And not knowing the town yet, I couldn't find the street." The voice was wheedling, the story too determinedly plausible. By moving slightly I could see into the hall and was not surprised to recognise the gipsy-looking girl for whom the butterfly brooch had been bought; nor was it difficult to imagine how she had been spending her time instead of delivering Julian's message.

"I wonder at them taking on such a girl at St Aidan's," Mrs Windross said. "It was six o'clock when Julian asked her to call. He'd give her a shilling too, I dare say."

Janet let me out and gave me a lantern for company. No sooner had she shut the door than agitation seized me. I had stayed far too long. Even by running all the way, I couldn't hope to be home by nine. Absurd as it was — I kept on telling myself how absurd it was as I flew along Buckingham Street and out into Market Way — I was afraid of father. The prospect of facing his anger appalled me. Yet what could he say, what could he do to a grown-up daughter who prolonged her free afternoon by a few minutes? Never having disobeyed him in my whole life, I simply did not know. The mere thought of his furious "Hester" unnerved me.

At the dimly lit entry to Nidgate I stopped to draw breath. The shops there were still open. A constellation of brass balls shone faintly above a lamp-lit pawn-shop. There were customers round a pieman's tray. The street was safe enough and it would shorten my journey by almost ten minutes, bringing me to the steps at the bottom of Silvergate. Banishing the thought of the rat-infested warehouses, I plunged into the gloomy thoroughfare and almost at once caught the cool scent of the river.

It was a stroke of luck to see just ahead of me the familiar figure of Bella, the match-seller from the market place. She was going home with her little girl in her arms. I came close behind and soon caught her up.

"You're out late, miss, by yourself."

I spoke to the child. She was clutching the simplest kind of doll, a flat painted face on a little stick.

"What have you got there?" I asked, forcing myself to walk at a reasonable pace and behave like a rational being.

"A gentleman give it to 'er," Bella explained. "She won't be parted from it. Never had such a thing given 'er before. Ever so kind he was."

Her feet were too bad for her to keep up with me. I went slightly ahead. Still, we made our way along Nidgate together almost to the end when she unexpectedly bade me goodnight and went into a beer-shop 'for a penn'orth of vinegar' as she delicately put it, leaving me to face the worst part of the walk alone.

I braced myself and ran on past the cobbler's shop. The reassuring tap of his hammer followed me to the last gas-lamp at the top of the wide shallow stairs going down to the wharf. I smelt tar and wet wood and the unfathomably mysterious smell of the water. On the top step with my hand already on the iron rail, I stopped. From below came the sound of voices — blows — heavy breathing. Men were fighting down there. Silence fell — and then, bringing my heart into my mouth, came a heavy splash and the sound of feet running towards the stairs.

I groped my way back to the blank wall of the cobbler's shop, closed the lantern shutter and retreated into the shadows, standing with my feet in a puddle. But I saw the two men who came tearing up the steps. I saw their faces in the gas-light, their expressions agitated, concentrated on escape. The first was a big fair man with a beard. The second was Josh Blakey. They moved so fast that I didn't see where they went or which alley took them in. They simply vanished into Sparrow Chare.

At any rate they had gone and would not, presumably, come back. I pulled myself together. It served me right. I had had plenty of warning. There would be a certain satisfaction in telling Julian that Josh Blakey's reformation was not quite complete. A wild rush down the steps and along the wharf and I would be almost home. With the nagging thought that they had been fighting, and had not been fighting each other, that there must be, or have been some other person, I nevertheless went quickly down, stepping lightly almost without a sound.

Presently there would be moonlight. Already the clouds were opening on luminous rifts of sky. But there were black shadows in the gaping entrances to the old warehouses and under the arches of the bridge where the Audley, swollen with recent rain, flowed swift and strong and almost silent in its long, unbroken thrust forward. Then at the very edge of the wharf as if half risen from the river, I saw in the darkness a darker shape; and above the quiet beat of water heard a human sound: a painfully drawn breath followed by a groan of laborious effort.

By whatever quickness of intuition I knew him, I never doubted who it was even before I saw his face in the light of my lantern. He was lying right in the water where they had pushed or thrown him. By a belated stroke of the luck that seemed quite to have deserted him, he had fallen close to a flight of steps, submerged now that the water level had risen, and these must have been supporting him. He had hauled himself up to grasp the edge of the stone landing stage and was clinging to it desperately. I went closer and saw a dreadful wound on his forehead. With agonising difficulty he was dragging himself by inches up the unseen steps.

I knelt down on the wet stones. If his face had been pale before, its pallor now was deathly. His eyes were darker than the water below as he raised them towards me in appeal, drawing me to him, binding us together in a strange intimacy as if we were both drowning: as if on the uttermost margin of existence we had met.

And yet, equally, he terrified me, most of all when with painful effort he put out a feeble hand for help. I leaned forward and for the first time saw his hand ungloved. (They had taken everything they could tear from him). In the watery moonlight and swaying lantern flame I saw that it was horribly disfigured, the flesh shrivelled, the skin bleached a leprous white, so that it seemed the hand of an outcast.

My start of revulsion may have been his undoing. I could not bring myself to grasp his mutilated hand. I have never been sure whether I only recoiled or whether I pushed him from me. Lying awake for many a tormented hour, I have never been sure. Certainly I did not help him and truly I believe he was past help.

His hand relaxed. It slipped back out of reach. The life went from his limbs as if he became all weight. He slid submissively into the water and vanished as suddenly and completely as if a hollow had opened in the deep river-bed and an invisible force had dragged him in. I felt the sinking in my own flesh. Then the displaced water rushed back and slapped the wharf.

Distracted, I lay down in the mud and leaned out as far as I dared and stared until the surface of the water writhed in serpentine coils like a huge mourning bracelet. There was no sign of him, nothing where he had been but the subdued and shifting pattern of grey and black water and further out the stealthy current flowing strongly in mid-stream. I remember fetching great whimpering sighs, longing with all my power of longing, now that it was too late, to save him.

I got to my knees and at the same time was aware of a change: a new transforming element. A calmness stole over the river. A softness came into the air like a benediction. The clouds drew off. The white face of the moon looked up from the water. I felt an agony of regret; a pity so profound that I could never speak of it — never. In all my life I had felt nothing like it, nor ever have again save from the same cause. I pitied him not only for his death but for whatever circumstances had brought him to it. I had not known him. I lost nothing by his death. What I experienced was pure, selfless compassion.

What had he wanted? And of whom? Our strange relationship could have been no more than accidental. He could know nothing of me whose contact with the world scarcely reached beyond the narrow walls of Silvergate. My foot, when I got up, touched tinkling glass; a watch; the one thing the ruffians had dropped. The outer case of enamelled gold had burst open. I knew at once that it was valuable. This, then, was the piece of jewellery he had wanted to sell. As Thomas said, his presence in Silvergate had been quite reasonable.

I hesitated, wondering despairingly what to do with it. My impulse was to drop it in the water after him. It must have been precious to him. But it was beautiful. It would have been an outrage to my upbringing to treat it badly. A kind of horror of the river and its merciless power to absorb and conceal, made me draw back from it. From sheer indecision I put the watch in my pocket and immediately suffered all the guilt of being in possession of stolen property.

Shivering, sighing, half demented, I dragged myself away. On the first of the steps leading up to the bridge, I turned, fancying that something had stirred. It was only the suck and ebb of water against the wharf. With the mortal sadness of a passing-bell the Abbey clock struck nine. Before the last stroke died away I was at home. Father glanced round as I slipped upstairs. A minute later I heard him bolt the door.

5

IT WAS MY plain duty to report the stranger's death to the police. I was never in any doubt about that. It must be done at once; or almost at once.

Instead of telling father there and then, instead of forcing him to take off his blinkered spectacles and look at me and listen, I felt only relief that he had scarcely noticed my return. Each step on each tread of the stairs took me further from the moment when I should have told him. Each passing minute made it harder to tell. And yet to go to the police without first telling father was unthinkable. During the long, sleepless night I rehearsed a number of openings.

"Father, I have something to tell you."

He would look up from the adjustment of a delicate watch movement with a quick frown of surprise, expecting some startling announcement, but not as startling as it would, in fact, be.

"I saw a man drowning. He had been almost beaten to death."

No words could convey the actual experience. That had happened in an altogether different world, increasingly remote from reality and, as I was to discover, a world to which increasingly I belonged. But father's fury would be immediate and inescapable.

"What were you doing down there on the wharf alone? Haven't I told you a dozen times? We'll have that fellow from the Courier pestering us . . ."

What would the newspapers make of it? Miss Hester Mallow, daughter of the town's leading watchmaker — alone in the dark — in one of Wickborough's most unsavoury quarters. Generations of Mallows had contrived to live quietly in Silvergate without ever being involved with thieves or vagabonds or committing any offence more serious than evasion of window tax. It was I, Hester, who would be at the centre of the new notoriety.

"Had you ever seen the man before?" the police would be sure to ask. "You had spoken to him?"

There would be significant looks. There would be a scandal like the scandal that had driven poor Amabel Craig to Australia. Amabel's fate had worried me long before I knew what the word 'scandal' meant. My head burning on my pillow, I experienced one of the random flashes of memory that come in moments of stress. Someone — was it mother? — had taken Louise and me to a service in the Abbey. We had come out into the sunshine. It must have been summer. We were wearing white dresses and chip bonnets with blue ribbons. People were talking. "It's the scandal," said a voice laden with gloom and regret. "She'll never live it down. Amabel of all people. It'll break her father's heart. She can never live in Wickborough after this." "What's happened?" I demanded in alarm, racked with pain for Amabel, whoever she was. "Hush." We were hurried home. It was a secret thing. Worse than a war or a plague, it couldn't be faced. And all at once I remembered Louise, a still centre in the eddy of distress. She was turning over the pages of *The Keepsake*. There seemed to be a bright light. The sun? What was it about Louise? Then I lost her again and returned with new anguish to my own troubles.

It was only a matter of time for of course I must tell. A scandal however damaging was of little importance compared to the offence. A defenceless man had been brutally done to death. I had seen the villains who did it. It was my duty to bring them to justice.

38

At breakfast, heavy-eyed and feverish, I watched father dealing efficiently with the tiresome necessity of eating. He treated it as an interruption to his work and hated to be delayed.

"You've not eaten a bite Hester. Are you well?"

"Yes, father. Quite well."

If only I were ill; desperately ill; dead!

"I've a great deal to do today and there's the meeting of freemen this evening. Will you see to my clothes?"

"Yes, father."

I must find a more suitable time. The absolute necessity of finding it kept me awake the next night and troubled me all the following day without bringing me to the point of confessing. Gradually the soothing idea came to me that I would tell Julian instead or at least first; and then with his support, tell father.

To confide in Julian was so obvious and natural that I almost did. On the Saturday morning I set off with my shopping basket and contrived to be near the gates of St Aidan's just as he came out on his way to the Close for an hour of Greek with his tutor who had his rooms there.

"Hester! What are you doing here? I'm glad to see you. Can you walk a little faster, love? I'm late. And I've something to tell you." He rushed along, bursting with energy and high spirits. "Good news. Several things. But first, what do you think? A letter from the Bishop. He's invited me to the palace to talk."

"About the dissertation?"

"Yes, but it will give me an opportunity to discuss my future as well, I hope."

"I must see you, Julian."

"Yes, of course."

We had come into the market place. One or two heads turned. Had anyone heard the pleading note in my voice? It must look as if I were running after him in every sense. But I must get it out somehow. Then by one of those capricious accidents that seem deliberately arranged, Julian gave me the very opportunity I needed.

"By the way, you remember Josh Blakey, the red-headed brute? Well, I went round to his place yesterday.

39

Weaver's Yard. Thought it wouldn't do him any harm to know that somebody was keeping an eye on him. You'll never guess. He's gone. Cleared out. Look out, Hester." He drew me away from the threatening hooves of a dray-horse. "Let's get on to the pavement. The wife's a decent woman. I recognised her. She's been to one or two Temperance meetings at the Mission, as well she might with Josh for a husband. He didn't go home on Wednesday night." We had come to the archway leading to the Close. "I must go, Hester. Tell you all about it on Sunday. As a matter of fact, the poor woman seemed relieved. 'I pray to God he'll stay away, Mr Windross', she said. There's a brood of red-haired children. We must try to help them. What a world!"

He quoted something I took to be Greek. It brought him to his tutor's gate. Now was my chance. Greek or no Greek, I must keep him a minute longer. I had actually begun 'Julian', when I thought of Mrs Blakey's prayer. What good would it do the children if I set the police on the track of their father? I hesitated. The gate slammed to. With the despicable cunning of cowardice, I seized on the excuse. The Blakeys would be happier if I kept quiet.

"I say." Julian had come back. "You must have travelled like the wind on Wednesday night. I managed to go home after all, not long after you left. Yes, I know" — I must have looked stricken — "Rotten, wasn't it? But I thought by racing through the Chare I might just catch you as you came down Silvergate and tell you about the Bishop's letter. When I came up from the wharf, there was a light in your room."

"You didn't see . . . ?"

"Not so much as the tip of your wings. You must have flown. It's twice as far through the market place."

"That's why I . . . Only father said I . . ." I groped for a suitable opening, distracted by the need for haste, the need for secrecy, the need to tell. "Oh Julian, it's such a dangerous place."

"You're nervous, Hester. That business with Blakey has upset you. You're too much alone . . ."

He left me bitterly regretting that he had not reached the wharf a few minutes earlier to share my ordeal. Seeing him had intensified my feeling of having been set apart from normal life. With the iron gate between us, it was I who felt imprisoned. He was free in the civilised company of bishops and tutors. I would never be able to make him understand what it had been like.

My life lost its simplicity. All that had been bright and clear became confused and dark. The weight of my secret increased with my inability to tell it. To recreate the sordid scene and my own part in it was bad enough. It was shameful to have been involved with such people in such a place; but worse still was the nagging fear that I had been more than a witness. When the stranger had put out his hand, had I pushed it away when by grasping it I could have saved him? Remorse and fear brought me more than once to my knees. Between the weakness of not having helped him and the baseness of having repulsed him, there was little to choose.

From time to time I resumed my imaginary dialogue with the police.

"And why, Miss Mallow, have you been so long in coming to us with this story?"

For it would sound like a story. With the thought came my first moment of ease. Without proof it was no more than a story: my naked word. I alone knew what had happened. Even those two villains knew less than I did and no one else was involved. Thomas had thought my behaviour strange when I mentioned having seen an intruder in the yard because he had not seen the man. I almost convinced myself that no other person besides Josh Blakey, his accomplice and myself had ever seen him. The thought of Thomas was oddly consoling. In my desperation I might even have confided in him; but he was away on one of his regular visits to the seaport where we bought our supplies of jet. By the time he came back, events had taken a different turn.

There had been something weird in my encounters with the stranger. That was now accounted for. It had been a case of second sight. He had borne about him like a prophetic cloud the foreknowledge of his own death. For some reason I had been singled out to share it. How else could the sympathy he had roused in me be explained? I had not known how to act. I had failed him.

Conclusions which strike me as crazy now seemed quite logical then. At last, wearied to death, I lay down on my bed in the middle of the day and slept until it was dark. When I awoke, it was as if years had passed. The conflict was over. I would never tell. It was literally too awful for words. Language in which to tell it could not be found. I yielded to my first instinct to keep the whole sad business to myself. The relief was enormous.

After that it was the watch that troubled me most, the one concrete piece of evidence that the incident had ever happened. Scrubbing despairingly at yet another ruined dress in the privacy of my room, I found it in the pocket and instantly got up from the floor and bolted the door. My impulse was to hide it for ever from sight. At the bottom of a drawer under a pile of night-dresses? But then I could never bring myself to wear any of them again. Behind the loose brick in the chimney? My hands shaking, I felt about for my childhood hiding-place, brought down a shower of soot and found the cavity. Quickly, as if the police were already at the door, I knotted the watch in a handkerchief, laid it inside, replaced the brick and spent a few minutes clearing up the soot.

It was while I was pouring out water to wash my hands that I saw how conspicuous the hiding place was. The loose brick stood out a good half inch. The discovery so frightened me that I put down the ewer with the intention of hammering home the brick with the poker. But the noise might disturb father. Besides, the cavity might be found when the chimney was swept; and how stupid to have wrapped the watch in one of my own initialled handkerchiefs!

Furtively I removed the brick and having unwrapped the watch, looked at it again, unwillingly. It was a lady's watch, exquisitely made. Professional interest overcame my loathing of the thing. The outer case was of gold, enamelled in translucent blue and white with an inset medallion depicting the draped figure of a woman holding a lyre, her hair in a Grecian knot. The inner case was also of gold with a London hallmark of the year 1777. The face of the dial was enamelled white with delicate gold hands. The numerals were in black, Roman for the hours, Arabic for the minutes. Pressing open the back, I found a watch-cock of intricate scrolls and floral shapes and the inscription of the makers: James Upjohn & Co, London.

"Hester! Where are you?"

Not once in six months did father leave the shop to find me. Now I heard him not only come upstairs but go into the parlour next door.

"Here, father, in my room."

In a frenzy I looked round for a hiding place, could be satisfied with none, thrust the watch deep in my pocket and opened the door by an inch.

"I'm washing my hands."

We met on the landing.

"There's a boy here with a message from the Guildhall. It's about the clock. One of the jacks is sticking. It must be the one we had trouble with last year. I must go at once. I don't like to ask it, but would you come down to the shop?"

There was nothing to do but wait. I sat on the high stool behind the counter with my hands idle in my lap until unwelcome thoughts drove me to slide open the partition at the back of the window by a few inches and look out. I was rewarded by an interesting little diversion. It was market day. Silvergate was thronged with shoppers, many of whom paused to look in the window. A young couple lingered. I recognised the young man from the counting-house who had bought Thomas's brooch, gave him a stern mental rebuke for wasting his employer's time once more and turned my attention to his companion to find — lo and behold! — the gipsy-looking young woman had been supplanted by a fresh-faced country girl. She was listening to her escort with respectful attention and an occasional adoring upward glance. I too looked at him

43

with new respect. He was fickle but this change of heart was for the better; and it really must have been a change of heart because the girl was wearing on the bodice of her pink cross-barred sarcenet dress (surely her best!), the butterfly brooch.

It was not until they had gone that I realised how short a time had passed since the sale of the brooch. In those two weeks he was not the only one to have changed so deeply that the time before seemed like a lost age. He was wise to have parted from the other girl. She would have brought him ill-luck as she had to me. If she had delivered her message in time I would not have been on the wharf at a few minutes to nine on Wednesday evening.

From either side of the glass partition came a shaft of light. One glanced on the locked doors of the watch cupboard; the other brightened the green-baized counter. In each, myriads of air-borne motes moved in mysterious patterns. I began to listen to the clocks, each ticking in isolation from its fellows, all intent on the same unwavering purpose until they too formed a mysterious pattern, a structure of sounds; or rather a forward moving current propelling the listener towards some crisis.

They arrived triumphantly at the hour of eleven. The varying chimes had died away when the commonplace ring of the shop-bell announced a customer: Alderman Kebb.

"I wouldn't trust it to anyone but your father, Miss Hester." He laid it on the green baize: an ancient repeater in a shagreen case.

"It has been left to me by my great-uncle in Worcester. There may be a lot to do to it . . ."

He chatted while I put the watch in a box, labelled it and locked it away in the right drawer.

"Shall we have the pleasure of seeing you at the Musical Evening? The cards should be out shortly."

"We haven't received ours yet, Alderman Kebb, but yes, I do hope to be there. Pray tell Mrs Kebb I shall look forward to meeting her — and Sarah."

Innocent, carefree Sarah with nothing to think about

except what to wear at the Musical Evening! My own happy innocence seemed a lifetime away. My spirits would never soar again. The watch in my pocket seemed to drag me to the floor. Oh, to be rid of it!

I stooped to replace the bunch of keys on the secret hook under the counter and was inspired. The opportunity was heaven-sent. Thomas was still away, father out. I had the shop to myself. The best place to hide the stolen watch was here among all the paraphernalia of watch-making; not in some isolated spot where, if found, it would proclaim itself as having been hidden; but among others where it would never be noticed, at least not for ages.

At the far end of the shop, beyond father's cubicle and Thomas's bench was a fitting of wide, deep drawers, one of them set aside for old, broken watches kept for their parts. A hurried glance up the street; no sign of father. In nervous haste I unlocked the spare-part drawer.

It was gloriously full almost to the top with a con-glomeration of glasses, keys, cocks, wheels, columns, hair-springs, stems, cogs, whole movements and discarded cases undisturbed for months, even for years. I thrust the watch to the very back of the drawer. If it should be found no one could connect it with me. Locking it away, I was conscious of a little heart-ache as from an act of disloyalty. Now there was nothing to connect me with its owner, either.

It was the Musical Evening that absolutely clinched my decision to keep my secret. The invitation card, deckle-edged and engraved in gilt, arrived next morning.

"The Mayor and Aldermen of Wickborough request the pleasure of the company of Mr O. Mallow and Miss Mallow at a reception to be held in the Milton rooms on the evening of Thursday, 4th May, at eight o'clock. Carriages at eleven."

The reception was an annual event attended exclusively by freemen of Wickborough, their families and friends. It was the highlight of the summer, rivalled only by the Christmas Ball. The card, propped against Minerva on the mantel-piece, symbolised all that was most respectable in the social life of the town. To be associated in any way with the police or the newspapers before the Musical Evening was out of the question.

It fell to me to write the reply in my best copperplate and long loops.

"Mr Mallow thanks the Mayor and Aldermen ... and has pleasure in accepting for himself and Miss Mallow ..."

"You'll want to see my dress, father."

I ventured to mention it one evening after supper. He was leaning back in his chair, his eyes closed, and he only nodded assent. But he did at least sit up when I came dispiritedly back from my room and stood before him. The dress was charming. Even in the midst of all my worries, I loved it: a muslin apron front over taffeta of pale apricot lavishly trimmed with bunches of matching velvet ribbon. I had white gloves with fifteen buttons, silk stockings, and for my hair a plait of velvet ribbon entwined with lilies-of-the-valley. The dress was not too low but low enough to leave my neck bare. I had put on the black ribbon with the ivory medallion, and awaited father's verdict. It was unexpected.

"You are pale, Hester. You need a holiday; a change of air."

The suggestion astonished me. I had never had a holiday away from home.

"You could go to your Aunt Tamar Lind. Codlin Croft is a snug little place. The country air would do you good. You're very much confined to the house here."

Codlin Croft was no more than a name, Aunt Tamar no more than a distant memory. She had come to see us once after the death of my mother, her much younger half-sister, and had impressed upon me one piece of advice. It was when she was leaving that she put into my hand a gold coin.

"Every girl," she said, "should keep a sovereign in her pocket, just in case. Always keep a sovereign in your pocket, Hester. You simply never know what might happen."

"What sort of thing, Aunt Tamar?"

I waited with a thrilling sense of adventure but she only laughed and patted my cheek.

"Make a little bag for it and pin it in your pocket. Then you'll be safe, whatever happens."

Intrigued, I did exactly as she advised; made a little bag of chamois leather and sewed the sovereign inside. Who could tell from what disasters it would save me? To move it from one pocket to another became an unthinking habit. I never thought of the sovereign as negotiable; had long ceased to think of it at all, or of Aunt Tamar. Beyond a vague feeling that to be whisked away to Codlin Croft would be a welcome escape from the present gloom of Silvergate, I could summon no interest in father's unusual concern for my health, as I modestly displayed the dress. He was looking at it absently.

"Oh, the dress. Yes. Very suitable." It was not the most encouraging of adjectives. Without the blinkered spectacles, away from the green-shaded lamp, his face was unfamiliar. "You need an ornament: a necklace or a brooch. Come downstairs tomorrow and we'll find something."

I understood, of course, that his concern was for the prestige of the firm of Mallow, not for me. All the same to have secured his attention to such an extent made me nervous. I took comfort in the thought that he would probably forget.

But when I went down next morning, feeling more normal in my plain house dress and apron, he left his work at once, took off his spectacles and came to the counter where he had already laid out two trays of jewellery; simple pieces, most of them. Wickborough had a good many prosperous tradespeople and well-to-do clergy in those days and farmers' wives drove in to buy wedding gifts and christening mugs. My father's business flourished. But there was little demand for expensive jewellery.

"This pendant?" He laid it out on a piece of black velvet and looked at it gravely, treating me as he would a customer. It was a tassel of gold with a single pearl.

"I like it."

"Too small, I think. This coral would match the colour in the dress. The mount is well done. What do you think? There, look in the glass."

I held the necklace against my brown dress. Perhaps he misinterpreted my subdued manner and thought me dissatisfied for to my surprise he burst out:

"You should have had some of your mother's things to choose from," and immediately turned away and put on his spectacles. "You can be looking while I get on."

He left me to finger the pendant listlessly and pin a brooch to my dress. Since he remained absorbed in his work, I went behind the counter and pulled out a tray of rings, brooches and cameos. I picked out a ring at random. It was hexagonal, enamelled black on gold. Inside, on four of the facets were engraved the syllables: Re-mem-ber me. The other two facets had been left plain so that a monogram and date could be added: or a name.

There was no one to remember him but me. I put the ring on my finger. It fitted.

"You don't want that, do you?"

"No, father." Startled, I answered with the promptness of guilt. He looked at me keenly. "I was only trying it on." I hung my head, on the verge of tears.

"What is Julian doing these days?" he asked abruptly. "I haven't talked to him lately. When does he take his final examination?"

"On June 21st. That's the first day." It had been a landmark too long for me to be mistaken.

"It will be another year at least before he is ordained."

"Yes, father."

"And a long time before he's settled. There" — as I laid the ring back in the drawer — "keep it if you want it. You can take any of these cheaper things so long as you make out a bill and enter the amount in the ledger. Have you chosen a necklace? Well, you can think it over."

In my room I tried on the ring again. Of course I couldn't wear it on the third finger of my left hand where it looked best. Did I want to wear it at all? "Remember me," it said mournfully, reproachfully. Slowly I pushed it over the knuckle of my third right finger, as a pledge. It seemed the least I could do. By keeping to myself the secret of his death, I deprived him of other mourners.

No sooner had the unspoken vow to remember him taken shape than I dropped him from my memory as completely as if he had never existed. He faded, in the light of a totally unexpected event which transformed my life as dramatically as if I had stepped from darkness into bright day. Indeed, I felt it with a rush of returning vitality in all my being as one welcomes the return of fine weather.

An unusual bustle in the street drew me to the parlour window. There was always excitement when a cab came down Silvergate. Pedestrians had squeezed themselves into doorways to watch as the horse came gingerly down over the steep cobbled way between the overhanging gables. It drew up at our own door. A customer? The driver got down, dragged from under his seat a leather trunk, set it down and hammered on the house door. Then with a touch of gallantry he opened the door of the cab and gave his hand to a young lady.

Mrs Wragge was beginning on the long descent from the kitchen. I ran down ahead and opened the door. At the same time father came out from the shop.

The young lady stood on the unshadowed pavement. She was dressed in pale grey and she seemed to shine like silver.

"Hester?" she said, hesitating. "Father." She put up her veil. "It's Louise."

And then I remembered her. I remembered the particular thing about Louise that had eluded my memory. How could I ever have forgotten? I saw it with the breath-taking freshness of discovery: her astonishing beauty.

6

IF I WAS enraptured, father was struck dumb. He stood as if paralysed as Louise and I embraced.

"You've come home," I said with a sense of enrichment. "You've come home. Oh, Louise!"

"I wasn't sure that you were Hester. You were only a little girl."

Her voice was a husky treble with a tendency to die away at the end of a sentence. It gave a touching quality to everything she said. We were of similar height and build but she seemed slighter and more delicate than I. Though she was more than four years older, I thought of her from the first as younger than myself.

"You must be dreadfully tired," I said. "Such a long journey. Mrs Wragge, my sister has come home."

We stood hand in hand, waiting for some response from father.

"Well, I'm sure," Mrs Wragge said over and over again, smoothing her pinafore and waiting for the official welcome to end before taking in the luggage. Passers-by stepped off the pavement to avoid us. At last father pulled himself together and held out his hand.

"Well, Louise. This is a surprise. You didn't think of writing to let us know?"

How cold it sounded! I guessed instantly that Louise had been afraid to write in case he forbade her to come. After all, he had sent her away, a mere child, with a heartless disregard for her welfare. Had _he_, I asked myself indignantly, ever written to _her_? Not once, so far as I knew.

I took her cloak and valise and led her upstairs. Father followed, leaving the shop door open. It was clearly a crisis. We went into the parlour.

"Have you any particular reason for coming home?"

The churlishness of it, before she had so much as sat down! I whispered to Mrs Wragge to lay the table at once.

"The cabman," she whispered back. "He's waiting for the fare."

Not daring to irritate father by asking for it, I took a shilling from the blue teapot and gave it to her.

Louise stood facing the window with her back to the big oak press looking so beautiful that the parlour sank into a shameful drabness. Two tears rolled down her cheeks.

"Mrs Maple died."

The little break in her voice conveyed the utter tragedy of Mrs Maple's death even more poignantly than the tears.

"Dear me!" father said. "I'm sorry. You should have let me know. We'll talk about it later. You'll see to things, Hester?"

A sound from the unattended shop sent him hurrying downstairs.

"He's glad to go," I thought. "How can he treat her so stiffly? His own daughter."

My warmth must make up for his coldness.

"I can't believe it." I hugged Louise again. "That you've come back. I've thought of you, often, but never pictured you here, always at Blairgouroch."

So far she had stood quite still like one of the goddesses on the mantel-piece. (I saw them, all at once, as plump and matronly.) Now, slowly, she drew off her gloves.

"Without Mrs Maple, how could I stay there, Hester? We were always together."

"You were quite right to come home, Louise dear. And for me it will be wonderful. You can't imagine. And you'll be quite safe here."

It was strange that I should put it like that, responding unconsciously, no doubt, to some half recollected phrases in her letters. The notion of keeping her safe already obsessed me. Almost without speaking, she communicated the need to be protected. I understood exactly how it had been at Blairgouroch. In the quiet stillroom among the glowing jam-pots, or in the housekeeper's room, presiding over the spice-cabinet, she had felt safe. Outside,

51

the sullen sea might buffet the rocks but indoors at Mrs Maple's side, there had been nothing to fear.

I watched spellbound as she took off her hat and timidly (it was outrageous that she should feel timid in her own home) sat down in the balloon-backed chair by the fire. Her travelling dress, uncreased and fresh, was altogether so simple and tasteful that it made me want to burn all my clothes. Newly alighted from her coach, Louise had for me both the pathos and glamour of Cinderella. Oh, there could be no doubt of the part she had played in our childish games. She had been the princess, the damsel in distress.

To put her at her ease I talked soothingly of little things.

"You must have been on the way a long time. When did you leave?"

"Monday," she said sorrowfully, "Monday morning."

It would have been unkind to press for details she was too tired to give. The huskiness of her voice gave to every word she spoke a melting pathos so that it scarcely mattered what the words actually were. When she had rested and drunk a glass of wine, I took her to her room.

"You'll like to have your own room?" I said doubtfully. "Mrs Wragge and I will soon have it ready."

"I remember it."

"And you'll remember the view."

I opened the window. We leaned out, our heads together. To the left, high above the huddle of old roof-tiles soared the splendid towers of the Abbey. A scattering of rooks floated in the blue air.

"It's pretty," Louise said.

From the corner of my eye I saw that she was not looking up at the Abbey but down at the parsley in the drain-pipe.

"It's nice to sit down there by the rockery on a sunny morning. The door opens into the alley." I caught my breath. Just for a second, he was there again, standing with his head bent under the lintel, with his strange air of not existing in his own right but for some other purpose, like a milestone or a sign-post. But the panic was gone in an instant. Louise had already banished my nightmare as she would banish every dark and sordid thought. She had come in time to release me from the atmosphere of squalid crime that had so deeply troubled me: an atmosphere so alien to the rare, cool climate in which Louise moved, that it was unseemly to think of it in her presence. "You remember the alley? We went that way to school."

"Do you know, Hester," she drew in her head, moistening her lips with an appealing look of diffidence, "I would rather...Is there another room I could have? Unless it's a dreadful nuisance."

"Why, of course."

In its time the house had accommodated a much bigger family as well as several apprentices and servants. There were plenty of unused rooms. It would just be a matter of airing one of them and moving furniture. We made a tour of them all, I talking, explaining and suggesting until I was hot and hoarse; Louise following, quiet and un-hurried, and looking as immaculate as if she had stepped out of a bandbox. It had always been so. As we opened one door after another, I remembered more and more. While Julian and I had rushed about, planning, arguing, grimy, dishevelled, Louise had stayed somewhere in the background, keeping her pinafore clean and doing it to perfection.

"They're none of them good enough," I said in despair. We had come at last to a front attic with no outlook: nothing to see from the tiny dormer window but roof-tops and a cloud or two; a withdrawn, enclosed place high above the street.

"I suppose it would be a bother to turn it into a bedroom. But I could carry up my own hot water."

"You mean — you like this?"

Louise sat down on a wooden chest under the fanlight. Subdued light from above kindled the golden tones in her light brown hair and gave an ethereal purity to her complexion. If she had floated heavenward through the shaft of dusty light, I would have been grieved but not surprised.

"This is where I like to be. Really, Hester. If I may."

We made it attractive. It became the most interesting room in the house. I had not seen its possibilities. We had the chimney swept and cleaned up the fireplace, which proved to be a pretty little eighteenth-century affair with a canopy of fluted steel and a tiny hob. Louise must have done most of the work herself. Mrs Wragge was too busy to do more than lecture the sweep and an express order for hair jewellery kept me occupied for two or three days, at the end of which I found the attic charmingly transformed with fresh chintzes, a patchwork quilt and crochet work table-covers brought from Blair-gouroch; and Louise herself seated in a rocking chair, showing no trace of her exertions. The room would be cold in winter but in those sunny spring days it was warm under the roof. We spent most of our time there, looking of necessity inwards.

"That's the only drawback," I said. "It's impossible to see out."

"Or in."

Louise never elaborated or overstated. Now she simply made this odd remark and left the subject alone.

Not that one missed the view, having Louise to look at. Yet she was without vanity or affectation of any kind. Her dresses were as simple as the elaborate fashions of the seventies permitted. Her hats, bonnets and shawls were of the plainest kind. The drawers in her tall-boy were filled with pretty things, given her, I imagined, by ladies whom she had occasionally helped to dress; but she would pick off the lace from a gown or peignoir and sew it on her petticoat rather than on a sleeve or collar where it showed, and she seemed happiest in a severely plain house-dress.

"I'm used to being indoors," she said when I urged her to come shopping with me. "Mrs Maple and I went out very little, usually in the carriage when the family didn't need it and Mr Roach wanted to exercise the horses."

Besides, at Blairgouroch, apparently, there had been nowhere to go.

"Still, you liked it," I observed.

Louise looked puzzled, distressed even. The distress, like everything else, became her.

"I liked being with Mrs Maple," she said at last.

As we talked in the seclusion of the attic, I came to understand more clearly how great a loss she had suffered in Mrs Maple's death. The two had been inseparable in a relationship ideally suited to Louise's temperament. Mrs Maple had been all-powerful, decisive, strict and kind. She had advised and taught; Louise had listened and learned. They had inhabited a finite world of things: linen, needles and thread; hem-stitched pillowcases; lace insertion for bed valances; carefully measured spoonfuls of tea — China, Indian and green; jealously guarded cinnamon, nutmeg and allspice; wafer-thin bread and butter: lavender bags: candied peel and home-made wines.

When Mrs Maple died quite suddenly while they were measuring out ticking for pillow-cases, the axis of Louise's world crumbled and vanished. Only the things remained.

"I didn't know what to do," she said again and again. "That's why I . . ."

"You came home and I'm so glad."

Was she glad too? It was perhaps too positive and robust a word to apply to Louise, suggesting an overflow of spirits incompatible with her controlled manner. That is, I thought of it at first as controlled and often felt ashamed of my own exuberance. Louise did everything with an economy of movement that gave to her smallest action a classic grace. She spoke with the utmost brevity; and yet, in her sad little voice gave the impression that the few short sentences she used were no more than clues to the deeper truths she left unspoken, just as, by no more than turning her head she conjured up new visions of beauty. It was like being reminded of another existence one had known and forgotten.

In trying to set it down simply without exaggeration (it is impossible to exaggerate what was, in its way, perfection) I am at a disadvantage. Beauty, even Louise's, fades with time. I am left only with the idea of it. No likeness ever did justice to it. Its appeal was not sensuous but of a spiritual kind: a beauty not chiefly of colouring despite the dreamy blue of her eyes and the delicacy of her complexion. It was the contours of her face that caught and held the attention: the bones, fine and austere, softened by childishly curving cheeks and mouth; and because it was beauty and not just prettiness, her face suggested more even than could be seen in its exquisite composition of features, skin and colouring. Its whole was more than the sum of its parts. It gave one a glimpse into the very nature of beauty: an assurance of the existence of something more beautiful still: an ideal; so that in Louise's company one felt the presence of this other factor as though she were the medium through which it could be reached.

It is necessary to remind myself of all this; to sit quietly in this fire-lit parlour where we used to sit; to look at the oak press, the pink candle-shades, the still figures on the mantel-shelf, and see them once again changed like every other object in the house, by the presence of Louise; or to try to see them so. Otherwise it is difficult to account for the havoc she caused.

As the days passed, her influence extended beyond the attics to the other rooms. She was wonderfully neat and methodical. Without effort she reduced things to order: not that the house had been untidy, but we were busy people. I had often regretted the lack of refinement in our house-keeping. Louise supplied it, though she seemed puzzled when I said:

"You've made things somehow more elegant."

She saw the house purely in terms of the things in it and by moving them a little, tidying some of them away and bringing others into prominence, achieved an effect she herself was apparently unable to feel.

"I've brought the Worcester jug to the front of the cabinet," she said, looking round for an explanation, "and I've covered the coal box with that piece of tapestry work. You had it as a table runner. The antimacassars needed washing. They look better."

56

Her brief catalogue of facts surely did not account for the change.

"What a difference!" Mrs Wragge said and added solemnly, "But with those looks she won't be with us long." I sighed in agreement. It was only too obvious that Louise would marry. But Mrs Wragge had in mind a longer parting. "That's a face fit for nowhere but heaven. She looks very nigh like an angel already."

I would have felt depressed, had not Louise enjoyed excellent health, except for a touch of nervousness natural enough after the shock and upset of Mrs Maple's death. She was not one to express her feelings. But one morning she came into the parlour where I was twisting a thick and difficult lock of hair into the shape of a heart to fit a locket. I watched her as she tidied her already matchlessly neat work-basket.

"I thought it would be different," she said suddenly, "from the way it used to be."

"Do you mean the house? Home?"

"Yes. The way you wrote about it, you made it seem different from the way I remembered it."

"What was it like, before you went away?"

From the red plush sofa, thence to the darker red curtains and over the ornaments on the whatnot, Louise's blue eyes travelled slowly and at last fixed themselves on me with a dreamy, visionary look.

"It was just the same," she said with heart-breaking sadness. "The floor has always had that hollow bit just there. That's why the door won't stay shut. But that vase," with a look of beautiful resignation she singled out the loving cup with an inset picture of the Abbey, "was one of a pair."

The practical content of this speech was so widely at variance with her look and manner that I floundered with a sense of incongruity, almost losing the thread of our conversation.

"But my letters —" I tried in vain to remember just how I could have misrepresented my home — "did you like having them?"

"I used to read them to Mrs Maple." The blue eyes

clouded with tears. "Some of them two or three times."
From a pocket in her work basket she produced them,
each meticulously folded to precisely the same size and
tied with ribbon.

Still, in my literary fervour and without intending it,
I must have misled her. She was not entirely happy: not
in the way that I, thanks to the novelty of her company,
was once again happy. It worried me. Searching anxiously
for the cause of Louise's lack of spirits, I found it in
father. Any man, one might have thought, would be
grateful to have such a daughter restored to him: a
daughter so useful, modest and lovely to look at as
Louise. To send her away at the age of sixteen had been
monstrous. Equally monstrous was his attitude to her
now. Nothing she did could please him. Of course it was
unwise of her, when she had dusted his books, to re-
arrange them in order of size. He saw the change the
moment he came into the parlour that evening: each
shelf symmetrically arranged: a row of books of
uniform height flanked by an equal number of larger
volumes.

"What in heaven's name have you done to my books?"
I quailed for Louise.

"They had to go there, the bigger ones," she said
bravely, "There weren't enough of them to have a shelf of
their own."

"Hester!"

"Yes, father."

"Be so good as to put these books back as they were,
first thing in the morning."

Louise helped but her help consisted in handing me
each book as I feverishly tried to remember where it had
been.

"He likes them arranged according to subjects," I
explained.

Louise sighed, quite at a loss.

"That's better," father said. "If you're going to spend
all your time with your sister, Hester, at least have the
goodness to keep her out of the shop. I positively will not
have her there. There's no need for either of you to come

58

down, for that matter. You have the rest of the house at your disposal."

Consequently he and Louise seldom met except at meals, which at our house had always been silent events. But father's injustice rankled with me if not with Louise. Like me she was afraid of him, but she never complained.

Once, briefly, I had the pleasure of seeing her really happy. We were rummaging in the back attic for an old chair we both remembered: a low sewing chair. With a new cover it would be useful in Louise's room. I went ahead up the twisting stair and was immediately distracted from all thoughts of the chair by the sight of Dash, the rocking horse. Half-smothered by an avalanche of ragbags and dust sheets, he had gone on galloping — though motionless — all through the years of neglect, eyes glaring, fiery nostrils dilated, as they had been when Julian and I rode him from the battlefield at Waterloo. He had later survived the Charge of the Light Brigade. Once, with suitable meekness and a humility not easy for him to assume, Julian had even ridden him into Jerusalem while I spread palms before his feet, all the more energetically for not being sure what palms were. And Louise? I felt sure now that of all our games she must have been the inspiration and centre piece: only, having made elaborate plans to rescue her, the fair damsel in distress, in carrying them out, had we forgotten her? Why, when she was in so many ways unique, had she been so easy to forget?

"Oh, look, Hester."

This time the little break in her voice was one of touching joy.

"Yes," I said. "He's still here. Dear old Dash."

I looked round to find Louise holding the counting frame with a smile of tenderness I had not seen before. Indeed she clung to it and when we had found the chair and she had carefully replaced the things we had moved, tidiness in the attic being out of the question even for Louise, she took the frame to her room and cleaned it thoroughly.

"It was always your favourite!" I remembered her

59

sitting on a stool, sliding the balls along the strings and counting raptly. "Why did you like it?"

To me it had been and was still a tedious contrivance.

Louise fingered a blue bead and then a yellow one.

"I don't know," she said wistfully. "It made me happy. I knew exactly what to do and there was always the same number of beads on the string."

She was happy, then, when there were no decisions to be made and no surprises. It was the same with her music. I had given up playing long ago, keeping in practice only with hymns, which would some day be useful, indeed essential, for a clergyman's wife. My taste was for difficult grand pieces far beyond my powers of execution. My failures discouraged me. Louise on the other hand had a small repertoire of simple tunes. She played them with absolute correctness several times a day, earnestly practising what she had long ago mastered and never varying the performance in the slightest degree. "I shall not see the snowdrops" was one I recall, and "The day of the victory was drawing to a close."

She played them in the evening too until I realised that in a short time she would drive father to distraction. He did not protest. Young ladies must play the piano and where else but in their father's parlour? But he leaned back in his chair, his eyes closed in such a ferocity of patient endurance that I trembled for Louise as she sat innocently between the pink candle-shades, conscientiously pressing and releasing the pedal with her small foot. She never sang. The sentiments did not interest her, only the order of the notes.

"Can you prevail on Louise to play her tunes during the day when I'm working?" Father had followed me to the door of my room. "I don't hear them downstairs. Otherwise I shall have to spend my evenings in the shop as well. If I hear 'Why do summer roses fade' once more, I swear to you, Hester, I shall sell the piano."

"Why yes, of course," Louise said when I tactfully passed on the message. "I can play in the afternoons. There are so many other things to do in the evening. Quiet things."

She sat in the corner by the book-case behind father's back with her own lamp and table so that he must often have forgotten that she was there as she painstakingly decorated a wooden box with polished cowrie shells. She had brought a great bag of them from Blairgouroch. Once I held one of the bigger shells to my ear.

"Listen, Louise. You can hear the sea."

I held it out to her.

"No, no. I don't want to." She pushed my hand away, smiling, but her distress was real. The sea was too big: it was immeasurable. She had hated the sound of it; or feared it. Hatred was beyond her emotional compass.

But she was not beyond the range of a storm or two. A few days before the Musical Evening, catching sight of the invitation card on the mantel-piece, I made an interesting and not too welcome discovery.

"The invitation is for you, Louise."

She looked startled.

"You see. It says 'Miss Mallow'. I'm only Miss Hester. Now that you've come home, as the elder daughter, you must go."

I grew quite solemn about it, glorying in the tremendous sacrifice. To be capable of such unselfishness: was not that rather unusual? It suited my mood at that time to yield to Louise whenever possible. I had even missed two visits to Buckingham Street rather than leave her alone. She made so few demands. She had suffered, been lonely. She must go in my place and take up her rightful position in Wickborough. Her appearance would cause a sensation. Already I basked in reflected glory though I would not be there to see it.

Enthusiasm clouded my judgment, not for the first time.

"Have you something suitable to wear?"

"Do you really think I must go? Oh yes, several things."

We looked at her dresses: a white tarlatan: a lilac silk under grey muslin: a cool blue with white roses worked in silk: all of them simple but with an expensive elegance that gave me a new insight into the social life below stairs at Blairgouroch. Had Louise worn them in Mrs Maple's room of an evening? No, not these though Mrs Maple had liked her to dress well and occasionally there were dances.

"I suppose Mrs Duncan and the other ladies gave you their things sometimes."

Louise was checking the number of buttons on the body of the white tarlatan and did not reply.

The lilac silk had taken my fancy. I urged her to try it on. She had reluctantly unhooked her skirt when Mrs Wragge came puffing up the stairs.

"The master's wanting you, Miss Hester."

Seizing the opportunity, I sped purposefully down the various flights and with a confidence I rarely showed in father's presence, burst into the parlour.

"Father, did you realise? It's Louise who must go to the Musical Evening. Look. It says 'Miss Mallow'. I'm helping her to decide on her dress."

He had been looking pale and tired. Now he flushed with anger, snatched the card from my hand and dashed it into the hearth.

"Have you taken leave of your senses? Isn't it bad enough to see you dancing attendance on Louise every minute of the day? How dare you make decisions for me?"

The wrath I had always dreaded and never experienced broke upon me now when my intentions had been of the purest. It was unjust, unreasonable.

"You aren't fair to Louise."

How did I dare to say it?

"Perhaps not." He was suddenly calm again. "It isn't like you, Hester, to reproach me."

The outburst of temper had wearied him. He seemed to me almost an old man. He leaned forward, one arm on the back of the sofa. His black alpaca jacket had long since faded into green and had taken on with the years the same curve as his shoulders, as if it too had developed a stoop from ceaselessly bending over clocks and watches. His beard was as much grey as brown. Once again I had the impression that my father had come out from behind the shelter of his spectacles and appeared as a stranger.

Whether the change was for better or worse, I didn't stop to consider. The sheer injustice of his attitude to Louise disgusted me.

"But if I schooled myself to treat Louise as a good father should," he said slowly, "it would make no difference. No difference at all."

There. He had admitted that he was not a good father. Why should he have to school himself to treat her kindly? It was the easiest thing in the world to be kind to Louise. I left him staring down gloomily at her fresh cushion covers and flounced upstairs.

Louise was sitting in her petticoat on the edge of her bed, looking so forlorn, so beautifully forlorn, that I almost wept.

"He says I'm to go to the Musical Evening."

"Then I'll put on my skirt again. Two of the hooks needed stitching, as it happened."

She expressed no disappointment. I thought it noble of her; and she helped me to dress for the reception without showing a trace of the envy she must surely have been feeling. I felt none of the usual excitement. My resentment towards father had grown no less when we met in the parlour to wait for the carriage. Louise was buttoning my gloves. Father had had his beard trimmed and looked imposing in his evening clothes, but glum.

It was a symptom of my state of mind that I had forgotten the problem of a necklace. Father solved it by holding out the coral pendant.

"You didn't like any of them, Hester?"

"I'm sorry, father. I forgot."

"No matter. This will do, I think," and he added with a touch of bitterness, "since we have nothing better."

Louise put it on for me and adjusted the chain so that the pendant lay in the dead centre of my bosom. She had already spent a full hour on my chignon. Now she adjusted a strand of hair and handed me my fan, one of her own, of ivory and ostrich feathers. Father's eyes sharpened with interest when he saw it but he said nothing.

We heard the carriage coming, and at the same time a

knock at the door. Mrs Wragge had been waiting downstairs to let us out.

"They're just leaving, Mr Windross, sir, the master and Miss Hester."

"I shan't keep them a minute."

The colour must have come to my face. Julian would see me looking at my very best. Father went down. I heard them speak as they passed on the stairs. I stood in the doorway in my muslin and apricot taffeta, my coral and gold, my velvet ribbons and lilies of the valley, and though he could not see them, my white silk stockings.

Did he *see* me at all?

"Hester! I hoped to catch you before you left. Where have you been?" He hugged me as he had done many a time since we were little.

"You've seen the bishop?"

I straightened my lilies.

"He's a marvellous old gentleman. We talked about the dissertation for a solid half hour. He will accept me for ordination when the time comes. My character and academic record, it seems," he said with an attempt at modesty, "have not met with disapproval. Now we can really make plans."

My fan fell to the floor as he seized both my hands. We looked at each other rapturously, sharing a vision of the future as we had shared so many and so much. In my case, from a delightful confusion of images emerged a clear picture of the little parsonage at St Mary-on-Audley, its stone nymph now bathing in a rosy light.

"Are you ready, Hester?"

"Yes, father. I must go, Julian. But I was forgetting. You haven't seen her yet."

"Louise?" Julian's voice expressed polite interest.

I turned back into the parlour, my hand on his sleeve. No premonition came to me of any shadow deeper than the soft dusk at the window and in the corners where lamplight could not reach; no warning of an anguish as sharp as any the old room can ever have enclosed. Louise was sitting quietly by the fire in her plain grey dress.

Having forgotten her for a few minutes, I saw her again with a new, breath-taking awareness of her beauty.

"Louise!"

I knew from the change in Julian's voice that he had seen it too; that this was something else we were to share. I knew from the way he looked at Louise, his face transfigured, that he had never in all his life looked at me. Because I loved him and understood him better than I understood myself, I knew with a terrible sense of desolation that I had lost him.

7

I HAVE NO recollection of the Musical Evening. It passed, the first of many evenings, in misery so intense that no influence from the outer world could reach me. The loneliness was complete, the change of direction so cruelly sudden that I almost foundered. The years ahead and the years behind were equally lost to me. It was as if both past and future had been snatched away in the same moment. There was no consolation to be found in either hope or memory.

The sight of Julian transformed had taught me in an instant the difference between affection and love. I had completely misunderstood our relationship. My role had been that of confidante, comrade, companion: no more. The future I had helped him to plan had been his, not mine.

Since there was no cure for it, I endured the pain. The suffering was constant. It lasted so long that I find it difficult to recall the sharp agony of its onset. It is always so with pain. The happiness of those earlier days is easier to recall: those earlier days being the time before Louise came home.

Yet mercifully even in the depths of my grief, I never blamed her. There was no credit to me in this. She could not help it any more than I could, or Julian. If I felt, in my finery, overdressed and coarse compared with Louise, that was no discredit to me either. Compared with Louise, everyone looked coarse and overdressed. Her extraordinary appearance was simply a fact in our joint history. She was so lovely and innocent of any ill-will that it was some time before I perceived yet another advantage she had over me. She was good at accepting facts. They enclosed her horizon, cutting off her view of anything so intangible as my feelings.

"You may keep it, Hester," she said when I went to her room next morning and silently laid the fan on the bed. "I have three others and it looked well with your dress."

"No, thank you. It's a little too grand for Wickborough." There was no need to tell her that I had bundled my dress into an ottoman with the intention of leaving it there for the rest of my life. To speak at all was a painful effort. Only a self-torturing impulse could have made me ask stiffly, "How did you spend the evening?"

"I finished the other side of my box. I'm wondering" — her husky voice and the soft droop of her mouth expressed a tragic anxiety — "if I shall be short of the larger shells."

"Did Julian stay long?"

"He left at nine so he must have been here for an hour and a quarter," Louise said accurately and added, "It seemed a long time."

"He always liked to talk."

With a revival of pain I heard myself speak of him as of someone I had known long ago.

"I don't think he talked much. If you don't want the fan, I'll put it away."

She produced a sheet of silver paper and reduced the unmanageable ostrich feathers to a neat parcel.

I went and threw my lilies in the dust-bin. Thomas had come home and was eating a late breakfast in the kitchen. He looked brown and well after his ten days by the sea.

"You should have seen Miss Hester in all her glory

last night," Mrs Wragge said. "She looked like the lady of the manor in her silks and glad rags."

"There's no need of silks and glad rags to make Miss Hester look like the lady of the manor," Thomas said gallantly. "But a holiday at the sea would suit you, Miss Hester, and bring back the colour to your cheeks."

It hurt my pride to seem lackadaisical. I exerted myself and told him what had happened to his butterfly brooch.

"I understand that young fellow has come into a snug little sum of money from his grandmother," Thomas said. "It won't last long. He's a philanderer so far as I can make out. Off with the old and on with the new in no more than a fortnight! There'll be no settling him until he comes in for a wedding ring and even then . . ."

I found the topic suddenly distasteful. Thomas may have noticed my downcast manner. He talked about the whaling ship he had seen come into harbour and described the gulls and the fisher girls gutting herring on the quay. I thought of myself at the prow of an ocean-going vessel putting out to sea, alone with the swooping sea-birds. My life now would be lonely. I summoned all my strength to face it. Others had been lonely. Half-listening to Thomas, I played with my ring, pulled it off and read the message. "Remember me." He had been lonely too.

I got up abruptly, interrupting Thomas in the middle of a sentence. He and Mrs Wragge exchanged looks. "Excuse me," I said and went out down the alley to the river. The banks were wooded on this eastern side of the bridge. From a seat by the footpath I watched a swan and cygnets among the reeds of the opposite bank and through the arches saw the tumble-down warehouses sway in the water with a deceptive charm. There a man had come to his bitter end. In the warm air of morning when the Audley was blue and green from reflected sky and trees, it was possible to think of him calmly. The sympathy and fear he had aroused in me had never quite been reconciled, but sympathy prevailed and with it something else: a perception that for all he had suffered there could be more that he had escaped: that to become one with the river might not be the worst thing that could

67

have happened to him. There was actually relief to be found in thinking of him instead of Julian.

The relief was shortlived. Almost at once Julian appeared. He sat down beside me without speaking but I was too well used to his moods to miss the smouldering enthusiasm he was trying not to show. He would speak of something else first.

"Yes," he said when we had stared silently at the swans for a minute. "Considering it's the cruellest river on earth, the Audley is extraordinarily beautiful."

"How is it cruel? You mean — dangerous?"

"Very. There are deep cavities and peculiar rock shapes in that stretch below the weir . . ."

"Is that why they never find people when they — fall in?"

"Mm. I expect so. They never do recover the body." The words were casual. He was not unfeeling, only pre-occupied and innocent, never having seen a man dragged down by one of those hungry currents or heard the smack of water on stone when he was gone. "Rum thing, Louise coming home after all this time."

"It was unexpected."

"There's something I can't understand about your father. It hadn't occurred to me before. As a matter of fact I'd forgotten all about Louise." He laughed at so unbelievable a lapse of memory, then frowned, trying to look detached and judicial. "Wasn't it odd that he should send her away to earn her own living? What on earth was he thinking about? To make a lady's maid of her? Can you believe it? When I saw her . . ."

"Father paid Mrs Maple for looking after Louise." Except from a sense of loyalty to the family, I had no wish to defend him. Besides, Julian had good reason to know that father was not mean. "She was to learn how to do things properly."

"Well, when you put it like that perhaps it wasn't such a bad idea."

"She really is an excellent housekeeper."

With this small act of martyrdom I got up, unable to bear the change in him any longer.

"Mother made a particular point that you should bring Louise on Sunday."

His attempt at speaking casually was a hopeless failure.

"Thank you. I'm sure she'd like to come."

He took a deep breath. His eyes were bright with the imaginative fervour that had never failed to kindle mine.

"What a morning! Has it ever struck you, Hester, how wonderful it all is?"

"What?"

"Oh, I don't know. The unexpected way things happen, like a sheet of lightning. In a flash the world changes. You realise all at once that you were waiting for something. Then it comes. You discover in yourself a completely new identity." He developed the idea. "So many facets of oneself . . . all of them fragmentary. Then suddenly, there it is, the central core, the real self, the end of the waiting . . . and every mortal thing," he dropped his voice in reverence, "is wonderful. The river, the swans, Burton's rotten old boat down there."

"The Abbey?"

It soared above us, breasting the air. With sailing clouds behind, it was the Abbey that seemed to move. I turned and saw it again in the river, rippling among reflected leaves.

"Yes, the Abbey. Rather." Julian spoke absently and I felt a sudden apprehension. Was it possible that Louise, frail and indifferent, could influence him more strongly than all that splendid edifice of enduring stone?

"Should you not be at a lecture?"

"Yes. One solid hour of Hebrew. An utter waste of time! Still, I'd better go. Sunday then? Unless — You're busy in the evenings, I suppose."

"Yes, and so are you."

"Well, I could slip out for an hour or two, just to call."

He waited to be invited. Then when I said nothing, he pulled my hair and rushed up the alley to the Close.

For Mrs Windross's sake I felt obliged to resume the old routine. Visits to Buckingham Street became an ordeal. There cannot have been many of them but while they lasted the weeks seemed to consist entirely of Wednesdays and Sundays, so keenly did I dread their coming. Louise gave no sign of either enjoying or disliking them. On the first Sunday she walked with Mrs Windross. Julian and I followed, feeling on my part at least, a new constraint. Even Julian's eloquent flights grew shorter and his silences longer, filled no doubt with thoughts of Louise.

Mrs Windross was plainly troubled. In my anxiety to ward off any kind of confidential talk, I became awkward and tongue-tied with her too.

"Is Louise to stay indefinitely in Wickborough?" she asked once when we were all four walking to St Mary-on-Audley.

"I believe so."

The weather was delightful; the banks were alive with birds, the meadows deep in cowslips. Her eyes like mine were fixed on Louise's slender figure in its plain blue and white cambric dress as she walked ahead with Julian.

"Do you think, Hester dear," Mrs Windross spoke hesitantly, "that you could drop a hint to Julian about his studies?"

"What do you mean, Mrs Windross?"

"I mean that he's not studying at all." Having raised the subject she became agitated. "He's simply not working. I'm dreadfully afraid that after all these years he's going to spoil things."

I reassured her. He had worked hard. A few weeks of neglect could surely not ruin his prospects.

"But his examination is in no more than a month. If he wasn't my own boy I'd say he'd gone out of his mind." Tears rolled down her cheeks. "I must say it, Hester, and you're the only one I can talk to. You know what it is. It's Louise. He can't think of anything else. Do you know — I hardly like to ask — does she encourage him?"

"There's no need."

"Oh, I know that. She's as lovely as a picture. I'd forgotten, you know. She was a pretty, quiet child but she'd gone right out of my mind. But what I meant was, does she want him? There seems a coldness in her." Mrs Windross looked at me hopefully. "Now then. They've

70

stopped on the bridge. I don't want them to see me like this." She mopped her eyes. "You talk to them, dear, and I'll hurry on."

I walked to the far end of the bridge. There was just room in the embrasure for Julian and Louise. The birches had come into leaf. Through their long branches I caught a glimpse of the nymph standing desolate in the shade. In the border forget-me-nots were fading.

"There it is, Hester," Julian said. "We've often looked at it, Louise, and thought it the perfect place to live."

"It will be damp." Louise looked anxiously at a spider caught in the fringe of her sunshade. "So close to the water. Julian, could you please...?" Julian removed the spider. "And there are no other houses or shops, only the church."

"Isn't that the most important thing for a parson?" Julian laughed but he looked depressed.

"For a parson, I dare say."

Louise went on. For once Julian let her go.

"Would you say, Hester, that Louise had a prejudice against the Church? As a way of life, of course, I mean."

"I don't think so."

"She hasn't said anything to you?"

"No. Julian, you must give your mind to your examination and do well. Your mother will be dreadfully disappointed if you don't and so will I."

"She's told you I'm not working. It's true. I can't tie myself down to all that dead, arid stuff. It's lost all meaning for me, if it ever had any."

"Of course it had meaning for you and it's the only way to get what you want."

"No, believe me." He looked quite wild, I thought. "What I want is something altogether different." He put his arm round me. "Don't worry, Hester. I won't disappoint you after all the help you've given me. Remember, you used to hear me recite Virgil in the old days and great chunks of Church history? You've always been like a sister to me; and that's another reason for rejoicing at the way things have turned out. I mean you really would be my sister, Hester love. Tell me — no, don't

71

just try to bolster me up — tell me honestly. Do you think she'll have me? Louise."

He stood upright, modestly pretending to brace himself for an unpleasant 'No' but expecting, I knew, a whole-hearted 'Yes, Julian, I do.' In his expansive moods his confidence was boundless. He had never doubted the successful outcome of any of his schemes; nor had I until now; and even now — I looked up at him, tall, well-featured, open-hearted, clever, and looked away. Who could resist him?

"There it is! Look! Under the alders there. That's a good omen, isn't it? Good heavens, Hester, you're surely not crying because you missed the kingfisher!"

His sudden concern cut me to the quick.

"I'm tired," I said.

We caught up with the others by the first cottage. Mrs Windross had just gone inside. Louise stood by the gate with her back to us. I had recently made an interesting discovery about her or rather about her looks; and the very fact that I had so soon learned to separate Louise from her looks was significant. But what I had actually observed was that it was only in her presence that one felt the spell of her beauty. If she went into the next room, one forgot it; or so it was with me. With others it may have been different. In any case, the continual re-discovery of it brought each time a new enchantment.

She turned. Under the pale sunshade only her eyes and lips had colour; but the lines of her cheeks and mouth were so soft, her whole aspect so delicate and harmonious that again I almost caught a glimpse of some region of the spirit which Louise for a moment made attainable. It was a region altogether beyond Louise herself. That, I was beginning to discover, was a problem: the extent to which things were beyond Louise.

Without being invited, Julian called on three evenings in the following week. Father roused himself to talk politics. With a certain relentlessness he denounced the Turkish atrocities in Bulgaria. I sewed and listened. At her own little table, encircled with light from her own lamp, Louise stuck shells on her box with mouse-like self-effacement. She and Julian were never alone. At nine o'clock he left, looking excited and harassed. When his examination was mentioned, the harassed look became one of agitation and one evening he left before the clock struck, saying desperately that he must get back to work.

"He's going to make a mess of things." Father grimly unfolded his newspaper and having taken a little time to find the right column, stared at it unflinchingly until bed-time.

"It's such a relief." Louise's eyes uplifted in the lamp-light, were misty with quiet joy. "There will be exactly the right number of shells. Only two left over and I can find room for them on the lid."

Was she too self-contained to speak of her feelings? Ideas and emotions had not figured, I think, in Mrs Maple's conversation. It was as if Louise had no vocabulary to express them so that I began to wonder whether, in fact, she had ideas and emotions.

But during the next week or two I felt increasingly sorry for her and exasperated with Julian. It was surely tasteless and even ill-mannered of him to call almost every day and at odd times, whenever he could slip away either officially or unofficially. He must often have flouted the regulations, which were strict: St Aidan's was, after all, a theological college. His slackness and unpunctuality could only be harmful to his prospects as an ordinand. I began to dread the sight of him fluttering down Silvergate in his academic gown like an unwelcome crow. It was at that time that he began to lapse into the untidiness that grew on him distressingly: the very last thing to endear him to Louise.

When she was not in her room Louise spent a good deal of time at the parlour window, that is to say, not actually in it but behind the curtain, where she could look out without being seen. Even so, Julian was often upon us before she could retreat. She had a curious way of looking at him (it must have been discouraging to a lover) as if he were miles away, almost out of sight. Rousing herself to the need to make some remark after minutes of silence, she would look at him without recognition. It was not deliberate coldness. Louise was incapable of any kind of affectation or subtlety. She had, goodness knows, never needed to adapt her behaviour with an eye to its effect on others, that effect having been invariably one of instant enslavement. It was puzzling then to account for her constant vigilance. It was becoming a habit. Even when he left, she went at once to the window apparently to watch him out of sight.

Julian appeared not to notice the coolness of his reception. He exerted himself to be pleasant and amusing, like an eccentric entertainer performing to empty stalls where the audience should have been. Then he would glance across at me and I would see how hollow-eyed he had become: how lost. The word when at last I hit on it was so appropriate that I felt afraid for him.

"It's clear enough, Hester," he found an opportunity of saying one evening when Louise went to fetch a skein of silk, "that she has no objection to me personally. I don't think I'm such bad company."

Such a mixture of anxiety and conceit seemed to me both pathetic and absurd.

"We don't really want your company at all," I said. "You could put it to better use at St Aidan's."

"My idea," he said, taking no notice, "is to make myself indispensable to her and then — It's no use talking vaguely. That wouldn't appeal to Louise. I know her quite well by this time. My plan is to show her how strong my feelings are by giving a tremendously practical proof of them."

"Julian!" My sharpness startled him. "You mustn't think of giving up the Church for Louise. Do you hear? It would be madness. If you ask me, you've gone temporarily out of your mind."

My harangue — for I said a good deal more — relieved my feelings, whatever its effect on him. He did at least appear to be listening. Then I drew breath for the last fateful sentence. It undid any good I might otherwise have done him.

"Besides, how can you be sure that if you gave up the Church, Louise would marry you?"

To my dismay I saw in his eyes the gleam that always heralded one of his more extravagant schemes. As a result of just such a gleam we had once fasted for three days to show our contempt for the flesh and had made ourselves ill.

"There's only one way," he said, "of being absolutely sure."

Louise came back. He talked of other things but he was obviously hatching some ill-conceived plan. I was irritated enough to feel resentfully that his plans had always been ill-conceived and to despise myself for ever having had any part in them.

But in all this time he found no opportunity of speaking to Louise alone. The agony was prolonged for all three of us. Father attacked the Turks with growing hostility and seemed oblivious of the suffering in his own parlour. For my own part, the feeling of impending crisis came from the hourly expectation that Julian would make his proposal of marriage. We all knew that it was inevitable.

"They're so unsuited to each other," Mrs Windross wept. She was always weeping at that time. "He's lost all sense of direction. If only she had stayed away! Oh, it isn't her fault. Of course she'll accept him. I shall have her for a daughter-in-law when I so very much wanted — Well, I took it for granted . . . I must day, Hester dear," she dried her eyes once more, "I think you're wonderful. He must be blind."

The choice of word was wildly unsuitable as we both knew.

"Perhaps you wouldn't mind, Mrs Windross, if I didn't come on Sunday?"

"Oh, don't, pray don't leave me alone with them." She melted into tears again. "I find her so difficult to talk to."

"Julian will talk to Louise."

"It's selfish of me, Hester. You have your feelings too. You've always been like one of my own and I don't know what I should do — shall do without you."

"We'll always be friends."

A headache, then, kept me from church on Sunday. Unfortunately for Julian it had the same effect on Louise.

"I shan't go without you."

She sat quietly by my bed and from time to time laid a handkerchief soaked in cologne on my forehead. In such a circumstance she knew exactly what to do. Mrs Maple had suffered from headaches.

I was wondering how to escape from my self-inflicted imprisonment when Mrs Wragge crept in to say that Mr Windross had called to see Miss Mallow.

"It's Julian." Louise stood for a full minute by my bed, waiting I dare say, for a word of advice or encouragement or even discouragement. I buried my bogus headache in the pillow.

"Tell Mr Windross my sister is not well." Into Louise's voice came a faraway echo of Mrs Duncan's. "And I am not at home."

I spent the whole endless day in my room. It was twilight when, having bathed my face and dressed, I went into the parlour. Louise was at the window. The side casement stood open. Half hidden by the curtain, she was peeping nervously into the street. Her attitude and manner were familiar. I recognised them — the recognition was strangely un-nerving — as my own. In just such a surreptitious way had I too looked out, expecting to see the tall figure of a man on the opposite pavement.

Our experiences could have nothing else in common. In Louise's case it must be Julian she dreaded to see. There could be no one else. Moreover if she was so very anxious to avoid him, there could be no danger of her accepting his proposal when at last it came. The thought should have been comforting. But with a chilling sense of fatality I recalled how my own adventure had ended. If I had been sufficiently detached, if I had been far-seeing enough to be capable of such a prayer, I would have prayed that Louise's adventure might have an altogether different sort of ending.

She turned back into the room, looking as I must have looked on those previous occasions: disturbed: and more than that. Had my face ever worn that look of intense and painful preoccupation, the expression of a mind attuned to other factors than those to be seen in the homely room? I surprised in myself a feeling of sadness. It was sad to see her behaving like a creature of shadows. She was meant for sunshine and admiration.

"It's all right, Louise. He won't come this evening."

She started, drew a great shuddering breath and covered her face with her hands. It amazed me that Julian should trouble her so deeply. She had never shown the smallest interest in him; had scarcely seemed to notice him.

"It's Sunday, remember. He will stay at St Aidan's this evening." I put the kettle on the fire and unlocked the caddy. "A cup of tea will do us good."

"Let's take it up to my room, Hester. Please."

She carried the tray, I the candlestick. Setting it down on the chest of drawers, I noticed a lighter square on the wallpaper above.

"You've moved one of the pictures." I recollected that the Sunderland ware plaque had hung there: a ship, a garland of flowers and in the centre the simple statement: 'The Lord sees thee'. "Where have you put it?"

"In the drawer."

"I used to find it comforting when I came up here to look for something. It made me feel safe. Didn't you like it?"

"Oh, no." Louise shivered. "I can't bear the thought of being watched."

She seated herself in the rocking chair and poured out tea. Reluctantly I sat down at the other side of the pretty, empty little grate. The day had seemed never ending. The same touch of abnormality was to infect the evening. We spent it there in the attic where it was impossible to look out — or in: perched together, alone, like birds in an eyrie, cut off from the world.

Louise was never talkative and gradually as night blotted out the blue dusk beyond the skylight and the single pane became a dark mirror reflecting our candle flame, we lapsed into silence. In this secluded situation it was irrational to feel — as I increasingly did — exposed. Just because they were invisible, I was aware of the chimneys pointing up and the roofs sloping sharply down with the energy of living things close at hand. Whether from the influence of Louise's unaccountable dislike of being watched, or from the memory of the Sunderland text, I was afflicted with an uneasy sense of something watchful outside; some formless, watchful intelligence welling up from the deep river-bed, flooding the cavernous recesses under the jettied houses and shops of Silvergate and brooding in the angles between slates and chimneys. One could never escape it, I thought, with the sensation of being looked for and found; and not only found but searched into and known — and stayed with and never left. But by whom?

One thing was certain. It was no use asking Louise. She was making ribbon bows to sew on the four corners of a muslin pin-cushion, bows of identical size and shape. The candlelight, so cruelly disposed to seek out unlovely hollows and pouches in the face, found no imperfection in Louise as she gave her whole attention to the blue ribbon bows.

8

LOUISE'S REFUSAL TO receive Julian on that Sunday afternoon failed to discourage him. The rebuff was too gentle. He was too hopelessly adrift to notice it. It was early the next evening, if my memory serves, that he called again, looking as if he had not slept for several nights. I knew the symptoms. I too had grown used to lying awake.

This time he had come to tell us that he and his mother would be out of town for a few days. Mrs Windross's sister who lived on an isolated farm ten or twelve miles away had contracted a sudden illness. They were to leave in an hour or two. I had the impression that the hired carriage was already waiting at their door. Nevertheless Julian stayed, talking disjointedly until father reminded him of the perils of driving on country roads in the dark, whereupon, as if we were parting for years, he shook hands all round, holding Louise's until she was obliged to withdraw it, then ran downstairs, his pockets bulging with the books he would be too light-headed to read.

Relieved of his nerve-racking presence, we remained subdued. Louise's silence was so profound as scarcely to be accounted for even by the intricate design in which she was sticking pins into her pin-cushion. Sure enough, as we said goodnight, she laid her cheek against mine and whispered:

"Do you think father would let me go away?"

"But you wanted to come home?"

"Only because there was nowhere else to go."

"You'll grow used to Wickborough again, Louise dear. It's all so different from Blairgouroch and you've only just come."

"I've been here fifty-two days."

I would have smiled: it was so like her to know the precise number of days — but her face was strained with a touching look of anxiety. Not that she lost a fraction of her beauty by it. The tension simply emphasised the delicate chiselling of her features.

"You couldn't live among strangers. You must stay here with your own family." I spoke soothingly as to a child.

"I wish someone would tell me what to do."

With her candle raised, she might have been conjuring up the departed spirit of Mrs Maple. I wished that unfailing source of wisdom could have been spared to us for another decade or two! I was not qualified to take her place, especially in solving Louise's immediate problem. It would have been kind and sisterly if I had said, "Julian will look after you. He wants to." Louise looked so pathetically in need of protection that I might actually have said it, had she not suddenly exclaimed:

"Listen!"

We were standing on the narrow landing. Behind Louise her own stairs curved up into the dark. Behind me a succession of half flights led down to the basement, so

79

that we seemed just then to be nowhere at all: plucked out of space; but not out of time.

"You can hear them right up here."

I had long since ceased to hear them but now I listened and heard them again: wall clocks, bracket, lantern, mantel and carriage clocks and our own long-case clock on the floor below.

"There are so many of them and father is always mending them and making more. What's the use of mending all those clocks?"

"But surely nothing could possibly be more useful and necessary than a clock . . ."

I stopped, feeling the absurdity of a remark so obvious; and yet something had been required, some response to what I recognised in Louise's manner as a trembling despair. I tried again.

"After all, Louise dear, they're only measuring time."

"I used to sit on the stairs and try to count the ticks. It came to hundreds and hundreds and then I would start on another clock. There was no end to it, no answer. Once I fell asleep there in the curve of the stairs where you can lean against the wall and when I woke and heard them still ticking, I could hardly bear it. It was dark and the air was full of clocks. I used to think they had something to tell, some frightful thing; and it's worse than ever now that there's this feeling of waiting . . ."

We listened. Sure enough there did seem a heartlessness, or was it a hopelessness in the compulsive ticking, an alarming urgency as if even the ticking could not go on for ever but was leading up to some change, some huge explosion of events disjointing the earth. The disturbing fancy was powerful enough to shake my hold on reality so that the commonplace sound of someone walking down the street seemed ominous; and yet, on reflection, the sound was not commonplace. Silvergate at ten o'clock at night was generally as silent as the grave. Those were a man's feet taking long strides down the street to the river but without haste, as if — at the horrifying thought my flesh crept — he had all the time in the world and more: as if he had all eternity in which to walk.

Louise had heard him too. The street and the river below could not have for her the sinister associations they had for me. We had come to this speechless, candle-lit moment from different directions: and yet I had never felt more strongly that we were sisters as we stood side by side in the same attitude of rigid attention and — there was no doubt about it — in the same mood. I had communicated to her my fear. Whatever heritage of blood and tissue and nerve we shared, it roused in each of us simultaneously an identical response. So I thought, with a thrill of awe no less intense for being what I now know it to have been, the outcome of a delusion.

It seemed to me then that the corruption lay in me. Tainted with secrecy and guilt, I had infected Louise and with the delicacy of innocence, she was the more severely affected. For no sooner had I recognised our feeling as identical than I felt a difference. Though nothing would have induced me to go to a window and look out, I could still acknowledge my fancies as superstitious nonsense, whereas Louise ... She no longer trembled. It was as if the flow of her blood had been arrested by catalepsy. I actually felt in my own body the change in hers, with the same sense of a spirit taking flight as if she had suddenly been frozen to death at my side: an experience so startling and strange that I momentarily forgot the cause of it. It was as a gesture of rescue, as if I had unexpectedly found Louise in a situation of acute peril, that I took her cold hand.

"It's a workman going home, or a policeman. There's nothing to be afraid of."

I said it to comfort her and was at once aware of having blundered. I must have sounded tactless and patronising. It was ridiculous to suppose that Louise could be upset by the sound of footsteps on the cobbles. My own nervousness had distorted my judgment and even my senses. I would be seeing apparitions if I went on in this fashion.

Louise sighed and went up to her attic. There at least she was out of reach of the clocks or any disturbing sound; but then in a sense she was always out of reach. Indeed, the feeling that Louise inhabited a sphere remote from the rest of us was confirmed the very next day by a peculiar scene which had its effect even on father.

He had come upstairs some time in the late afternoon for a letter he had mislaid. Somehow since Louise's arrival, I had given up the muffins though Thomas and Mrs Wragge still had theirs. Louise and I ate fingers of toast and thin slices of seed-cake in the true Maple tradition. I was bending over the kettle when father came in and went straight to the writing table. Louise had just cut two exactly equal portions of cake. She put down the knife.

"Father." He half turned, absent-mindedly, from his letters. "I want to ask you a favour."

Father put down the letter rack and faced her. The appealing break in her voice, the misty softness of her eyes, would have melted the hardest heart; and as if these were not enough, with the utmost simplicity but so dramatically that I positively gaped, Louise went down on her knees. I remember how delicate her hands were with the soft lace falling over them as she clasped them in front of her.

"Father, please let me go away."

Her grey skirts had fallen obediently into sculptured folds. Every line of her figure, every curve of her face was beautiful in its appeal. In this posture she seemed more than ever different from other people. My eyes filled with tears. Looking for a similar response in father, I saw that his expression was certainly serious; indeed, grave.

"Where could we send you, Louise?"

He spoke as if she were an item of property difficult to dispose of.

"If she would have me, I could go to Aunt Tamar's. I used to want to go there when I was younger. Please, father, may I? Please, I beg you."

Divided between distress at the prospect of losing her again and the fear that father would be brutal enough to refuse, I waited.

He neither answered nor urged her to get up. With the same simplicity Louise bowed her head and waited too. After a breathless minute I took my eyes from her and saw to my surprise that father's thoughtful gaze was resting, not on Louise, but on me.

"It might be as well for you to go, Louise."

I put my arm round her and drew her to her feet. Father watched dourly.

"Yes, Hester," he said. "It might be a good thing if Louise went to her Aunt Tamar's. What do you think?"

I could only shake my head in doubt.

"The two of you" — father's return to irritability made the atmosphere more normal — "are altogether too much. I'll write to Tamar now."

To my surprise he took out writing paper and dashed off a letter without the smallest hesitation.

"You can post it, Hester."

As I left the room, he said: "You don't change, Louise."

"No, father," Louise said sadly; or perhaps it was the quality of her voice that made the words seem sad. One could never be sure.

"You didn't tell me," I said later, "that you were going to ask father to let you go to Aunt Tamar's."

"I've been thinking of it for a while. I can't bear it here, Hester."

Without her I couldn't bear it either. How dull the house would be when she had gone, leaving the old life in ruins! As we waited for Aunt Tamar's reply, my restlessness grew. I was indoors too much. The house, always a living thing, took on an extra life as if to stifle my flagging spirits. Now that Louise had drawn my attention to them, I could not forget the clocks. They hammered on my nerves. The warm weather drew out the suffocating smells of chimney smoke, and of ancient damp and heavy fabrics. I used to long for darkness when the tradesmen's calls and the rumble of wheels would cease. But when night came I lay awake, and faced my future: a long spinsterhood of plaiting hair into bracelets and keeping house.

One wakeful night I heard them again: the slow footsteps of a passer-by walking in the middle of the cobbled street from the print-seller's to the river; a lonely soul wandering homeless while Wickborough slept. As I lay, stiffly alert in the dark, a shape attached itself to the sound: a form reared up from the feet: a black, slender figure in an unbelted ulster and a narrow-brimmed hat. Could he possibly be there again, still there? Sweating with fear, I reminded myself that he was dead. I heard the first solemn stroke of his death knell as the Abbey clock began to strike the hour.

A policeman or a workman going home late, I told myself sensibly when the tolling notes had died away. But I pulled off the black and gold ring and dropped it like a hot coal into the pastille burner on the chest by my bed. I needed no memento. I would never forget him; and in a very short time a reminder more potent than the ring was put into my hand.

Aunt Tamar's letter came at the end of the week. I think we all three felt anxious as father slit open the envelope.

"You're fortunate, Louise. Your Aunt writes that your visit would be an answer to prayer. That's the way she puts it. Her prayer, I suppose." How could he be so flippant, having seen Louise actually on her knees? Now, without any change of expression, she looked radiant. If Mrs Wragge had seen her, she would have been more than ever convinced that Louise was on the point of departing to a better place, and not Aunt Tamar's. "She has been in poor health for some months and there has been difficulty with servants." Father read from the letter. " 'If Louise could come for a visit, it would be of the greatest help to me. I quite long for it.' "

So it was settled. Louise would pack at once. It was providential that Julian should be away. By the time he came back she would be gone; but the prospect of telling him was more than I could contemplate. It was easier to face father. Summoning all my courage, I went down and found him alone.

"Father," I said nervously. He had already put on his spectacles again and was brooding over Alderman Kebb's watch.

"I have no hair-spring suitable for this," he said

irritably. "It's a Dutch watch masquerading as an English one. See here, a London hallmark on the case, but the movement..." He looked at it with disgust.

"Father."

"What is it?" he asked testily and took off his spectacles.

"I know. You want to go to your Aunt Tamar's too." I nodded.

"You deserve a change. Things have gone badly with you. Do you think that going away with Louise will make them better? Do you want to be with her?"

"Just to go away, father," I said, weeping, "for a little while. To be in the country and..."

"I can't spare you, Hester, but I can't refuse you. The change will do you good and by the time you come back, it may have brought a change of heart too."

His understanding was too much for me. Embarrassed by the tears now flowing too freely, I thanked him and groped my way to the stairs.

"Only...there's the question of my work, father. You said you couldn't spare me."

"I wasn't thinking of your work. The plaiting can be put out as piece-work and should have been long ago. Thomas and I will manage. He's my stay and support, is Thomas."

He was pulling open drawers in search of the piece of mechanism he needed. It made me uneasy to see him in the little used corner beyond Thomas's bench; but I felt no real apprehension. There was nothing whatever to fear. Nevertheless, I grew hot, just as if there were. In such uncomfortable situations, do one's thoughts influence events? Father had pulled open the drawer of old watches and spare parts and was rummaging in its depths.

He stopped. He made no exclamation but a stiffening of his head and shoulders showed that his attention had been arrested; strikingly arrested. He stood quite still.

Instinctively I turned to the staircase to escape.

"Hester!" Surely he could not have found it so easily; and if he had, could not connect it in any way with me. "Come here."

In the dim greenish light his face was colourless. He was deeply moved. Under the circumstances almost any emotion would have surprised me. I was certainly not prepared for sentiment. He held the blue and white enamelled watch, not just with the interest of a craftsman but tenderly.

"It's beautiful," he said, and sighed. "Still beautiful. I've been very much to blame. God knows, I should have learned not to leap to conclusions."

My own train of thought prevented me from following his. Indeed how could I have interpreted his sadness, the loving care with which he rubbed the gold case on his handkerchief, his regretful shake of the head as he pressed open the inner case and saw the broken glass.

But then how could he have understood my feelings: my horrified recoil from this souvenir of the murderous wharf? If only he had known, if only I could have brought myself to tell him, he would never have said:

"I wanted to give you a piece of jewellery, Hester, something worthy of you. Here it is." He had taken a soft-haired brush from his pocket and was delicately dusting the movement. "I thought — It was a sad mistake. Heaven forgive me for it, and yet there was every reason ... I thought it had been — Well, no matter. Somehow or other here it has been all these years. You see, it was meant to hang on a gold châtelaine with enamelled pendants but that's long since gone." He unlocked another drawer, found a heavy gold chain and attached the watch. "I'll repair it for you, of course, but try it on."

"Thank you, father."

It hung like a millstone round my neck. If he had ransacked the chests and storehouses of the entire globe, he could have given me nothing I would have hated more.

"You remember it?"

What could I say? I hesitated. His next remark was so astounding that at first its meaning escaped me altogether.

"How could you remember? This is the Upjohn watch. I bought it as a great bargain in a London sale room in the early days of our courtship, for your mother. It will make me happy to see you wearing it. This was your mother's watch, Hester."

I remember how dark it was; how suddenly the clocks raised their voices to a deafening chorus; how a feeling came to me of the vast complexity and mystery of life, as if the Audley had changed its course and, charged with all its secrets, now flowed through the narrow house. I remember too my swift, astonished realisation that the stranger's connection must have been with my mother. But I do not recall any feeling of surprise that she had kept secrets from my father. In the seven years since her death she too had become a stranger to me.

Father was smiling a little as if the sight of the watch had revived an old ardour. I blessed the instinct that had made me keep the whole incident to myself. If my mother had been false to him or had deceived him in any way, he must never know. His unspectacled eyes were softer and younger. His misunderstanding of the situation made him vulnerable. I felt the first stirring of sympathy for him but the very thing that inspired it prevented me from showing it. Besides, on the brink of parting, it was too late.

9

WE LEFT EARLY the next morning and travelled by railway to Wickborough Junction, thence in an old-fashioned waggonette to Bidewell. From there to Lullerbeck the lanes were too narrow for any large vehicle and the one cab at the Fleece was out on hire. Leaving our luggage at the inn to be called for, we walked the rest of the way.

The afternoon was warm. We took our time, sharing, I think, a mood of detachment such as released prisoners must feel. To stroll between banks of lacy hedge parsley with occasional glimpses of buttercup fields beyond was enough. We neither of us cared when we arrived at Codlin Croft or whether we arrived at all. The one drawback was that out of deference to Aunt Tamar we were both wearing bonnets and had left our parasols at the inn. How we longed for wide-brimmed hats!

"Did you mind when I told you that I was coming too?"

Louise smiled.

"I'm glad, Hester. Just imagine if I had had to walk all this way by myself."

As might have been expected, the smile was charming enough to supply whatever was lacking in the response.

"It really is," she said, "a very long way."

"And yet you seem pleased."

"I'm pleased that it will be so private."

Having spent half the night packing, I was beginning to feel tired and footsore. It was a long time since I had walked so far. A dreamy sensation of having wandered for years between flowering hedgerows made me almost forget where we were going.

"If you hadn't asked father first, I don't believe I would have dared to."

Louise shook one of the four flounces of her grey and white jaconet and released a tuft of thistle-down.

"I knew he couldn't refuse when I went down on my knees."

She spoke with such confidence that I laughed.

"One would think you had done it before."

"And so I had."

"When was that?"

"Before I went away the first time. He gave in then and I felt sure he would again."

Louise never raised her voice but this quiet revelation brought me literally to a standstill.

"But I always thought father sent you away."

"Why should he do that? No. I begged him to let me come to Aunt Tamar's after mother died. Then somehow he heard of Mrs Maple again and I went to her instead."

"You were pleased it turned out like that?"

"Well, otherwise I wouldn't have known Mrs Maple."

Father had had good reason, then, for saying that Louise did not change. What did change was my view of father. I had misjudged him. The thought troubled me, as did Louise's calculating way of speaking of him as if he had no interest for her apart from his capacity for being used.

She had taken the opportunity of our halt to wipe her clouded shoes free of dust on the long grass. In her light dress with its pink shaded ribbons, she seemed so perfectly in harmony with her surroundings that she might have risen, one of summer's fairest growths, from among the ox-eye daisies and silver-tasselled grasses that grew from the high bank. A yellow butterfly alighted on her bodice just below the shoulder.

"It's pinned itself there, like Thomas's brooch."

The similarity was delightful but Louise did not smile. "Thomas's brooch?"

"Thomas Griff. He's taken to making insect brooches. I told you in my last letter."

Louise shook her head.

"I didn't know. You never told me."

She dislodged the butterfly, ready to walk on, but I hesitated, feeling puzzled and again troubled.

"You can't have received the letter. What could have happened to it? It would be at the end of March that I wrote. I told you about Julian's dissertation."

"What about it?"

"Oh, I don't know. The title, and how good it was."

"The letter must have been lost in the post."

I did not protest. Instead I tried to remember when Louise had last written to me. She had not written at Christmas. The discovery that she had gone away by her own wish made a difference. What had seemed the hurt silence of a banished daughter now looked much more like indifference.

We went on. One country lane melted into another without producing a signpost. Occasionally a startled rabbit scuttled across the way, leaving us startled too. Step by step I became more conscious of being alone with Louise, really alone for the first time; and for all the summer fragrance through which we passed, I could not rid my mind of the troublesome fancy that I was going in the wrong direction and should be going back to Wick-borough: home, to father. It was surely ridiculous to feel, between the quiet fields, the hovering presence of danger.

I glanced sidelong at Louise. It dawned on me that I scarcely knew her. Father had never talked about her nor had Mrs Windross, and Mrs Wragge had come to us after Louise left. Thomas had never known her. All I knew of Louise came from my own short experience of her. There could be many things about her I did not know.

But then Louise knew me in much the same limited way, except for my letters. The possibility that she had drawn no conclusions about me and had no wish to do so did not alter the fact that I had secrets from her. For instance, I had not yet told her about the watch. I was reminded of it when she looked at hers and said, "Half past three," in the husky treble that gave a melancholy charm even to the hour.

As father had not had time to repair the watch, I had left it behind and certainly had no wish to burden Louise with its sinister story. Walking through changing green vistas of woodland and pasture, I experienced as many changes of mood. Father began to appear in a different light; to be right where I had thought him wrong. I could also have misjudged my mother. She might simply have lost the watch long ago and been afraid to tell. No one would ever know how it had fallen into the stranger's hands. I could almost have believed that he had been nerving himself to bring it back; but why? That was a problem to be pondered at leisure. Meanwhile I must tell Louise that father had given the watch to me. It would seem an act of favouritism. She, the elder, should have it. On the whole I felt justified in putting the matter aside for a time.

We came at last to a field gate bearing the name 'Codlin Croft'. On the other side, a path led us across a rising field, round the edge of another, and past a group of Scotch firs. There we saw the house among trees just below the ridge. Five minutes' walk brought us to a wicket gate in a low thorn hedge. I remember hesitating, my hand on the latch, and looking back down the long bridle-path which was to prove so memorable a feature of the place. Louise reached across and opened the gate. I followed her up the path between larkspur and mignonette. The door opened.

"Maggie's girls," Aunt Tamar said, and drew us in.

By a natural process of attraction we became part of the place at once. Aunt Tamar and the house itself absorbed us. It is difficult to think of them separately. Some indefinable assurance of welcome waited in the white-panelled hall and in the low-beamed rooms half seen through open doors: in the coolness of stone floors and wistaria-screened windows; in the warmth of Aunt Tamar's greeting. It was a homecoming rather than a visit.

She was a slim little woman with large dark eyes and smooth grey hair under a lace fanchon. She still wore, though in modified form, the crinoline fashionable in her heyday and so moved more easily than we did, dragged down as we were by our heavy petticoats. There was nothing in her manner to suggest that she had been expecting only one of us.

"I hope you don't mind, Aunt Tamar. Father said I might come too for a little while."

"Then you are Hester. I wasn't sure which was which."

She looked from me to Louise, tactfully dividing her attention equally. She must have remembered us from the early days when she had come occasionally to Silvergate.

"It was good of Oscar to spare you both. I shan't want to let you go."

Every detail of that first holiday is still fresh to me: the country smell of the rooms, a smell of pot-pourri and wood smoke: and out of doors the scents of roses and mignonette from a garden rising through flowerbeds to vegetables and beyond the cabbages to rough pasture, gorse and bracken until at last the heather took over on the blue crest of the hill. It was to me that Aunt Tamar came for conversation. She was inclined to over-exertion and easily tired. We sat in the garden a good deal and I read to her; or watched the swallows soar and swoop; or listened to bees murmuring in the Solomon seal. Drifting through the warm afternoons and long twilights, I recovered. The sense of being at peace was heaven-sent but I shall never cease to be grateful to Aunt Tamar for it. Looking back on that interlude of sunny days, I can almost recapture their special quality of luminous contentment, the more precious to me now because it was so shortlived.

Occasionally Louise and I went shopping at Bidewell in the moth-eaten landau which Aunt Tamar had been in the habit of hiring for such outings for many a year. The actual shopping fell to me. It was I who combed the shops to match embroidery silks and sought out the blacksmith or the glazier. Louise preferred to sit in the landau in a shady cul-de-sac off one of Bidewell's streets. (There were only two.) Hurrying back to join her, I had more than once the feeling of returning to a rarer air. Louise had always the ability to impose on her surroundings a suggestion of delicate refinement. The cushions might bulge at the seams. The coachman's caped overcoat, worn as a sign of respectability even in the hottest weather, might be threadbare and even torn, but no one could sneer at the ramshackle equipage with Louise as passenger. It was a pity, I felt, that so few people had the pleasure of seeing her.

Sometimes Aunt Tamar asked me to call at the Fleece where the carrier left parcels. Once or twice I had a fancy to take tea in the riverside garden there but Louise did not respond to the suggestion. She was so quiet and unobtrusive that it would have been ungracious not to let her have her way.

I enjoyed catching glimpses of visitors to the Fleece through the upper half of the glass doors to the dining and smoking rooms. In the summer months the inn attracted a sprinkling of artists who came to sketch the ruined abbey further up the river. But my acquaintance stretched no further than the boot-black, Ned, who also did errands for the carrier: a willing boy who spent his spare time in a sunny nook of the courtyard, engaged in the unlikely occupation of reading. When I first saw him he had a coverless copy of *Burke's Peerage*.

"They were going to throw it out, miss," he told me, scandalised. "You can find out a lot from a big book like this."

On my next visit I gave him a threepenny copy of *Robinson Crusoe* which he enjoyed so much that it became a habit to keep him supplied with reading matter. As soon as I set foot in the Fleece, he used to materialise and hang about hopefully but without ever putting himself forward, so that I became quite fond of him.

Aunt Tamar's servant problem was an unusual one. It was not that the maids left but that she couldn't get rid of them. They stayed until they were so old as to become a burden. Susie had just been eased out of the house and settled, at Aunt Tamar's expense, with a grand-daughter. Lettice, who had stepped into her shoes, was older than her mistress: too old to be bothered with the two young sisters recently taken on to be trained as house and kitchen maids.

In such a situation Louise knew exactly what to do. First thing in the morning she went to the kitchen and laid the foundations of a smooth-running day. Without saying much, she established a routine and left Tilly and Edith gaping in admiration. Small crises did no more than rear their heads and wither at her approach. After two or three days there were no more crises. Louise was able to concentrate on the bead mats she was making, the colours mathematically arranged in perfect rectangles.

"Tilly has the makings of a good maid," Aunt Tamar said. "She's a kind, thoughtful little creature."

"She's careful in her weighing out," Louise said, "and doesn't waste anything."

By their deeds rather than their moral qualities did she know the maids, in so far as she knew them at all. She seemed not to notice Tilly's adoration. At first it amused me to see the poor child slavishly imitating Louise as she moved gracefully about the kitchen. She was sensitive enough to feel and admire Louise's cool detachment; too sensitive to be cool and detached herself.

In Aunt Tamar's household there was no rigid barrier between family and servants. The moods of the kitchen quickly penetrated to the parlour and the spirit of the parlour filtered down to the kitchen. When it was somehow discovered that Tilly's birthday was on the same day as Louise's, 17th June, the astonishing fact raised the two younger maids to an ecstasy of wonder. Sympathetic vibrations thrilled from top to bottom of the Croft. Such a coincidence . . . Tilly had had a funny feeling . . . what would Mother say? Miss Mallow of all people. Aunt Tamar and I were drawn unresistingly into the little eddies of delighted exclamation.

Louise took it calmly. Was she aware that after the first incredulous outburst, a deep and unnatural silence descended on the kitchen? Did she notice how carefully the door was kept closed with Edith on guard to open it by no more than a chink, when necessary?

She must have known that the two girls spent all their afternoons washing and stoning raisins and chopping peel, even if she had not noticed that *The Englishwoman's Cookery Book* was removed from the book shelf in the morning room each day and mysteriously returned each evening. On 15th June the plummy odours from the oven were as striking to the senses as Tilly's drawn and pallid cheeks.

"She's paying for it herself, poor child," Aunt Tamar said, "but of course I shan't let her."

We neither of us mentioned it to Louise for fear of spoiling what could scarcely be a surprise. I had a silver brooch for Tilly in the shape of a lover's knot. Louise had made an immaculate parcel of half a dozen lawn handkerchiefs. Aunt Tamar gave each of the maids a half sovereign on their birthdays. She laughed when I showed her my sovereign in the chamois leather bag.

"You'll see," she said. "Some day you'll bless me for it."

The cake was a triumph. For years to come, until they were old and grey, Tilly and Edith would remember it. I remember it well myself in all its dark richness on Aunt

Tamar's best fluted glass plate. Impossible to keep it until the afternoon! It appeared incongruously on the breakfast table with a paper-lace birthday card inscribed with respectful good wishes to Miss Mallow from Tilly. With admirable restraint Edith had not added her name. The day belonged to Tilly and Miss Mallow whom the stars had miraculously united.

Lettice went out, leaving the door slightly ajar. A breathless, expectant hush made itself felt in the hall.

"It looks very nice," Louise said. "It's kind of Tilly." She glanced out of the window. "I think we should net the strawberries in the top bed."

She poured out the coffee.

Aunt Tamar and I exhausted ourselves in praising the cake and at the top of our voices. We went on perhaps a little too long. As the minutes went by I felt with positive pain that anti-climax had set in and went to the door in time to hear the kitchen door click shut.

"Louise," I said desperately, "I'm sure Tilly will be expecting . . ."

"Do you mean —" Louise showed a touch of alarm "— she's had her presents, hasn't she?"

"It was such a very special gift, the cake. Couldn't you — she'll be longing to hear that you like it."

"I'll ring . . ."

"Or you could go and thank her," Aunt Tamar said.

"Yes." Louise was always amiable. "I'll go along and thank her." And when she had finished a leisurely breakfast, she did. I heard her.

"Thank you for the cake, Tilly. It seems to have baked well, though we shan't cut it until this afternoon. You and Edith must have a piece. I wish you many happy returns of the day," she added in her tragic little voice. "We'll clarify the dripping, I think."

When I went into the kitchen five minutes later, Tilly was still crying.

"She's been that worked up over it," Edith said.

Tilly's flushed face imprinted itself even on the pages of *The Heir of Redclyffe* which usually absorbed Aunt Tamar and me in the afternoons. But on the whole, thanks to Aunt Tamar's influence, I shed the feeling of responsibility for Louise, at least for a while. It had been instinctive, unreasonable. Louise's nerves too must have recovered their tone. The improvement was shown in her choice of a room; at least I believe it was her choice. It harmonised so well with my own preference that I have forgotten. At any rate I was delighted with mine at the back overlooking the garden. Louise had a smaller room over the front door. She could sit at the window and see right down the bridle-path to the gate opening on the lane.

The track was so long and our lives were so quiet that the sight of a visitor coming to the house caused a sensation.

"Somebody's coming, ma'am," Lettice would say. Not that she could see so far but Tilly or Edith had told her and the news spread. The excitement was prolonged by the steepness of the path. Visitors approached slowly and were gradually identified as the postman, the rat-catcher or a tramp begging his way to the Union at Bidewell. We spent a week at the Croft without seeing anyone but old Mrs Hidkin the herb-woman. She carried a tray round her neck with linen bags of camomile, hyssop, comfrey and woodruff to lay between the sheets. She also took orders for osier work.

"It's my son that does the baskets and such," she told me as I sniffed the elusive scents of the herbs, each smelling almost like something else so that sense and memory were constantly intrigued. "He lives down here in Lullerbeck."

"You don't live in the village then?"

"No. I come from Sleedale. Over the Rigg."

She was drinking home-brewed ale in the kitchen when Louise came in to count out the silver forks for Edith to clean, and measure out the powder and spirit.

"Your sister, miss?" she whispered. "My! Once seen never forgotten I should say of her." She got up reluctantly. "If ever your rambles take you into Sleedale, young ladies, you'll look in and see me? It would make a change. There's nothing but sheep up there."

96

I promised that we would take a walk in her direction one day.

"Just over the Rigg. You can get to it quickest through Mrs Lind's garden."

She went home that way herself, through the top gate and out into the heather.

"There's some one coming, miss," Tilly said one afternoon as I sat in the garden. "A gentleman coming ever so quick."

I went through the house to the front porch and saw Julian. He had been more than usually occupying my thoughts. The next day would be the first of his final examination. We had looked forward to the date for so long that it was impossible not to think of him. It seemed perfectly natural to see him in the flesh. At the same time I wondered uneasily why he had chosen to spend the last day on a journey into the country and whether he would be able to get back in time.

Aunt Tamar had joined me by the time he appeared at the door. It was a help to have her there. After even so short a parting, I saw how the change in him had quickened and I said, "This is Julian Windross, Aunt Tamar," as though introducing a distant acquaintance.

He was just sufficiently in command of himself to behave politely to Aunt Tamar; to beg her forgiveness for calling uninvited; to presume on her acquaintance with his mother and his long friendship with Mr Mallow.

Into the quiet parlour he brought a spirit of unrest. He sat with his eyes fixed alternately on the door and the french window leading to the verandah. When Aunt Tamar's small talk showed signs of coming to a puzzled halt, I mentioned the examination.

"Ought you to have come? Today, I mean."

"I always meant to come today," he said testily. "This was to be the day."

The assumption that I would know why seemed a further proof of his disordered state of mind. Aunt Tamar had taken up her tatting and was watching him with interest as she manipulated the shuttle.

"I'll call Louise," I said, taking pity on him.

She was at her window, having watched him all the way up the bridle-path.

"Can't you tell him I've gone away? Don't leave me alone with him, Hester, I beg you."

"I'll try not to."

Julian was already on his feet when we went down, his back to Aunt Tamar though she was talking to him. I saw her look of surprise change to one of comprehension as he said, "Louise, Louise," as if he had been lost and now saw some faint hope of rescue.

We all sat down. The scent of stocks and cut grass drifted in from the garden. Doves cooed in their cote. Shadows of lightly stirring branches moved on the carpet. A shower of petals fell from the vase on the top shelf of the étagere. Louise rose, carefully picked them up and placed them in the velvet and gold-tasselled waste-paper basket. With a long-handled brush she anxiously flicked a speck or two of soot from the cascade of white horsehair filling the fireless grate. Then she sat down again in her Prince of Wales chair of buttoned green velvet and resumed her bead work.

Such a scene of domestic harmony and charm — particularly if one happened to be sitting opposite Louise — can rarely have been equalled. Yet Aunt Tamar confided to me afterwards that she had never in all her life seen young people looking so wretched. She must have meant Julian and me.

From time to time he looked desperately out through the shaded verandah to the garden and made a preparatory movement as if about to get up or burst into speech. At last Aunt Tamar rang for tea and suggested that Mr Windross might like to wash and refresh himself. I glanced anxiously at the clock. There was one train from the Junction to Wickborough at half past seven. Even if he caught it, he would be late home.

In the little stir that followed as Lettice and Tilly brought in the tea things, Julian took Louise by the arm and led her firmly into the garden. We waited. In their white napkin the warm scones cooled. On their silver dish

98

Lettice's feather-light cakes drooped a little. Twice Aunt Tamar lifted the pot to pour out and put it down again before Julian blundered into the room, groped his way to the door, then recollected himself.

"I'm sorry, Mrs —" He had forgotten her name. "— ma'am, but after all I must leave at once. I do thank you — most warmly — for receiving me."

I went with him into the hall. Unseeing, he took his hat and went out but he came back to say conscientiously, "Goodbye, Hester." I watched him stumbling down the path, his head bowed like an old man.

"Oh, Aunt Tamar," I said. "Julian isn't himself. He isn't like that at all, truly."

She poured out a cup of tea with an air of relief as Louise came slowly in from the garden.

"Would it be interfering," Aunt Tamar said, "to ask what the young man wanted?"

"He wants to marry me."

"And you?"

"I said no." With a tiny flurry of spirit Louise added, "He won't listen. He came today to make a sort of bargain." Her lips drooped. Her brows met in the rudiments of a frown and grew at once smooth again leaving no imperfection in her clear skin. It was Louise's nearest approach to a look of disapproval. "He said that if I would marry him some day, he would give up his career in the Church. He said that if I would promise, he wouldn't take the examination."

"What difference would that make?" demanded Aunt Tamar.

"It wouldn't make any difference to me." Louise sipped her tea.

"Julian thinks of it as a sacrifice," I explained, "to give it all up for Louise."

"I don't want him to make a sacrifice." Louise adjusted a spray of maidenhair fern and pushed the crystal vase to the exact centre of the table. "He doesn't seem to understand that I wouldn't marry him even if he wasn't going to be a clergyman. I can't." Then, as if some explanation

99

should be given she added simply, "I don't really like him very much. I hope he won't come back."

"He's quite mad." I pushed back my chair. "Someone must talk to him. May I . . .?"

"If you think it will do any good, Hester dear."

I crammed on my hat and caught him up at the field gate; at least I called and he waited there.

"I'll walk part of the way with you."

He nodded. We trudged through the dust in silence. In my house shoes I tripped occasionally over a loose stone.

"I've thought of nothing else for days," he said. "It seemed a practical gesture."

Had he really thought it a gesture likely to influence Louise?

"You must try to forget about it for a while and concentrate on your examination. You've always wanted to be a clergyman. You have a calling." He sat down hopelessly on a boulder. "You haven't time to sit there. Your train . . ."

"It doesn't matter. There's something I haven't told you, Hester. I haven't been honest with you or Louise. The fact is, I shan't take the examination in any case. It would be hypocrisy to go on and be ordained. I have no calling." I looked at him, appalled. "Oh, I honestly thought I had until . . ."

"Until you met Louise?"

"Yes. My feelings for her have shown me how superficial my life has been. If my belief had been strong enough I wouldn't have been bowled over so completely by Louise. You know what St Paul said. 'Nothing can separate us from the love of God.' It isn't true. Louise can do it. She has come between me and God and I'm glad. I wouldn't want God if I could have Louise."

"How can you talk such wicked nonsense?"

"It was the beauty of the Church I loved: the candles, the language — nothing else, I see that now. Whereas when I'm with Louise I seem on the verge of finding the real meaning of life."

"But if she doesn't love you?"

100

"I love her so completely that to tell you the truth it doesn't matter whether she loves me or not. Naturally I want her to but most of all I want her, as my wife. To have her always with me."

I went with him all the way to the station, enduring the back-breaking journey in the waggonette. Not that my company did him the least good but I got him into the train and by loading him with messages for his mother and my father, gave a touch of normality to our leave-taking.

"It's good of you to listen, Hester," he said, realising as the train moved, that I was there. When he had gone I stood for a long time, too despondent to leave the platform until the ticket collector coughed and rattled his keys at me. It seemed as good a reason as any for moving away when I had no reason, no purpose, no hope of my own to direct me.

10

I CLAMBERED INTO the waggonette and sat dispiritedly waiting for the driver, half aware that a cab had arrived to pick up a passenger: a man who had been pacing up and down. I had vaguely thought of him as having come off the Wickborough train and would have thought no more of him had not he, or his driver, spoken the words 'Codlin Croft'. I looked round quickly, too late to see his face. The cab rattled off. It was five minutes before the waggonette followed.

As we lumbered along the rough road, dropping a passenger at a farm gate or cottage door, I wondered who the visitor to Codlin Croft could be. I had been unable to form any idea of his age or station in life. Aunt Tamar would have told us if she had been expecting her lawyer or a professional visit of any kind. I knew that she had a much loved brother Samuel who lived at Tunbridge Wells but the old gentleman was in poor health. The man had got into the cab quite nimbly. Could he be Uncle Samuel's son, Andrew? By the time we had reached the Fleece, I calculated that the visitor would have arrived at the Croft.

Sure enough, I had walked no more than a quarter of a mile when I met the cab coming back, empty. But when I trailed, hot and weary, into the parlour, Aunt Tamar and Louise were alone, peacefully twisting old letters into spills.

"My poor Hester! Come and sit down. Lettice will bring you a tray."

"Has he gone then, the visitor?" Since Aunt Tamar looked blank I explained.

"You must have been mistaken, dear, and I'm glad. Two uninvited gentlemen in one day would be rather too much."

She looked round. We were alone. Louise had noiselessly placed her spills in the vase and gone out.

"It was upsetting." Aunt Tamar patted my hand. "Julian seemed dangerously over-wrought. When a young man puts his career at risk . . ."

"He has lost his faith. Whatever will become of him, Aunt Tamar?"

"Time will tell. You can't imagine how glad I am to be old. The suffering young people bring on themselves is too awful to remember. When a man wants something as much as he appears to want Louise, then he'd best have it. That," she added, "is the best cure. Poor girl! Beauty like hers is a terrible disadvantage. It produces effects she is incapable of understanding. She doesn't see that lovely face or any other as lovely, only other people looking at it. I've always been plain. Oh, yes," when I protested, "and it isn't such a bad thing to have to exert oneself to be loved. All the same Louise is rather unusually — thick-headed."

She pronounced the word with such alarmed surprise that we both laughed. It was a luxury to talk to her. In time I would have confided in her but time was denied us.

And yet, how easily and pleasantly it went by! At Silvergate my life had been dominated by time: by the striking clocks, the Abbey's quarterly chimes and father's strict routine; but here, when my light tasks were done, time was measured by the drying of dew on rose petals and the cuckoo's changing tune as June passed into July, lilies and hollyhocks came into bloom and Louise brought us smoothly through the soft fruit season, luring the wasps efficiently into one syrupy jar while she filled and sealed the others.

It was in July that Mrs Windross wrote to me: a sad, bewildered letter. Julian had not only absented himself once and for all from St Aidan's; he had given up all thought of entering the Church as a career and indeed never entered it at all even for worship.

"He says it is all an illusion. Dr Thorkeld called to see me. He was very kind and wondered if Julian was suffering from a nervous illness. He will help him to find a position as a tutor in a family but it will be poorly paid, I think. Thank God we have means."

I folded the letter, feeling that I never wanted to go back to Wickborough. I would have been content to stay for ever at the Croft with Aunt Tamar. I have a photograph of her in one of the silk dresses she wore in those leisured afternoons. It was brown, I remember, the flounces edged with black lace to match the square of lace on her smooth hair. How could she think of herself as plain? Her large eyes, even allowing for their fixed stare into the camera during the long exposure, have a look of humorous understanding. If only I had known her sooner and longer! But the photograph also shows the delicacy which in real life one overlooked, until a bout of activity reduced her to a helpless invalid. She would rest for a few days and recover but each time with a loss of strength.

Louise was turning her thoughts to the preserving of plums when the news came about Uncle Samuel's illness. We found Aunt Tamar in tears over the telegram.

"I must see him again, before it's too late," she said. "We've been parted for too long. I must see him once more."

Louise supervised the hasty packing. I walked to the inn to order a conveyance and made up my mind to go with Aunt Tamar if she wanted me. I am sure now that she did and wish that I had gone. When I suggested it her face brightened but before she could answer, Louise said, "Please, Hester, don't leave me here on my own."

I hesitated, melting again into the old mood of protective affection. She was — or rather she looked — so defenceless.

"No, dear," Aunt Tamar said. "It would not be suitable. This is an isolated place. You must both stay. I can't tell you how it will ease my mind to know that you will be here to look after things, and it won't be for long."

In the end it was Lettice who went with her. We squeezed into the four-wheeler and rode as far as the field gate, then watched until the curve in the lane took her out of sight — for ever. We never saw Aunt Tamar again.

To part with her for even a week or two reduced me to tears.

"I shall miss her dreadfully." I sniffed into my handkerchief.

"They should be at Tunbridge Wells by half past nine this evening," Louise said, dry-eyed.

But we both wept when the news came. Grief and exhaustion had brought on a heart attack. Aunt Tamar outlived her brother by only a week. They were buried in the same grave.

"Where shall we go?" Louise asked when we had read the letter from Andrew, explaining that Aunt Tamar had left everything to him.

"Why, home of course." I was at that very moment writing to father.

"I can't go back to Wickborough."

All the sadness of Aunt Tamar's death found expression in Louise's small voice. As it died wistfully away, Wickborough took on the remoteness of a lost city. It was so moving and she looked so beautiful that it was easy at first to overlook the fact that none of the sadness was for Aunt Tamar.

"It needn't be at once. You see, Cousin Andrew says it will be some time before Aunt Tamar's affairs are settled." I read the paragraph aloud. " 'I should be deeply obliged, though without any right to ask such a favour, if you and Miss Hester would stay on at Codlin Croft, should Mr Mallow be agreeable, until I am able to come and arrange for the sale.' He's written to father too."

"And afterwards — it will be so difficult to know what to do."

The helpless little air of doubt clouded my vision. In restrospect it is the tenacity of purpose I can see. Of many things Louise was oblivious but not of the change in her prospects caused by Aunt Tamar's death. The problem must have occupied her constantly. Her dislike of the house at Wickborough must have been stronger than I had imagined. She was determined not to go back. At intervals she would look up from her bead work with a look of tremulous appeal. I never knew whether it was a fault in one of the beads that was troubling her or the uncertainty of her future until she said, "I simply don't know what to do now that we can't stay here."

Now that we were quite alone, I became more closely identified with her than ever before to the extent of adapting my train of thought to hers; and gradually, as the geometric shapes in the bead mats emerged with infallible precision, I saw with fatalistic despair where her thoughts were leading.

"The only thing for a woman is to have her own home."

She added the last blue bead to the apex of a triangle and fixed it firmly with her thread so that it could never escape. She would marry Julian in order to have her own home. I was almost sure of it.

It was very quiet. The house had changed. Since Aunt Tamar had gone so abruptly, it seemed no more than a repository of the things she had left behind. But it did not remain so. It can be dangerous to stay on in an enchanted place when the good fairy has left. Other influences creep in. Even with the windows open, a chaffinch pecking on the verandah and fresh flowers in the vases, there seemed an oppressiveness in the air as if a cloud hung about the upstairs rooms and would presently make some disastrous move. I felt it most in the evenings and took to standing in the porch and looking down the empty bridle-path. The hills were massive as they had never been before and strangely active. In the twilight they drew together in a denser blue but in the dusk they turned black and came nearer. Then I would hear Louise making her nightly tour of the house, closing the windows and barring the shutters.

We had left the shutters open when Aunt Tamar was there though any protection she had provided must have been fragile indeed. All the same I did feel a little nervous without her and Lettice, who had stayed at Tunbridge Wells to make herself useful in the bereaved household.

Father must have told the Windrosses of Aunt Tamar's death. As a result we suffered another visit from Julian. It interrupted and temporarily drove from my mind a curious little conversation I had with Louise. She had made some remark about the disadvantage of not having a home of one's own and with a new wave of sympathy I realised that this was the third time she had lost the protection of an older woman. There had scarcely been time for Aunt Tamar to take Mrs Maple's place as the strong support to which, ivy-like, Louise must cling, when she too was snatched away. I said something of the sort.

"Yes," Louise sorrowfully replied, "and it's almost the anniversary of Mrs Maple's death."

"Not yet, surely. It was only April when you came home."

An extraordinary change came over her: a kind of rigidity. Only her eyes moved as she looked at me with lips parted as if she were going to say something really important. But the voice that gave the stamp of truth to everything she said, however trite (and it must be admitted that Louise's remarks were often trite) said only:

"It feels like years."

"Here's a gentleman in a gig, miss," Tilly reported and presently Julian drove up.

His appearance was smarter than it had been for some time. The mere act of getting down from a gig gave him a prestige he had certainly lacked on his last visit. But the weeks of idleness had done him no good. He looked haggard and peevish but from the first moment I caught the old light of elation in his eyes and guessed that he was borne up by some new project; guessed too what it was.

All the signs were ominous. Louise came down without being called and herself supplied Julian with cake and wine.

"You'll be coming back to Wickborough soon?"

Julian's question came out heavily like the first shot of a cannonade strategically planned.

"As soon as Cousin Andrew comes."

"You'll be glad to take up the old way of life, Hester."

To my surprise, he was right. It would not be the old life but it would suffice: I was needed at home.

"And Louise?" Julian's change of tone from one of friendly interest to warm sympathy pierced me to the heart. In the struggle to keep my composure, I missed Louise's brief reply.

"If you were married," Julian had quickly suppressed the warmth and brought out the next shot without finesse, "No, don't go, Hester, I'm only putting the facts — there would be no need to go back to Silvergate. You could have your own home. I'm not without money." He actually launched into an account of his assets. "Not enough to live on for a lifetime but I could easily support a wife at Buckingham Street. You're not extravagant. You're good at making your own things." He cast a puzzled glance at the beadwork and swept on, "We could live very well." . . .

My discomfort in being there was brought to an almost feverish pitch by the conviction that this time Julian would succeed. I listened in horrified fascination as he presented his argument, using the same cool reasoning power he had no doubt applied to the famous dissertation. He made his proposal without affection, much less passion. That was his only justification for making it in my presence and that was exactly the way to appeal to Louise. There was a perverse relief in seeing him once more at his best. How clever he was! And how well, after all, he knew Louise!

"You'd rather be mistress in your own home than have

to depend on Mr Mallow. The only other thing, so far as I can see would be to take a position utterly unworthy of you — to be at the beck and call of strangers." Then with a flash of insight that seemed to me quite diabolical he said, "You would have your own parlour at Buckingham Street, naturally, and your own pianoforte."

We waited for the words that would settle his future — and hers — and mine. Incredulously I saw that Louise had lost her unruffled calm. She was moved. The prosaic statement of facts had affected her as no loving outburst could have done. Julian had found the way — not to her heart, no, not that — but to whatever faculty supplied the motive force of Louise's actions. Here was the obvious solution to her problem.

No trace of self-interest marred her features. They conveyed as usual an idea of perfection, almost indeed, they fulfilled it. But behind the lovely mask, her small, rigid mind must have been as near as it could ever be to a state of tumult. Otherwise she would never have been goaded at last into telling the truth she had so long concealed.

"How can I marry you when I'm married already?"

11

WE WERE ALL three thunderstruck; Julian and I by the experience of seeing Louise turn from maid to matron before our very eyes; Louise by the fateful mistake of having told.

"I never meant to tell." She burst into tears. "I didn't want anyone to know, ever."

After the first moment of shock, I felt — and was ashamed of it — a great throb of relief; shameful because it was obvious that Louise was wretchedly unhappy, but impossible to repress. Not only was I selfishly glad that Julian would still be free: I saw Louise's marriage as his salvation. With a certain detachment, then, I who had been the most miserable was able to observe the misery of the other two.

My complacency was pricked by the sight of Julian's face.

"It was wrong of you, Louise," I said, "not to tell — and dreadfully unfair to Julian. Why on earth did you try to hide it?"

"You don't understand," she wailed, "how awful a thing it is. It frightens me even to think of it."

She had been afraid ever since she came home. It was possible to see that now. Uneasily I wondered why she should have been so very frightened. The most important factor in her marriage had not yet been mentioned.

"Where is your husband and who — who is he?"

My brother-in-law, I thought, unbelieving.

"He's called Nicholas. Nicholas Vince. I ran away from him."

"He didn't" — Julian had covered his eyes with his hand and did not look up — "ill-treat you?"

Louise did not answer. Into her silence we read the worst. She had dried her tears and sat sorrowfully gazing out of the window. What unimaginable horrors had those blue eyes looked upon?

"Oh, how dreadful! I had no idea. Why didn't you tell me, dear?" I put my arms round her, round Mrs Vince. 'This is my sister, Mrs Vince,' I heard myself saying to some unidentified caller.

Julian had got to his feet, looking most unlike a clergyman.

"Tell me where he is. I'll find the brute and make him answer for it."

He would enjoy it too. Remembering the incident with Josh Blakey, I said,

"You mustn't do anything so foolish, Julian."

"There's no need to go and find him," Louise said. "He'll find me. Wherever I go, however long it takes, he'll find me. He'll never let me go."

Poor girl! She must have been living in constant terror. No wonder she had been a little insensitive to the feelings

109

of others, wholly possessed as she was by dread of this fearful man.

"Where did you live, Louise, after you" — Julian's lips trembled — "were married?"

"In Cairlie." Louise spoke with extreme reluctance. "It's quite a little town, not far from Blairgouroch."

I thought of the man in the cab who had driven to the Croft but had never called, then reproved myself. It was so easy, for me at any rate, to give way to fantasy. Why should Louise's husband behave in so mysterious a fashion? All he had to do was to knock at the door and demand to see his wife. The thought was not consoling. It sent me there and then to the front door. I closed and bolted it.

Having unwillingly given away her secret, Louise gradually told us the facts. She had married after Mrs Maple died. Her husband was a lawyer's clerk, she told us with a shudder. It is no exaggeration to call it a shudder of loathing.

"I couldn't bear it. I ran away. Yes, almost at once. After two weeks."

As we sat talking the whole thing over in hushed, awestruck voices, I was aware of a familiar element in our situation. The scene had darkened, the music grown more sombre: otherwise we might have been children again with Louise as the fair damsel in the tower, Julian and I as the gallant rescuing knights. I forgot how often my role had been that of the slain dragon. How else could Julian always have been the hero? While we had fought and toiled for her, Louise had slipped away in her immaculate pinafore to count the balls on the counting frame.

Faced with a crisis, Julian and I drew closer.

"You realise what this means to me," he said in a low voice when it became imperative for him to leave. He had long outstayed the limits of a conventional call. "It simply destroys my whole life."

The remarkable thing was that now the first shock was over it seemed to have enlivened him. His distress was genuine but he had recovered some sense of purpose.

"We must do something for her," he said reverently.

Seen through the parlour doorway in the long perspective of the hall, Louise looked small and slight like a delicate piece of porcelain; but as always with the added grace that gave her the appearance of nobility rather than mere prettiness. "Can you believe that any one but a fiend in human shape could deliberately make her unhappy?"

"No," I said. "But you know, Julian, there's nothing we can do. She has left her husband and he is legally entitled to have her back."

"The fellow should be horse-whipped. Oh, I know you're right, but it would help if we knew more about him. I don't want to stir up trouble but someone ought to find out what he's about."

"It ought to be father." My heart sank. He would have to be told.

"Leave it to me." Julian squared his shoulders. "I shall go to this place, Cairlie, and just look round." Then with a pathetic change of mood. "Don't try to stop me, Hester. I've nothing else to do now."

With a last adoring look at Louise, he left.

The sky was overcast. We lit the lamps early. Louise made her round of the house, drawing curtains and closing shutters. Her constant watchfulness — I saw it now in that light — had infected me. I understood, now that I shared it, how the hourly dread of Nicholas Vince's arrival had worn her down. I understood too the hopelessness of it. She must know that her escape could be only for a time. He would come and take her back to a bondage that would last for the rest of her life. It puzzzled me that he had been so long in doing it. When I gently probed her on the subject of his cruelty, she seemed petrified and could only look at me, speechless, with eyes that had looked into depths I could not imagine. I must try to make her as happy as possible during the short spell of freedom left to her.

It was difficult. Instead, Louise passed on her distress to me. From that day I could not settle to any useful occupation but spent my time roving about the house and

111

garden, all the time debating whether or not to write to father. Each day must bring the dreaded moment nearer; yet I could think of no plan for dealing with Nicholas Vince when he came. As for Louise, she was incapable of planning. Only sheer desperation could have driven her to the audacious act of running away. Now she went quietly about her household tasks and began on another bead mat, giving no sign of the turmoil she had roused in me. But I had long since learned that Louise's appearance gave no clue as to her inward state. It was a factor on its own, existing independently of Louise.

We kept the front door closed, rather to the surprise of Tilly and Edith. However, they quickly grasped the idea that we were a household of defenceless women and derived a good deal of fearful enjoyment from it, giving little screams of fright when we occasionally met in dark corners.

Our one hope lay in concealment. Louise must not be seen if or when Nicholas Vince came. In this I felt that the maids would be more of a hindrance than a help since it was impossible to take them into our confidence. And yet it was through them that we heard...

I went into the kitchen one evening and found them sitting opposite each other, elbows on the table, in a delicious huddle of fright.

"I'm that scared, miss." Edith giggled weakly. "I daresn't go to bed. Tilly was telling me..."

"Don't be silly. It's past your bedtime. Tilly, you mustn't frighten your sister with ghost stories and such rubbish."

"He isn't a ghost, miss," Tilly said unexpectedly. "He's a real gentleman but funny in his ways."

"Who?"

"They think he must be staying at the Fleece at Bidewell. He drives out in a cab and gets down at the field gate or sometimes he walks to the village and stands about. Young Mrs Hidkin that has the shop, she was the first to tell me about him; but I saw him myself, waiting in the lane when I came back with the flour and I got through the hedge and came back by the field."

My instinct had not misled me then. This must be the man I had just missed seeing at the station. There could be no doubt as to who he was. His inexplicable habit of hovering just out of sight no longer surprised me. It was what I had come to expect of Nicholas Vince. Had he been waiting until Louise and I were alone? I went to her at once. "He's here." Her face blanched. "Or at least at the Fleece. You must stay at the back of the house. He can't get round to the verandah if we bolt the garden gate. But I don't know what to tell him."

"Tell him I'm dead. It will soon be true. If I have to go back, I shall kill myself, or him." The stark brevity of these dreadful words curdled my blood. "I can't bear ever to see him again, never mind be his wife. That's it, Hester. You must tell him I'm dead."

I was beginning to feel far out of my depth.

"We must go back to Wickborough," I said, "and tell father all about it."

Father would send a carriage if we wrote to him; and that was what we must do in spite of Louise's panic. But I felt unequal, just then, to all the complications of closing the house, dismissing the girls and arranging the journey, in secret moreover. In fact, we left it too late.

As it happened, I was alone in the house and taken unawares. Since the two maids were sisters, they took their monthly day off together and had set off early in the morning to walk the five miles to their home. Louise was at the top of the garden gathering windfalls. I went to the front door and he was almost there; a man in town clothes walking steadily up the bridle-path. Far down outside the field gate I saw the glint of coachwork. His cab, having gone on to the village to turn, had drawn up to wait for him.

He was near enough to see me. Louise and I had each brought the one black dress kept for just such a sudden bereavement as had befallen us. As the maids had remarked, we were sufficiently alike to be unmistakably sisters. Our colouring was similar. I believe he mistook me at first glance for Louise. His pace quickened but as he came closer, his expression changed.

113

He took off his hat and hesitated. His uncertainty surprised me. He was not the coarse, brutal man I had, with wild variations of detail, imagined. But when he looked full at me, there was a hardness in his eyes and his face, with the pale complexion of a clerk, was stiff with tension.

"Does the name Vince mean anything to you?" he asked brusquely, but not impulsively. I felt that he had chosen to frame the question in that way.

Face to face with him, I knew that there was no hope for Louise. He was a real person: a reasonable fellow creature: her husband: not an ogre or a savage beast. Nevertheless my instinct to protect her made me determined that this time at least he should not have her. For one irrational moment, remembering my black dress and Louise's instructions, I wondered if, only for a time of course, he might be led to believe that she was dead. Fortunately the thought was too horrible to entertain. Instead, I prayed she would not come in through the verandah and took the additional precaution of closing the door behind me and stepping out into the porch. "Yes, Mr Vince, it does. I'm Hester Mallow. I know why you have come. Louise has told me."

He looked at me sharply.

"She has?"

He took out a handkerchief and dabbed at his face. He was perspiring and nervous.

"She is not at home at present. Perhaps you would like to leave a message for her."

At once I felt ashamed. The conventional formula was unsuitable, insulting even, on such an occasion. He looked at me with contempt, as well he might. All the same, I was surprised to find that I could deal with him. He could have knocked me down, stormed into the house and dragged Louise out by the hair; but I knew perfectly well he would do none of these things. The wariness in his manner puzzled me but I was not afraid of him, dastardly as his behaviour had been. There was simply no accounting for the deviations in human nature, I told myself with new worldly wisdom. The most inoffensive-looking man could be in private a ruthless beast. I hardened my heart and remained coolly in command of the situation.

"I should have liked to see her."

"Have you come far, Mr Vince?" (Ought I to call him Nicholas?)

He made a gesture towards the lane.

"I have a cab."

"I ought to ask you to come in and take some refreshment. You must excuse me. We are a household in mourning."

He nodded and murmured some condolence. He had heard in the village of Mrs Lind's death.

"What shall I tell Louise?"

"That I must see her." His face flushed with agitation. "I must — and soon I tell you." His voice broke on a note of desperation. "When would it be convenient?"

How could I say 'Never'?

"If you would leave an address, Louise could write to you."

The suggestion seemed to me admirably sensible. He ignored it.

"If I may, I shall call again."

It was on the tip of my tongue to say that we would be leaving soon but I realised in time that this news would hasten his next visit. I bowed.

"Good day, Mr Vince."

He went away, leaving me doubtful and unhappy. Was it sheer gratitude for his existence as Louise's husband that made me see him in not too unfavourable a light? An uncomfortable feeling that with Louise I had been living in a feverish world of shadows, cut off from the obligations of real life, made me reluctant to go back to her.

As soon as I saw her, the feeling left me; or ceased to be uncomfortable. She had put her basket on a seat under the apple trees and was examining the fruit. With the soft breeze stirring the frills of her pink apron, in the dazzling interplay of sunshine and shade, she seemed scarcely a creature of earth but of air and light.

115

"Louise dear." I pitched my voice low. It must have sounded ominous. She turned quickly. "He has been here. Nicholas." I used the name deliberately to place him within the safe limits of the family circle. We would have to accept him. "He's gone."

I stopped, shaken by her look of sheer terror. It was as if the white face stared out at me through prison bars from a place of secret torture.

"He'll come back," she said.

"Yes. He says he must see you. It's only reasonable. After all you did marry him. You must have promised to cleave to him, forsaking all other." Then as she still looked sick and faint, I asked, "Why ever did you marry him?"

She had no need to reply. I could supply the answer. Because Mrs Maple had died and there was no one to tell her what to do. He would be persistent, like Julian.

"If I speak to him or see him even, he'll never let me go. I shall die, I tell you, and then you'll be sorry."

The words were infantile: their effect was devastating. I believed her. The outcome would be tragic and would break my heart. Reasoning was useless. I promised that if he came again he would find the house shut up as if we had gone away. If there had been time, this would have been no ruse. I was determined in spite of our promise to Cousin Andrew to close the Croft and go home.

Even the light breeze died away. The day grew still and warm. We ate a lunch of bread and cheese and lettuce in the cool kitchen and afterwards sat on the verandah, our black dresses a reminder that Aunt Tamar was gone and with her all the tranquil peace of such languid days as these. Again I was troubled by the feeling that Louise and I had withdrawn into a region without people and were waiting for a message from the world outside.

The eeriness of what followed was the greater, I think, because it happened in the sunshine of a summer afternoon. The blood is more likely to be chilled at twilight or in the dark. Not that there was anything blood-curdling in the event. It was the way in which the normal became abnormal through the distorting influence of fear; it was, most of all, the insane secrecy into which I allowed myself to be beguiled, that gave me then and long afterwards the sensation of having turned daylight into dark and not only in the literal sense.

For the third or fourth time I went through the house and looked down from the vantage point of the front porch. The hollows were full of blue haze. The long track wound down between gorse and bramble bushes, foxgloves and nettles, all shimmering in the heat so that I saw the whole landscape through a gauze veil; and I heard, like a warning from the hillside, the anxious bleat of a sheep.

Nicholas Vince was coming. I had not expected him again so soon. This time he was walking slowly. As a concession to the heat he had exchanged his hard hat for a straw one. It looked incongruous above the suit of dark worsted. He must have gone all the way back to the inn since morning. Was it impulse or persistence that had brought him back so soon?

He came on, small between the Scotch firs, tall between the gorse bushes.

"He's coming again, Louise. Nicholas."

I shut and locked both outer and inner doors. Louise closed and locked the windows opening on the verandah. We barred the shutters and drew the curtains, doing it all silently with the half paralysed frenzy of a dream when one's limbs seem heavy with invisible fetters. The sudden darkness was alarming, as an eclipse of the sun must be.

"Let's go into the morning room."

My own whispering was as frightening as the need for it. We crept through the shaded hall to the little room beyond the parlour. It projected from the house with a window facing towards the front door and fitted with slatted wooden blinds instead of shutters. In front was a tiny strip of garden enclosed by iron railings. Its gate was always padlocked, the plot being reached by a door from the morning room itself.

Louise had scarcely lowered the blind when Nicholas Vince pushed open the wicket gate and went up the path

117

to the front door. There was nothing imperious in his knock but it seemed loud enough in the extreme quiet to rouse the whole neighbourhood. With a clatter of wings the unsuspecting doves flew from the roof to the pear tree. He waited.

Louise and I knelt in the window, our arms resting on the horse-hair sofa, our eyes just high enough to see through the half open lower slats of the blind. From this limited viewpoint it was impossible to see his whole figure but we had an excellent view of his boots. I could feel Louise's heart beating as we crouched side by side. A fly buzzed desperately between the blind and the panes. Through the thin delaine of my blouse I felt the prick of horse-hair. But all my attention was fixed on Nicholas Vince's elastic-sided boots. They had their own eloquence: too narrow for country roads: dusty; bulging at the toe-caps; worn down at the heels. When he knocked again the knock was challenging but the boots fidgeting on the broad flags were anxious. It was the boots that changed him in my eyes from enemy to victim. The secrecy, the silent house, the unknown outcome, were all unnatural. I felt a growing distaste for the whole affair.

He stood back from the door and looked up at the house, its front softly draped in pink roses; then treading on the flower beds, he looked closely at each window as if hoping to find a chink in the shutters. Motionless in our shaded room, we could see him moving in full sunlight. I thought he muttered something before going back to the knocker and beating a loud rat-tat-tat.

"He'll go now," I breathed.

He lingered at the wicket gate, looking back at the house, his face grave and troubled. It was very quiet again. Then, terrifyingly loud like the screech of a witch, a yaffle called from the wood: a cry of unearthly mockery. He started violently as if there were trickery in the air and suddenly I loathed the whole situation. There seemed a dishonesty in watching him unseen from a darkened house. He with the sun on his face was a real person while we were no more than frightened shadows hiding from life. In another moment I might have pulled up the

118

blind or rushed to the door; but in another moment he had gone.

I stood up, rubbing my palms, pricked red by the horsehair. Louise got up too. In the half-light she looked like a beautiful ghost — or a sculptured figure for there was a lifelessness about her as if she had been mesmerised.

"It was hateful," I said in a furious whisper. "Why did we do it?" Then in my normal voice, "He had a right to see you. Your own husband."

"But it wasn't my husband," Louise said. "That wasn't Nicholas."

12

HER SAD LITTLE voice died away, leaving me to struggle with a development so unexpected as to take my breath away.

"Then who is he?"

"I don't know."

"Why didn't you say? We could have asked him."

"Oh, no. I only wanted him to go away. No, you mustn't, please Hester."

Her hand slipped into mine, her pleading look, restrained me from going after him; and after all, the dilemma was Louise's not mine. She would be the one to suffer if I did the wrong thing in a situation so fraught with uncertainty that it offered no clue as to what the right thing might be. All the same, my bewilderment mattered less than the surprisingly sharp pain of rebuff: a suspicion that Louise had not played fair: or more simply, a suspicion of Louise. It should have been impossible for her, as we knelt so close together breathing in unison, to let me blunder on in my mistake without so much as a nudge or a whisper to enlighten me. I felt it as a small act of betrayal, like being left alone in the dark. A brightness was dimmed for me, as if a creeping mildew had touched the roses on Aunt Tamar's porch.

At least I could raise the blind with a snap. With the same irritated energy I uncovered all the windows and dragged open the heavy front door. Even if I had run after him, it would have been too late. Through the distant hedge I saw the glint of the cab and the top of the driver's chimney-pot hat going in the direction of Bide-well.

Louise had gone out into the garden. I found her in the summer house leaning her elbows on the table with the same petrified air of having absented herself or been put to flight. I sat down on the grass.

"You must have some idea who he was."

She shook her head. I tried to recall the details of his first visit and felt guilty. I had misled Louise. I blushed for my folly in having concluded that the man was Vince, in never having doubted it. His coming, his mention of the name, the fact that we had been expecting him, his appearance . . . The whole stupid mistake had been mine; and yet even my stupidity did not account for his remarkable restraint in not correcting me. "Oh, no, I'm not Vince. My name is . . ." That was all he had needed to say.

In the light of Louise's disclosure, our meeting re-shaped itself. He had not, as I had assumed, come with a claim on Louise. Had I not felt, even at the time, that his manner was tentative and troubled? A persistent anxiety in him presented itself to my memory in the shape of his boots. But his eyes had been hard with purpose. He had wanted very much to see Louise. It occurred to me that he had been cleverer than I: more discreet. (Could any one have been less discreet?) He had told me nothing at all; he had wanted me to take the initiative because he didn't trust me.

Or was it Louise he didn't trust?

"There's another thing." I pursued the train of thought aloud, as much of it, that is, as could be shared with Louise. "If he could find you, by enquiring I suppose, why hasn't Nicholas found you by this time?"

Louise's tongue delicately moistened her sweetly curving lower lip.

"That's what I can't understand."

In the very depths of her eyes as she looked into the green shade under the trees, I caught a hint of panic.

"You're quite sure, Louise dear," — It was difficult to put the question tactfully — "that Nicholas would want to have you back? I mean, suppose he hasn't been — bothering."

To look at her was to see the utter folly of such a proposition. Moreover a doubt had been resolved. The visitor had not struck me as being capable of the brutality which had forced poor Louise to run away. Nicholas Vince must be a man of an altogether different stamp. To have had dealings with the man in the boots had been bad enough. The thought of Nicholas Vince frightened me so much that, like Louise, I would have fled to the ends of the earth to avoid him.

Suddenly it dawned on me that our visitor had not come in search of Louise at all, but of Vince. It was Vince he had asked for. His desperate need to see Louise arose from his desperate need to see Vince. How much easier it was to cast Vince in the role of villain! He had practised some vile fraud on the wretched man.

"Do you think your husband had wronged this man in some way? Could he have borrowed money from him?"

"I don't think so." She paused. "Nicholas hasn't any money."

I was aware that when I had time to ponder on it, this piece of information would prove to be important: enormously important: but there were many other things to think of. My instinct was to press Louise for details but by this time I had begun to find her economical use of words exhausting. Besides, she would never bring herself to tell me what it had been like to be married to such a man. Scenes all the more horrifying for their vagueness were best banished from the imagination.

"Does Nicholas know where father lives?"

"I didn't tell him. It all happened in such a hurry, our marriage, and then I knew at once I should have to leave him. He just thought of me as a connection of Mrs Maple.

121

Yes, he knew I had a family. Oh, Hester, he'll come for me."

"At any rate," I said heartily, "if he hasn't found you between April and September, there's no reason to think he will find you today or tomorrow, or even soon. Perhaps not at all."

"He'll find me," she said.

We were interrupted by the clang of a tin basin and the splash of water in the kitchen. To have those two good silly girls back again was wonderfully reassuring.

"My, it was hot," Tilly said. "Mother was for sending a pound of butter but it would have been nothing but grease. You've eaten nothing so far as I can see."

And the very next day brought a letter from Lettice. She would be back, God willing, in two or three weeks. There were two letters besides hers. One, from Andrew, contained further expressions of gratitude and the polite hope that we were not being inconvenienced by the length of our stay. He hoped to come to the Croft at the end of September.

He and Lettice had addressed their letters to Louise. Julian had written to me, a long letter. I suspected that he was lonely. He had made enquiries at Cairlie, obviously priding himself on his diplomacy. He had found the house in a quiet street and had asked for Mr and Mrs Vince. At first the landlady had had difficulty in remembering the name. A young lady newly married? Oh yes, she remembered Louise; but the couple had left almost at once. He was some sort of lawyer, she believed. Mrs Vince had left one day and Mr Vince, having packed and settled the account, had left the next. It had evidently been a sudden decision. That would be nearly a year ago. April? No, it had been at the back end of the year. It was dark when she came home and heard from Mr Vince that his wife had left. He had been sitting without a lamp and came suddenly out on to the landing, giving her a real fright. She didn't know where they had gone.

I read with a renewed and hurtful sense of having been kept in the dark; but at least I understood now why my last letter had not reached Louise. She had not come home until April but she had left Blairgouroch in the autumn. I gave her Julian's letter to read. Her eyes travelled slowly and conscientiously from line to line like those of an earnest pupil conning a task. Then she sat up as if ready to answer the inevitable questions to the best of her ability.

"It's quite a long time since you left Nicholas."

That was what I meant to say and may, indeed, have said but in some curious way my mind was diverted from Louise and that was surprising, especially when she sat so attentively, waiting for my questions. What was it that attracted my attention so that I forgot her? A curious sensation as of the nerves responding to a movement in the air. I remember raising my head quite sharply and looking out across the verandah — we were in the parlour — and up the sloping garden to where a tall fir tree stood black and slender against the clear morning sky. Some trick of memory, some intuition, or both, brought me almost to a new kind of comprehension, then left me on the brink of discovery.

"Who is it?" Louise's startled voice recalled me to myself. She had got up and was looking in the same direction. "You saw someone."

"No. Of course not. Where did you go when you left Nicholas?"

This time I did actually speak and as she answered, I seemed again to be on the point of taking some vitally important mental step forward, as if in counterpoint to her reply there were other words I almost heard; and yet the reply itself was interesting enough.

"I went to Edinburgh." Her gaze grew dreamy as she remembered. "I took first floor rooms overlooking Queen's Street Gardens. As a married woman I could do that, you see, Hester. It was pleasant there. I could watch the nursemaids and the children. There would have been a band sometimes in the summer." Her eyes clouded with tears. "But I hadn't enough money to stay. While I had money it was easy to manage without people to pester me. I had my own piano. I paid extra for that."

She told it all with touching innocence. If I had pointed out that she had never mentioned Edinburgh until now, she would simply have said "You never asked me." All I knew of Louise had been told in answer to my questions. How little she had volunteered! It was not her nature to talk, least of all about herself.

There were to be many times when I felt afraid. So far the fear had often been on Louise's behalf; but I was to feel increasingly afraid of some quality in Louise herself. It is easier to account for it now than it was then, when I was too ignorant, too hopelessly ensnared by the fascination of Louise, to be capable of understanding what I instinctively felt. I accepted wholeheartedly her account of the stay in Edinburgh. She would live there exactly in accordance with the principles of decorum laid down by Mrs Maple, never swerving from a course of strictest propriety. What was disturbing was the absence of any background of living persons, most of all her husband. Raptly moving the balls on the counting frame or playing her piano above an empty winter street, she had been the same Louise as she was still. Unpestered by people, she could have lived in an Arctic waste. Experience could not change her because having no feelings, she had no experience; but for one exception, her fear of Nicholas Vince.

She had eluded him, not for a summer only but for almost a year. The sheer mystery of his absence occupied my mind continually until at last I found a reason. It came to me, not in a blaze of light, but as a slowly growing clarification, the only one possible. By some cruel freak of Fate, Louise, who could have chosen a husband from an eager host of the best, had married an out-and-out villain; violent in his treatment of her: dishonest in his dealings with such unfortunate individuals as the man who had called. Either he was hiding from justice or — more likely — he had been arrested for one of his many felonies and put in prison.

Having reached this obvious conclusion almost with a gasp, I refrained just in time from passing it on to Louise. The disgrace of having a husband in prison would be too much for her. Besides the whole point of a term of imprisonment was that it came, eventually to an end. Why subject her to the misery of counting the days until his release? In vague uncertainty lay endless hope.

In all this, I thought of Louise; but in my heart a little secret spring of happiness rose unchecked. Julian might never marry me but he could not marry Louise either.

Because it was impossible to live in a state of constant anxiety, we grew easier, Days passed. The man in the boots stayed away. Codlin Croft could never be the same without Aunt Tamar, but just to be there, to sit on her chintz-covered chairs and see her tatting basket on its stool, to tend her flowers and poultry and answer letters that had come too late to reach her, made me feel close to her and postponed the final parting. That would be when Cousin Andrew came.

It is difficult to remember the exact sequence of events in a period when time flowed so smoothly as to seem, in memory, an unchanging current. It was before Lettice came home that my plan occurred to me. I'm sure of that. I remember thinking that if Lettice had known I was going to the Fleece, she would have given me some message for her sister who lived over the stables there, her husband being an ostler, whereas in her absence it was simply a matter of putting on a hat and saying that I was going for a walk, a habit that had grown on me as I discovered the beauty of the countryside, after a girlhood spent in Wickborough.

The plan was so sensible that I felt annoyed at not having thought of it before. I should have gone to the Fleece immediately after the unknown man's visit and simply had a talk with him, without telling Louise.

"I wonder if we could have a little chat," I would say, having found out his name, "about something of interest to us both."

It seemed a thoroughly competent choice of phrase. I would skilfully discover what he knew about Nicholas Vince: his background and history and whether there was more recent news of him than that contained in Julian's letter.

I chose my time carefully. After luncheon Louise often went to her room to occupy herself with the small pieces of sewing most properly carried out, according to Mrs Maple, in private. The fact that we were two sisters with the parlour to ourselves in an entirely feminine household caused no wavering in Louise's adherence to this blameless habit. Meanwhile I would walk to the Fleece and be back for five o'clock tea.

My chief anxiety was lest the man should have left. In that case I could at least find out his name. The thought drove me to put on my things in a spurt of haste, as if a few minutes would make any difference when days had been wasted, and I ran downstairs, feeling pleased at the prospect of an outing and in my pleasure, forgetting why I had of late been indoors so much.

All the more shattering then, as I glanced in the hall looking-glass, was the knock at the front door.

13

IMMEDIATELY, TILLY APPEARED. I swept her aside like a stray chicken, stepped into the porch, closed the inner door behind me, drew a deep, strengthening breath and opened the front door.

A tall, powerfully built man filled the doorway.

"Oh Thomas." I laughed, almost in tears. "Oh Thomas, it's just you."

I held out both hands. He took my right in his and shook it warmly.

"That's right, Miss Hester. It's just me. And who did you think it might be?"

He asked directly as if he thought the answer important. In his voice and quiet eyes I felt a personal concern, for me. Yet in his unruffled way he was pleased, for some reason. Because I had seen nothing like it for some time, I was aware of his happiness. It moved me. My voice shook.

"I meant — no one saw you coming."

"You wouldn't see me. I came over the fields." Glancing up, I saw that the concern was still there. "You keep a lookout then?"

"Come in, Thomas. I'm glad to see you."

"And you keep all the doors shut." He opened the inner one for me.

"It's cooler," I said quickly, "and it keeps out the flies."

"It would be an obstinate fly," Thomas said, "that would make his way through two doors like that." He paused to admire the oak panels and iron studs on the outer and the handsome brass lock on the inner before looking round the hall. "It's a gracious house, Miss Hester. A place to live at peace in."

Tilly hovered.

"It was just to take the gentleman's hat, miss."

The well-brushed beaver was Thomas's best, as were his coat and fine cambric shirt.

"Yes," he said with frank satisfaction, "you'll be noticing my new clothes. It was time, as you know. As a matter of fact, speaking of flies, I've made a guinea or two out of the insects. We sold a very nice spider yesterday. Jet body and gold legs." He went into details. "You'd hardly credit the folly of women with money in their purses."

"Did you come especially, Thomas, to see me — us?"

"There were two or three reasons, together. There's a mantel clock to be delivered at Lullerbeck Hall. Master didn't fancy sending it by the post office. I'm going there now and I'll stay to see the clock settled. I ate my dinner early at the Fleece and came out here to give you this." He felt in his pocket and produced a package wrapped in white paper. "Master seemed to want you to have it, even though you'll be coming home soon. I have the impression, Miss Hester, that he sets great store by the article in that paper as well as the one it's for."

I opened it reluctantly. Father had renewed the glass, removed all signs of damage from the case and attached it to the gold chain.

"It's my mother's watch."

"You'll be pleased to wear it then, especially as he seems so set on it."

He might have been prompting me but there was no reproach in his voice, only still, and increasingly, concern.

I put the chain over my head and was conscious of the weight of the watch on my breast.

"It was a sad thing," Thomas observed, and I felt him observing me too, "a sudden death like that."

The remark caught me quite unprepared. I felt the blood drain from my cheeks. He had found out then.

"Mrs Lind passing away so suddenly."

"Oh, Aunt Tamar. Yes, yes, very sad."

"You thought I was referring to someone else's decease?" Thomas said slowly.

"We miss her very much. It isn't the same."

"But you're feeling better for your stay in the country?"

"Yes, Thomas."

"And Miss Mallow? I trust she's well too."

"Yes, thank you. We're both well."

"Master Mallow asked me to find out how things are with you here and whether you need help of any kind."

"No, thank you," I said, looking at his broad shoulders and kind calm face, but avoiding his eyes.

"You've all the money you need, for instance."

I nodded.

"Is there anything I can do to arrange your journey home? Would you like me to bespeak a carriage when I go back to the Fleece, for the appropriate day?"

"Did you — were there —? It must be quiet at the Fleece now that the summer visitors have gone."

This feeble stratagem provided so unsuitable an answer to Thomas's question, as he plainly showed, that I felt obliged to blunder on:

"I only meant if there are no visitors there, it won't be necessary to order a carriage until nearer the time."

"There were one or two gentlemen in the dining room," Thomas said thoughtfully. "As to nearer the time, when will that be?"

I explained the position.

"Then as soon as Mrs Lind's nephew comes, you'll be

coming home; and more than welcome you'll be, as Mrs Wragge asked me particularly to tell you, not to mention Master." He hesitated. "He's slowed down a bit this summer. I don't like leaving him on his own too much. In fact I'd best be getting off to the Hall."

"Give father my love." I heard my voice tremble again and was surprised to discover that the message was heartfelt. "And thank him for the watch."

It was not perhaps a sign of the warmest gratitude to take it off. I put it on the table and nervously laid the chain round it like a frame. Thomas declined to take any refreshment.

"You were going out, Miss Hester?"

I explained that my errand was to Bidewell. He walked with me part of the way through the fields. It was he who talked, his slow voice a background to my anxious thoughts. An impulse to confide in him almost overcame me. He was the very person to tell: understanding yet impartial: full of common sense and kindness.

"She must go back to her husband," I imagined him saying. "That's what Mrs Vince must do. She's taken him for better or worse. But if you ask me — it's taken him nearly a year to think things over. He's in no hurry."

But it wasn't my secret; nor was it fair to put Thomas in the moral dilemma of having to keep it from father.

When we parted at the stile where the field path met the road, I felt lonely.

"It's been a privilege to see you, Miss Hester." Thomas stood bareheaded. "After all this time. Not that it's far from Wickborough. Easy enough to be here in a day if need be."

We shook hands again. He left me poised between reassurance and alarm. Thomas was not the only one who could cover the distance between Wickborough and Lullerbeck in a day.

To ask at the Fleece for a gentleman would be embarrassing, especially without knowing his name. I paused by the archway leading to the stables, summoning up courage to go in at the front door, when as if by magic, Ned came into view, sat down in the corner just inside the arch and made a great show of tidying his box. I went nearer and watched him shaking out his cloths and inspecting his brushes.

"You've missed it, miss, the waggonette for the railway. It went five minutes since."

"I didn't want the waggonette, and I'm sorry, Ned, I haven't a book for you today."

"Never mind, miss," he said bravely, and I felt remorseful. "There's plenty I can read again and I've got this." He produced a copy of the sensational news-sheet masquerading under the name of *Illustrated Police News*. "Like to look at it?"

The offer was made in a spirit of comradeship, from one student of literature to another. Not wanting to offend him, I glanced fearfully at the crude illustrations: an open coffin: a tall hat and an inch of forehead above the surface of a quicksand with the caption: Too late to drag him out, witness asserted. With Ned's eye upon me I dutifully skimmed the headlines above stories of corpses and exhumations, lonely farmhouses and shrieks at dead of night.

"It does you no harm, miss," Ned said solemnly, "to learn the ways of the wicked. Stories like that can put you on your guard, especially a lad in my place that hopes to marry some day. It's been an eye-opener to me to read what some of those women have been up to, aiding and abetting, urging on and covering up. And if you were to see them, they'd likely look as good and innocent nearly as yourself, miss."

In the few weeks I had known him he had become surprisingly articulate as if every word he had read and re-read with such ravenous interest had enlarged his understanding. I listened, amused by both his knowledge of the world and his innocent wonder at its ways.

"Take her, for instance." He took the news sheet from me, folded it back and pointed to the ghastly drawing of a female with snake-like hair and cruelly curving lips, under the screaming headline: 'She knew but would not tell. Murderer protected by woman's silence'. "She was as guilty as what he was. He was the one that did it but she was" — just for a second he hesitated then brought out the word successfully — "an accessory. That's a person that knows about a crime but hushes it up. Here, take it, miss. It doesn't take hold of you like Robinson but you'll find plenty to interest you."

"No, thank you, Ned. It isn't quite — to my taste. I don't believe it does any good to read such things."

He looked at me with quick understanding.

"You think it'll lower me?" he asked surprisingly.

"Yes, if you think too much about horrid things like that."

I reproached myself for not having brought him something more uplifting to read, feeling at the same time that Ned would lift himself up. The editor of the *Illustrated Police News* would not find in him an easy victim.

"How long have you been a shoe-black, Ned?"

"Only this summer, miss. Before that I had a crossing to sweep in Wickborough. Couldn't hardly read more than a few words in them days." He spoke of his unenlightened state with cheerful contempt, then went on confidentially, "It's my aim to go up in the world — as far as I can go. Something in the law mebbe. A judge."

From the catch in his breath and his quick look to see how I was taking it before he set about blacking a brush, I knew that I was sharing a secret dream.

"You did wisely then to learn to read."

"The best thing that ever happened to me was meeting Mrs Tafferty's lodger. I swept a crossing for him and we got talking. He was a gent that always had time to talk. He give me good advice. 'Learn to read and write, Ned, and you'll go up. Otherwise you'll stay where you are.' It was him that told me I could go to the Board School in Nidgate and he wrote a letter to the managers to tell them I couldn't afford the ninepence. They let me in for twopence a week. I learned like wildfire and here I am, going up."

Prompted by the preliminary and enthusiastic spit he now gave to the first boot, I remembered my mission.

"Do you have many boots to clean?"

"Not now. There's only one gent staying here."

131

"I believe I may have seen him. Does he drive out to Lullerbeck sometimes in a cab?"

"Mr Benjamin? No, he's gone. He left a week or two back. He came from Scotland, Mr Benjamin did."

"Has he gone back to Scotland?"

"Couldn't say, miss. Wickborough was where he went when he left us." Then as I turned away he said kindly, "Why don't you have a cup of tea in the garden here before you walk back to Lullerbeck?"

For a treat I did as he suggested, drank tea at a rustic table and in a cheerful mood walked back to the Croft by the river path. To have talked to Mr Benjamin would have been an ordeal. I was glad to have missed him. He slipped from my mind and with him Nicholas Vince. It was enough that Nicholas existed. So long as he stayed away, he did no harm and fulfilled the excellent function of preventing Louise from marrying Julian. In the privacy of my own thoughts I could be selfish. From selfishness I progressed to hope. In time, all would come right again. Julian needed me. It was in me he could confide, not Louise. Our lives were rooted in the same experiences, tastes — and beliefs? His loss of faith was merely a part of his general tiresomeness at present. With all my follies I was just wise enough to see that he had loved the Church for the wrong reasons. There was nothing to stop him from learning to love it again for the right ones. Except Louise.

In the shade of its alders I watched the Audley sliding smoothly south. In time it would come to St Mary-on-Audley and the quiet reach by the parsonage where the kingfisher darted low under the overhanging branches, a flash of living blue. Louise would not have cared about the kingfisher. "It's pretty," she had said, looking down at the parsley, not up at the Abbey. She did not discriminate between parsley and abbeys, between Julian and other men. It didn't matter to Louise where she was so long as she was safe, unpestered. With a gush of gratitude I thanked God that she would never be mistress of the little parsonage and some day when Julian recovered his senses . . . Watching the blackberries glow red and black

132

in the sunshine of declining summer, I forgot Louise's beauty; forgot too its power to enchant the eye each time one saw it again.

She was not in the parlour. The sun was low. On the round table lay mother's watch: a lovely thing of blue and white and gold. The lady with the lyre sat still, unmoved by the leaf-shadows that rose and fell on table and carpet and made the whole room tremble. Whatever hand had fashioned her had placed her beyond the reach of time in an element where she could not change. The surrounding enamel had not escaped a scratch or two but the lady was unblemished. How strange! The watch kept on coming back to me. There was no escaping it. Whatever its adventures, it was meant to be mine. I must wear it and I must tell Louise about it. I came reluctantly to these conclusions, put out my hand and paused. Had Louise already seen it ? The chain, which I had laid in a careless curve round the watch, now enclosed it in a perfect circle with a mathematically straight stem from hook to perimeter. It was so typical of her that I smiled.

"Louise!"

She was not in her room, nor in the garden. The maids had not seen her all afternoon.

"Tilly thought you'd both gone with the gentleman," Edith said, "when no one rang for tea."

But Edith thought she had seen one of the young ladies come out through the verandah when she was hanging out the tea-towels. From the wrangling that followed, it emerged that one young lady in a black dress and Leghorn hat could easily be mistaken for another.

"The one with the gentleman must have been Miss Hester," Edith said.

But Tilly was almost sure that the one with the gentleman had been Miss Mallow.

14

THE EVENING WORE on. Louise did not return. An anxious rummaging in her cupboards and drawers revealed that she had taken her velvet bag, purse, hairbrush and comb and, I thought, a nightdress and slippers. She had not, then, strayed from the garden and been pounced upon. On the other hand she had not left a note. That troubled me. She could not surely be so unfeeling as to have given no thought to my anxiety. That I should have come to so naïve a conclusion in spite of having known Louise for some time, was just another example of my failure to learn from experience. She had gone, in the same manner as she had gone from Cairlie and before that, so far as I knew, from Blairgouroch.

But I had learned that Louise would not lightly leave Codlin Croft and submit herself to the hazards of the outer world; not without good reason though the reason might be, must be, an unpleasant one. If there could be two young ladies, could there not also have been two gentlemen? Had Nicholas Vince silently appeared, unseen by the maids, stood over Louise while, trembling, she packed the velvet bag, and dragged her off to face the terrible reckoning in some secret spot? Had he been watching day and night until she was alone, seen me go off with Thomas and seized his chance? Even though nothing was too bad to attribute to Nicholas Vince, my reason almost reluctantly rejected these colourful fancies. There was no *need* for him to behave like that.

Without Louise in front of me to melt my heart and undermine my common sense by the touching droop of her lips or the pitiful break in her voice, I was able to keep my anxiety under control. Louise had a surprising knack of looking after herself. Well, it was not the faculty that was surprising so much as my feeling that it should be so. On reflection I found that every situation adapted itself quite naturally to the convenience of Louise.

In this mood I actually lay down on the sofa, my head on one of Aunt Tamar's cushions, and was about to consign Louise to the careful hands of Providence, should she be unable for once, to manage on her own, when my eyes came to rest on the mother-of-pearl and papier-mâché table where Louise kept her beadwork in a beaded bag. The table was bare, in so far as an object so lavishly ornamented could be called bare. Louise had taken her beadwork.

Strange to say, the fact made no difference. Louise could have taken her beadwork with the same sedate grace and arranged it in her velvet bag so that nothing was cramped or rumpled, whether she was going into the garden for an hour or whether she was fleeing the terrors of the damned. There was absolutely no means of judging her inward state from her appearance and behaviour. Indeed her appearance made judgment of any kind impossible.

Removed from it, I remained surprisingly calm. All the same, uncertainty kept me awake. At some early hour of the morning I drew my curtains and felt the cool dawn wind on my tired face. From the bracken beyond the garden came the melancholy bleat of sheep, a cry of loneliness and loss that made me scan the grey slopes anxiously in sudden fear that Louise might be out there exhausted and alone. A new impatience to find and help her made the hours until breakfast seem endless. Even then I was so unwilling to alarm the maids that I made a show of leisurely preparation before setting off for Lullerbeck to make enquiries.

Once through the field gate, since there was no one about, I ran all the way, only slowing down within a stone's throw of the half dozen thatched cottages round the green. Mrs Hidkin's daughter-in-law sold tea, sugar, needles and thread over a table covered with brown plush in her front room. She must have wondered at the length of time and the amount of animated chatter I expended on buying a paper of pins. She was not a talkative woman and her mind was on her stew-pot.

"My sister brought black thread, I believe, when she came in yesterday," I said, with an uneasy hankering after the frankness and honesty I seemed to have lost.

135

"The other young lady hasn't been here but once," the younger Mrs Hidkin said, "and that was when you both came asking for butter-muslin which I hadn't got."

"I was mistaken then in thinking she came to Luller-beck yesterday."

"She may have got the thread in Bidewell," Mrs Hidkin volunteered as she went back to her onions. "Her next door —" she jerked her head in the direction of her neighbour — "was telling me she'd seen the young lady go off to Bidewell yesterday with the gentleman."

Mrs Hidkin's respectful distinction between 'the' and 'a' gentleman was not lost on me. Whomsoever Louise had walked to Bidewell with, it was implied, must be a gentleman having some connection with the household. It was even possible that he had been seen in the village before, as Mr Benjamin had been. My fears revived. The notion that Nicholas had been lurking in the neighbourhood seemed not only less preposterous than on the previous evening but highly probable. We had exhausted ourselves in avoiding poor Mr Benjamin, only to be taken unawares when the real villain arrived.

At our own field gate I paused, wondering whether Louise and her companion had gone by road or through the pasture. Having come home by the river path, I had missed them. While I had been indulging happy dreams of my own future, Louise had been facing a very present trouble. After all my efforts to help her, at the actual moment of need she had been alone.

It was mid-day when I arrived again at the Fleece. Again Ned quietly appeared and again looked hopefully at the extra pocket I was wearing. With him, however, I was on terms of complete honesty.

"I promised to bring you a book, Ned, and I haven't. This is an unexpected visit to Bidewell. Did you see a young lady pass by, yesterday, or get into a carriage?" I described her as being of my own height and wearing a similar dress.

"There was nobody here all the afternoon except yourself, miss. They were all at Wickborough races except me and the kitchen girls and Mr Stilesworth."

It seemed likely that if Louise had been anywhere near the Fleece, Ned would have divined her presence, mistaking her for me and hoping for a book. I was halfway back to the Croft when it occurred to me that young Mrs Hidkin's neighbour had probably made that very mistake. She had seen me walking to Bidewell with Thomas, not Louise at all. Tired, hungry and despondent, I sat down on the bottom rung of the stile. My morning had been wasted. The calm, reasonable mood of the night before had quite left me. An unexplained absence opens a floodgate of disturbing possibilities. I was distressed, not only for Louise, not even chiefly for Louise, but by a growing sense that in the contest between Louise and her husband I had put myself on the wrong side, however much the thought of Nicholas Vince alarmed me.

The eye-strain which had ceased to trouble me when I gave up the fine hairwork, had come on me again. My head ached. The ripe corn swayed though there was no wind. A tree swelled to the width of two trees and shrank again. Closing my eyes, I imagined myself with Thomas, walking through the fields, and watched the mental image change. With a slight touch — but with oh, how significant a re-moulding of form and feature! — I became Louise and at my side —? To create the shape of Nicholas Vince was beyond me. Besides, no feat of imagination could change Thomas. Dear, good Thomas!

I went home and found no ease in a conversation with Tilly who was waiting for me in the hall.

"Beg pardon, miss." She was round-eyed. The situation had been thoroughly discussed no doubt, in the kitchen. Edith was hastily laying the cloth for a belated luncheon. "It come to me all of a sudden when I was putting the silver tea-pot back in the cabinet there that I must have seen Miss Mallow going up the garden. It would be about a quarter to three yesterday afternoon. I remember thinking 'Miss Hester's come back' and wondering where you were going, for there's nought up there but the path over the Rigg. But you hadn't come back so it must have been Miss Mallow."

In the middle of luncheon a possible explanation came to me. Louise had been in her room when Thomas called. She had not seen him coming because he had come through the fields. Hearing a man's voice, she had leapt to the conclusion that it was Mr Benjamin's or worse still, her husband's. She had watched her opportunity to slip out and literally run away, up the garden and out into the path through the bracken, because it led her away from the road, the house, the village. It led nowhere except . . . I had wasted my time on the wrong Mrs Hidkin.

The theory appealed to me because there was no place in it for Nicholas Vince. The absurd fact that Louise had taken her beadwork as she fled did not shake me. By this time I had accepted in Louise an eccentricity, to use no harsher word, of which her coolness was a necessary part. Her standards of behaviour were abnormal. I still believed then that she had standards. Now I can see that she merely behaved.

I put on my hat again and told the girls where I was going.

"Miss Mallow would have to stay the night," I said. "She would be tired."

I spoke with feeling. Scurrying to the village, thence to Bidewell and back would have provided sufficient exercise for one day. It was foolish to set off on another much longer walk when the afternoon was already well advanced: unsuitable too to go alone like a labouring woman. Nevertheless I set off grimly up the steep garden and through the gate to the rough stretch of gorse and bracken above, and so to the top of the hill where I stopped, realising what I had undertaken. A huge sweep of interlocking hills stretched, heather-clad, from west to north to east. Above their vast expanse soared a sky so wide and deep from horizon to zenith that its white clouds seemed no larger in their field of blue than the white sheep on the hills below.

Alone on the ridge, I seemed to shrink to so small a compass that I dared not move. To take one step into that silent, unwelcoming territory seemed an act of reckless courage. In primitive awe I covered my eyes and was even more conscious of the watching hills and waiting sky. Pretending to myself that it was only to rest, I crouched down on the heather and stared defensively at the dry stems of ling, deliberately limiting my gaze, until gradually, discovering that in the stillness ants were busy on the thin soil and in the silence bees were murmuring, I regained my usual size.

But it was the thought of Louise that gave me confidence to go on. If the solitude and the distance frightened me, what must they have done to her? Louise was afraid of the sea, the tall towers of the Abbey, the endless ticking of the clocks, the watchful eye of God, of anything she could not count or measure. If she had come to the ridge and gone on, how much greater must have been her fear of whatever she was running away from.

With no idea of my direction, I took the widest track through the heather. It led me away from the ridge and towards the east where presently I could look down into the cleft of a deep valley on my left. At the bottom of a long slope the young Audley foamed between fern-fringed rocks and young larch. Mrs Hidkin's direction "just over the Rigg" made no allowance for the twists and turns of the rough track. I had given up hope of finding any sign of human life when, miraculously, a jag of outcrop rock, one of many, proved to be no rock at all but the gable end and chimney of a house with its back to the eastern hill.

The sight was encouraging. Moreover, the further I went the less bare became the scene. Becks went tumbling down into the Audley through leafy little valleys of their own. There were patches of thyme and bilberry bushes, their small leaves already red. But it was not yet autumn. The air felt thick with the humid softness of late summer. The outlines of rocks and trees were blurred or so it seemed to me, but then I was tired and my eyes ached. The unexpected lurch of a sheep across my path made me jump and I jumped even more violently when a turn in the track brought me almost face to face with a shepherd sitting on a stone and smoking a clay pipe. He touched his hat and seemed inclined to talk but his speech was rough and I didn't catch all he said.

He was less surprised than I, having seen me from a higher point some minutes before.

"Yes, I saw you. 'She's back again, I thowt'." He stopped short and looked at me more carefully. "By sangs, it's another lady."

"Was that yesterday? You must have seen my sister. She's gone to visit Mrs Hidkin."

I spoke with confidence. My theory was confirmed.

"Is she poorly like — Mistress Hidkin?"

"No. I hope not. She asked us to call and see her."

He looked impressed, as he might well be, by the energy with which we cultivated Mrs Hidkin's acquaintance. The house — it still seemed a long way off — was indeed hers.

"Never in my mortal days," he observed as we parted, "have I seen so many folk on Sleedale Rigg. Year in year out there's nowt but sheep and me and Matty Hidkin — and Tom and his wife once a month from Lullerbeck. Three strangers in no more than two days! The world's changing fast."

"Three strangers!"

"Ay, a big chap walking fast not so long after the other lady went by."

"Where did he go?"

The shepherd shook his head. They had passed the time of day no more. The man had been in a hurry.

Another twist of the track and I was alone again. How quickly the scene could change. How easily the rise and fall of the land could conceal a sheep, a shepherd, a stranger! As easily as the murmur of running water could muffle a sound. I walked softly, nervously alert, half expecting at each turn of the track to find someone ahead of me; or standing by the wayside, waiting. From time to time I caught a glimpse of Mrs Hidkin's house below, each time more clearly until I could look down on its chimneys and into its square of green garden enclosed by stone walls.

My path crossed a narrower track leading up at right

angles to the ridge. Instead of hurrying on, I sat down. My limbs were shaking, from tiredness, I dare say, but also from an extraordinary nervousness. The situation was peculiar, as far removed from my normal experience as this remote spot from the narrow house in Silvergate. It was fraught with so many unknown factors that I found it difficult to single out any one of them and think about it sensibly.

One of the problems, however, was soon solved. I had been sitting there for a few minutes when a slight figure in black appeared in Mrs Hidkin's garden: Louise. She must have come out of the front door which was beyond my range of vision. She stepped into the shelter of two or three low-growing fruit trees and seemed to be leaning against the trunk of one of them, submitting dreamily to light and air like the stone nymph at St Mary; or was she expertly judging the condition of Mrs Hidkin's apples and mentally putting them into pies?

I didn't call out. Having come all this way, I didn't want to see her. The discovery was distressing. Now that I could look down on her and not at her face, I saw the small black form quite clearly as a threat to my peace of mind. Never, since she had stepped out of the cab and stood shining like silver on the pavement, never since then had I known a moment's ease. It was not only that she had taken Julian from me. She had changed Julian. She had changed me. We both loved her and through knowing her we had both been altered for the worse, while she herself had not changed one iota. Here was I, puzzled, anxious, tired, hungry, and there was she in the cool shade, having left the Croft without a word of explanation. Her choice of refuge was so incongruous that for a minute or two the assumptions on which my view of life was based fell away in disorder. I tried to remember why we were here instead of at the Croft or in the dear lop-sided house in Silvergate. I entertained a notion of madness. It occurred to me that Louise might be out of her mind, driven out of it by her fear of Nicholas Vince. The thought filled me with such irrational terror as to infect the whole landscape. The hills themselves quaked.

141

I had almost forgotten him. The memory restored me to a clearer vision of my surroundings; except that my vision was not clear. My head swam. My eyes played tricks with me again. Mrs Hidkin's chimney moved across the river, hung for a moment above the swelling slope on the other side, then moved back again and settled on its wavering roof. I tried to get up but my knees would not support me.

It was in half turning, with my hands pressing down on the heather, that I saw him: Nicholas Vince. I never doubted it. This time I was sure. He was quite close, less than a hundred yards away, looking, not towards me but down at the house, at the green square where Louise stood under the scanty shade of the trees.

I sat still, weak with fear. How had he come there so silently? Had he been there all the time? I couldn't quite see him in detail and dared not move to get a clearer view. He seemed to be dressed in grey — a lightish grey. There was something inhuman about him. That could have been my imagination but he was not what I would have expected. His posture was hawk-like, intent, thrusting forward but absolutely still. I could just distinguish a dark shape behind him like a pack or bag. He was leaning from behind a boulder so that only the upper part of his body was visible, particularly the sharp angle of his left shoulder and clear-cut forehead and profile, as hard as if they were cut in wood. These details were unimportant. The horror came from his silent presence and sinister stillness.

The house lay below, innocent as a sheepfold at the mercy of the wolf. I prayed that Louise would not move. My irritation had gone. My disapproval of her conduct melted into the familiar longing to protect her. I had misjudged her. She had been right. "He'll find me, Hester. I'm always expecting to look up and see him, watching me." And here he was, having traced her to this isolated spot.

Wild plans flashed through my mind. A scream of warning? But where could Louise go? Short of hurling herself from a crag she could find no escape. "Tell him I'm

142

dead." The husky voice sounded again in the depths of my heart. "It will soon be true." Pity for her sharpened my wits. So long as Nicholas Vince didn't see Louise in the garden, another girl in black would serve to distract that fearful fixed and wolfish gaze. He would see me and think I was Louise. He would see me running away and think I was running away from him. Excitement affected my eyes again. Surely he had moved. His angular figure bulged and seemed to turn. I blinked. He was as still as before.

The sick faintness left me. I got up in a single sudden movement and just in time. Louise had turned at the same instant and walked back to the house. Stumbling over my skirt, I recovered myself and took to my heels, waving my arms as I ran to make more commotion. In my flurry, remembering only that I must run away from the house, I took the narrow path to the left instead of the way I had come, each step taking me into unfamiliar country.

I risked a backward glance. He was not, after all, coming after me. Yet the rustle of feet was unmistakable. It was coming towards me. He must have made a detour through the heather to cut me off. He loomed above me on the path, gigantic against the sky.

"You mustn't hurt Louise," I cried out. "You mustn't hurt Louise," and fell sobbing at the feet of Thomas Griff.

Thomas said very little, so far as I remember, but presently I found myself leaning against a cushion of heather and sipping water from a bottle he had taken from his bag. I remember too the brief sensation of having come home after an impossible adventure: brief because almost at once anxiety returned.

"Has he gone?"

"There's nobody here," Thomas said, " so far as I can see."

He walked to a hillock a few yards away, looked about him and came back.

"I was running away," I began.

"Never mind what you were doing," he said, rather

143

sternly, I thought. "Just sit there and keep quiet for a
bit."

It was remarkable how quickly he re-shaped the distorted scene and removed its feverish elements. My heart-
beat became less frantic. I stopped shuddering and sobbing
and watched a fleecy cloud browsing in its field of blue.
Presently Thomas gave me a slice of bread and a piece of
cheese.

"How very strange — you just happening to be there
at that very moment. Where did you come from?"

"From Lullerbeck Hall. The clock went like a charm.
There was no need for me to stay more than one night.
For that matter it seems strange to find you here, Miss
Hester, by yourself and in such a state — of mind," he
added tactfully.

I was aware of cutting a sorry figure and sat up,
making an attempt to tidy my hair.

"I came to find Louise." If only I could tell him! But
one confidence would lead to another. Either the whole
story must be told or none of it. "She's at Mrs Hidkin's
down there."

"Then the best thing would be for me to take you there.
You need a rest."

"No," I said quickly. "Louise doesn't know I'm here.
I was just going down to the house when I saw him." I
got up. "Would you mind looking again, Thomas, just to
make sure? Has he gone down to the house, I wonder."

"Who?" Thomas said.

"There was a man, watching . . ."

He followed me to the hillock.

"Can you see anyone?"

"Not a soul."

For some reason Thomas looked sad and troubled.

"You don't believe me. Come, I'll show you where I
was."

Feeling safe with Thomas behind me, I went quickly
down the track, turned to the right and found the very
spot where I had sat: or almost the same spot. Only by
taking up exactly the same position and attitude as before
could I have recaptured the illusion that Nicholas Vince

was still there. Had I moved a foot or two, a few inches even, I would have seen him for what he was: a lightning-struck birch leaning from a boulder. A leafless, splintered bough stuck out in sharp profile from the bleached trunk. One of those broomlike outgrowths of twigs peculiar to birches had the look of a pack on square angular shoulders: or would have had such a look to a person half crazed by fear of a watchful enemy.

Still, even Thomas admitted that anyone might have been deceived.

"You see," I pointed, shamefaced, to the nose and brow. Even then the shape frightened me. I had given it life and could not yet see it as only a stricken tree resting on a grey rock.

"Yes," Thomas said soothingly. "Anyone might have been taken in especially if they had it in mind to see such a person in such a place."

The merest movement and Nicholas Vince was there again, all his obsessive desire for Louise expressed in the fierce forward tilt of his head and shoulders, all his determination to possess her again concentrated in the devilish sharpness of his wooden features. Even with Thomas there I would not have gone an inch nearer in case he moved at last, got up and went down with monstrous strides through the heather to Mrs Hidkin's house.

At the same time I could have died of shame and would have done, I felt sure, if anyone but Thomas had found me out in such a piece of folly. He had not spoken again. Belatedly I recognised his last words as an invitation to tell more. But I had not foreseen the direction his thoughts would take until he looked down at me with straightforward sympathy and said gently:

"Had you been expecting to see the same man?"

"The same?"

"As you saw —" he hesitated — "as frightened you in the yard in Silvergate."

"Oh no, no." I stared at him and shook my head violently. "No, no." I said it several times, more and more emphatically because it was so difficult to know what to say next. We had been involved in a similar situation before, Thomas and I. Then as now, he had found me shaking with fright over an apparition that only I had seen. In each case it had been a nameless man. From Thomas's grave look I knew that he thought me — odd. Who could blame him if he took an even gloomier view and feared for my sanity as I had come to fear for Louise's? Had not I myself found a touch of madness in the turn that affairs had taken?

It was time to extricate myself from a danger far worse than any that threatened in the shape of Nicholas Vince. With an enormous and I believe in the circumstances a creditable effort of will, I pulled myself together; and yet, in so far as I was able to scramble out of the morass of mystery and suspicion in which he found me, most of the credit was due to Thomas. His goodness and un-shakable sense restored me to the well-regulated life from which I had somehow strayed, as though across the silent moor came the orderly ticking of clocks: the quarterly chimes: the harmonious striking of the hour.

As if to endorse the idea, Thomas said: :

"I don't half understand what's been happening, Miss Hester, but it seems to me you've been walking in strange ways; and the best thing would be for you to walk out of them again."

The wonderful simplicity of this suggestion impressed me.

"It's only a question," he said, "of whether you want to join Miss Mallow down there or whether you don't. But if you'll pardon me for saying it, you and Miss Mallow may have had enough of each other for a while and it might be best for me to take you back the way you came." Then no doubt recalling the words with which I had so eccentrically greeted him, "As for anyone hurting Miss Mallow, from what I know of her it isn't likely." He glanced down at Mrs Hidkin's chimney stack. "She should be all right down there. She's a grown woman used to fending for herself whereas you look done in. I'll tell you what, if it would ease your mind, I'll walk down there and just see if all's well."

"She went there without telling me where she was going."

As the clouds of fantasy rolled away, I faced the silent spaces of Louise's life. She surpassed me in more than looks. Her powers of concealment far exceeded even mine. So far as I knew she had never misrepresented the truth but her omissions, once made good, had proved to be staggering, chiefly her ability to conceal her marriage. The enormity of that piece of deception amazed me all over again. Dimly I saw that Louise's limited remarks, to which her husky tones gave the significance of clues to a wider, loftier truth, might be clues I had entirely misinterpreted. The character of Nicholas Vince, for instance. But I was weary of him, utterly weary.

"No," I said. "We'll go back to the Croft."

When we had finished the bread and cheese, we left him there, leaning over the rock, watching Louise: a monster of the faery world to which Louise's magic had brought me. The skeleton form, blanched and bare, may still be there for all I know. I turned my back on him, leaving him to the moorland winds, and at the same time resolved to close my mind to all thoughts of Louise's husband. Wherever he was, languishing in prison or sailing the high seas, it was no affair of mine.

"You mustn't tell father."

"I'll tell Mr Mallow what I think fit," Thomas said. "No more and no less. But what I can't tell him is that you're looking any better for your holiday, Miss Hester."

From the ridge our way lay mainly downhill. Thomas entertained me with news of Wickborough and when that was exhausted he hummed and whistled 'The British Grenadiers'. Stepping out to the tune, I managed the walk well. It was dusk when we went through the gate into the garden. A robin sang. Above the scented fir trees hung a new moon.

"It's a peaceful spot," Thomas said.

And for a while I too felt the peace of the place return, as I remembered Aunt Tamar and forgot Louise.

15

RISING LATE AND going to bed early, I spent a good deal of the next two or three days in bed, almost recapturing the tranquil charm of the time when we had first come. Sometimes I pretended that Aunt Tamar was still there downstairs and even when the pretence faded into the recollection that she had gone, solitude was no trial to me as I watched the September days brighten and fade. I read a little and ate the carefully set meals that Tilly and Edith, breathless with anxious effort, brought to me.

Thomas, as he supped off cold pie and porter before going back to the Fleece on the evening of our return, had impressed on them my need of rest.

"You must rest, miss. That's what Mr Griff said," they told me separately several times a day, enjoying the atmosphere of lotus-eating repose as they had enjoyed the tension of the past few weeks and equally ignorant of the reason for either.

What they thought of the unexpected movements of their revered Miss Mallow I could not tell. When I told them she was staying with Mrs Hidkin, they accepted the fact as they would have accepted some innovation in the services at church. When Louise was mentioned, one of them would say:

"Miss Mallow must have rest. That's what Miss Mallow must have."

Having got into their vocabulary, the word was used a good deal.

By the third day idleness had begun to pall. The lull — as I was later to think of it — could not last for ever any more than Louise could stay indefinitely under Mrs Hidkin's humble roof. I must bring her back, but with certain adjustments in our relationship. There must be a complete clearing of the air. I would insist on her telling father that she was married and had left her husband. Never again would I lift a finger to help her to hide from him. Kindly but firmly I would wash my hands of them both and fix my mind on the improvements in my own

148

prospects. Whatever its disadvantages to her, Louise's marriage had nothing but advantages for me.

During those quiet days, in spite of my vow to forget Nicholas Vince, I did for the first time consider another possibility, then reproved myself for always looking on the black side of things. Besides, if he *had* unfortunately died, we would have heard of it. Louise would have been found and informed. A vision of solicitors, documents and respectable, grieved relatives represented my idea of Nicholas Vince's death, when, in time, he should be gathered to his fathers, wherever he was now. My recent experiences had mellowed my opinion of him by sharpening my attitude to Louise. I was inclined to let him out of prison and hand him over to a press gang or put him into a hospital, in so far as I dwelt on his adventures at all. He was fading into the past, like a fictitious character safe within the covers of a book.

One morning, then, within a week of Thomas's visit, I rose up, full of energy, put on my thickest boots, took a parcel of food and a bottle of cold tea and set off once more for Sleedale. The last wreaths of morning mist uncurled as I climbed to the ridge and faced the wide landscape, this time undaunted, even glorying in the empty sky and rolling hills of indigo and purple. Confronted by the open grandeur of earth and air, I felt my pettiness melt away. My spirit expanded to embrace a wider charity. Sympathy for Louise, a true impulse of the heart this time, made me eager to talk to her, though firmly of course.

Now that I knew where it was, Mrs Hidkin's house stood out like a landmark. If Louise had wanted to hide, I thought, she should have chosen a city. Among thousands of people an individual could be lost, as indeed she had been when she went to Edinburgh. The thought of that solitary winter always disturbed me. Louise had enjoyed it. Withdrawn in her upstairs room, she had played her tunes again and again for no one to hear; and she would never have stopped and come out into the world if she could have afforded to stay there. There was something uncanny in it and in her position here. The same motive had driven her to the opposite extremity: to this moorland dwelling so conspicuous as to be an invitation to any wayfarer, to say nothing of a determined husband looking for his wife.

But I had applied the same logic when hiding the watch and the principle hadn't worked. The watch had been found again; or rather, it had found me. It had the persistence of a living thing. Once again I wearied my mind in trying to unravel its involved history and reached no conclusion except that it had been destined, or determined to hang itself round my neck. I was wearing it now as much from a feeling of fatalism as for its usefulness. It hung between Louise and me, as it were, when we came face to face in Mrs Hidkin's kitchen.

Mrs Hidkin was putting out her herbs on stone slabs in an ivy-hung outhouse.

"There you are, miss. I thought you'd be coming."

Certainly she showed no surprise. After her first guest I must have come in every sense as an anti-climax. But on her own ground Mrs Hidkin was not quite at ease. She was flushed with more than fresh air and stooping over her baskets. There was a distracted uncertainty in the way she picked up the same bunch of camomile again and again and put it back in the same place.

"She came in here that night like a spent bird. 'May I stay here, Mrs Hidkin?' she said. 'It's a pleasure, love,' I said, and give her the best bed. She hasn't said nothing." Mrs Hidkin looked at me with sudden burning curiosity. "She's just sitting there like the Queen on the tea caddy." Then with elephantine tact she said, "You'll sit down for a few minutes before you take her back?"

"Thank you, Mrs Hidkin. We shall be leaving as soon as possible. My sister can't have realised the distance. She isn't used to walking. It probably exhausted her so much that she couldn't face the walk back alone. You've been very kind."

I gave her ten shillings.

"Ee, I never thought..." she protested, astonished at the amount. Louise would have known exactly how much to give her and it would have been less, but I was determined, under the new order of things, to take charge.

"I'll speak to my sister while you finish your work."

Louise was sitting on a Windsor chair, her hands folded in her lap. In the dark, low-beamed room with its tiny window, she looked ethereal, the pure lines of her face delicate to the point of transparency. At the last minute I hesitated. For a few days I had been free of her. Some mysterious prompting made me turn back to the daylight: to the unbroken blue above and the free flowing stream below.

Or perhaps it was an instinctive shrinking from a new element in the room: a hostility. It must emanate from Louise. She did not greet me by word or smile. Her range of expression was narrow. I had never seen her brow shadowed by anger. It was not shadowed now; but in some faintly recognisable way, she bridled. I sat down at the other side of the table. Unless I put the questions, there would be no information.

"Why ever did you leave without telling me?"

The answer came with a little rush of pent-up resentment.

"Because you deceived me. I found out that you had seen him — Nicholas. Why didn't you tell me?"

"You're quite mistaken. That was Thomas. Thomas Griff."

Her unexpected choice of words, a hardness in her manner of glancing away, were puzzling.

"Do you mean that you thought it was Nicholas who called?"

"I knew that was Thomas Griff. I saw you go out."

"Then . . .?"

"You have seen Nicholas, haven't you? Or found out something about him that you haven't told me."

"Do you mean that you don't trust me?" I demanded, flabbergasted. "How could I have seen him or found out anything? Why should I have kept it from you if I had?"

It occurred to me that I had to some extent deceived her by going to the Fleece. I explained.

"It came to nothing. The man had left. His name is Benjamin. In any case, it was only to help you. I would have told you but you had gone." The sensation that she was sitting in judgment on me so outraged my feelings that I could hardly speak. "Haven't I tried to help you and ...?"

I stopped in despair and with a confused impression that my whole summer had been devoted to caring for and about Louise. It seemed to me that I had given up to her without outward sign of grudging them, my dearest hopes, my inward peace, my thoughts, my energies. It was hopeless to expect her to see that before she came, my life had been quite different.

The tremor in my voice may have reached her. She half turned her head. Seen from this new angle, her face revealed a new, lovely tension between curve of flesh and structure of bone, a new flawlessness of skin, a new depth of blue in her eyes. But I saw no sign of recognition. She was looking at me as she might have looked at apples on a tree, assessing their weight and usefulness.

"Do you swear that you have never seen Nicholas — or heard anything of him?"

"Swear? How can you ask such a thing? Can't you just believe me if I say that I've never laid eyes on him and that all I know about him is what you've told me. And that's not much. Very well then. I'll swear to you if you like that I've never seen Nicholas Vince. I hope I never do. But if ever I do see him I'll tell you, tell you, tell you ..."

I spoke with flat, deliberate emphasis. The syllables came weightily from my lips, heavy with angry denial; and then I sat still as if listening to their echo. An extraordinary conviction of their importance came to me as if I had uttered a spell. An absolute promise, unmodified by any reservation, often seems to challenge fate. It was as if I challenged it then. The atmosphere changed. I had spoken so loudly as to set the air in the dim little room quivering: or there may have been a gust from the open door. In response to some vibration there came a loud crash. A picture had fallen from its hook on the wall opposite the window.

We were both shaken. I picked it up: a daub in sombre

oils of the late Mr Hidkin, a thin-faced man with dark side-whiskers. The artist's inexpert brush had given his eyes a glassy blankness as though, when painted, he had been already dead. I re-knotted the frayed cord and hung him back on his hook, an unwelcome intruder upon an interview already depressing.

Louise had sighed and put her hand to her head in a bewildered way. My mood changed.

"Louise." I talked to her gently and seriously, telling her that her troubles had made her unreasonable. "It's not surprising, dear, considering all that you've been through. It's all been too much for you." Reluctantly, for her sake, I dragged Nicholas from the pages of fiction and murmured something about his cruelty and brutality.

Her reply was to say the least unexpected.

"Oh, but Nicholas isn't cruel."

Where facts were concerned, Louise was not unwilling to have them right.

"But I thought . . ."

"I never said he was cruel."

I stared at her, astounded; and yet cruelty to Louise would have been even more astounding. That had surely been obvious all along. As usual I had jumped to conclusions, reading into her silence what had seemed the only possible explanation of her leaving him, instead of asking for practical information.

"Tell me about him," I said with desperate patience, as if the subject had cropped up for the first time. "What sort of man is he?"

"I don't know how to describe people. He's the sort of man who longs for a thing, or person, and can't think of anything else until he's got it." Dear Louise! She was describing Julian, or any other man unfortunate enough to cross her path. "He'll never let me go because he loves me." She presented the fact as having equal weight with other facts. "He loves me so that he cannot think of anything else or want anything else. That's why I know he'll find me. All the time I expect to see him waiting for me. You don't understand, Hester, what it feels like to be haunted."

As she, I suppose, must haunt him. The tragedy of it chilled my heart. It was unlike Louise to speak of an experience so intangible. Then I realised that for her no phantom was involved but a man of flesh and blood: a husband. I realised too that if he had not made her love him, he had at least made her feel for him in another way. There was a sort of triumph in that: in having extended Louise's capacity to feel.

"How could you leave him when he loves you so much?"

She didn't answer. With a phrase or two she had put an end to the brutal felon I had imagined as successfully as if she had murdered him before my eyes. Coarse-grained, purple-veined, loud-voiced, he perished. In the lengthening silence his place was filled, for me, by an impression of watchful sadness and the patient persistence of love: an impression so moving that I felt an aching pity: so strangely familiar that I could almost have given to the new Nicholas Vince a form and shape. It was like the uneasy stirring of shadows when a candle is lit.

"It was even worse at Wickborough. Every time the bell rang downstairs, I thought he might be in the shop. Every time I looked out of the window, I expected to see him standing in the street, looking up, watching for me."

I clasped my hands to stop their trembling. The voice was Louise's. The experience was my own. It was I who had looked up Silvergate towards the print-sellers' shop. My mind opened to a new range of harrowing possibilities, like a swift and terrifying glimpse into dark waters.

"I'd rather die than go back to him."

Mechanically I recognised the familiar need to comfort her.

"I can understand, I think, why you ran away from him. It must be dreadful to marry a person and then find that you can't love him, when it's for such a long time." There was a certain relief in resorting to this lame remark and so postponing other thoughts. "But I really can't understand why you ran away from the Croft for no good reason, only an absurd fancy."

"It wasn't an absurd fancy."

154

Nor was Louise's reply a childish contradiction but a confident statement. It frightened me. I had grown used to reading into Louise's bald speeches meanings of my own. Suddenly I realised that she meant exactly what she said, always: no more: no less. I knew her powers of concealment. Her areas of silence were wide and deep. With a startled conviction that she was drawing on them now, I waited for the words that were to shatter my peace of mind for a long time to come.

"It wasn't an absurd fancy," Louise repeated. "It was the watch."

Through the open door drifted the subtle scents of hyssop and rosemary, comfrey and fumitory and the rustle of Mrs Hidkin's pinafore as she moved from tray to tray turning the grey-green bunches. The crisp air brought in sounds of running water, of becks and springs hurrying downhill to join the Audley. Yet with all my senses tinglingly alert, I might have been shrouded in dense fog, so completely did Louise's remark confuse me; and in dense fog the smallest step forward can bring catastrophe, so that I positively dared not speak. But I undid my collar and slowly pulled out the watch, which so far I had worn inside my bodice. I took it off and laid it on the table.

"I saw it at Aunt Tamar's," Louise said.

"You remember it?"

"Yes, of course. It's mother's watch." She leaned forward and pushed delicately at the chain here and there, drawing it up in a straight double line from the ring and arranging the rest in an almost perfectly circular frame round the watch.

Still fog-bound, I hesitated, intensely aware of the need for caution.

"Father gave it to me."

"Father!"

She was afraid of him as I had been. I saw it in her eyes. My own fear of him had gone. In my confusion and doubt, the wooden cubicle seemed a refuge, the figure bent over the bench a friend I had treated too lightly.

155

"Did father say where he got it?"

"He found it in a drawer."

Louise shook her head.

"I was there when he found it," I said, steering my way between looming rocks.

"Nicholas must have been to Wickborough. He must have been."

"Why do you say that?"

"I took the watch," Louise said. "I took all mother's jewellery when I went to Blairgouroch. I took it without telling father. If I had asked him," Louise's mournful voice gave to the sad fact an additional sadness, "he wouldn't have let me. I haven't dared to tell him yet. He has no idea. I suppose he must have thought someone had stolen it."

The distinction between Louise's taking and someone else's stealing was clearer to her than to me but I doubt whether it was any consciousness of reproach in my manner that made her add:

"Still, the things are all quite safe. At least I thought they were."

It was dangerous to speak but absolutely necessary to know more.

"And you gave the watch to Nicholas?"

"No." Louise showed surprise. Had she ever given him anything? "But I had this other watch and didn't wear mother's so much. Nicholas kept it for me with the bracelets and rings and chains in a box he had. While we were in furnished rooms, the partners let him keep it in their safe. I had to come away without the jewellery." Then as if apologising for this thriftless act, "But I felt sure Nicholas would keep it safe for my sake. Only of course that was why I —" She hesitated — "Well, I had to take the money instead. Otherwise I couldn't have managed, could I? I had a little of my own. The ladies gave me money when I helped them to dress and I never spent it. There was no need when Mrs Maple was alive."

For the first time her eyes glistened with unshed tears. I tried to think of something to say. Any remark would serve to put off the decision I must presently make but it wasn't easy to find one.

"It was a pity about the jewellery," Louise said. "It might have been useful. That's why I took it in the first place. But now I don't care about anything except keeping away from Nicholas."

The watch too was cold and beautiful. My dread of it was justified. It was an evil talisman. Without it I might never have found out this awful thing I would so much rather not have known. Worse than that, the knowledge was crushing the very life out of me.

"I didn't want it," I said, hating not only the watch but my whole unwilling involvement in the dreadful situation.

Louise had got up at last and gone to the door as if to make sure he was not coming. Having looked in every direction, she stood back well within the porch where she could feel the sun without being seen.

"It's driving her mad," I thought. Fear was the only emotion she could feel and she was totally possessed by it. And yet her white face as she turned it towards the blue day was as smooth as the enamelled face of the lady with the lyre and far more beautiful. It had the same air of resisting change as though its beauty had been imposed upon it by a too skilful and relentless hand: an imposition Louise had to bear. The thought roused in me again the impulse to help her. What a blessing then, that I could! With a few words I could set her free from this miserable fear. Without them she would spend the rest of her tormented life in one hiding-place after another. Things had so fallen out, in this strange fashion, that I had become the instrument whereby Louise could be made happy again.

But I was not yet quite certain.

"Nicholas loved — loves you," I said. "Why should you be afraid of him?"

When she shivered without answering, I persisted, taking care this time with the tense.

"Is there any particular thing about him that frightens you? Surely you can tell me, your own sister."

I gripped the table, waiting for the final blow.

"It's his hands," she said at last.

There was no doubt then: no possible mistaking the fact that Nicholas Vince was dead. I bowed my head as one does in the presence of death. It was not his passing only that I mourned again, more bitterly even than when I had seen him die. The new hopes I had begun to cherish for my own future, they died too.

16

IT WAS THEN that I should have told her, at once, before the stark memory her simple words aroused became complicated by other factors.

"It was both hands then?" I almost said and with a gasp recovered myself. It served equally well as a gasp of surprise and launched me on my dubious course.

I too went to the door. Mrs Hidkin was busy in her vegetable patch. I took Louise's arm. We went out and found a wide boulder where we could sit side by side above the stream. Here in the fresh air it would be easier to tell than when we faced each other across the table in the crowded room.

It was with every intention of telling her that I opened my lips. What actually came out were the blunt words:

"What is the matter with his hands?"

The question was less straightforward than it sounded. It took me another step in the wrong direction.

There must have been days like this at Blairgouroch, inland, away from the sea with its infinitely variable power to frighten Louise. There would be a brown stream perhaps like the Audley: red berries on the rowans: heather still purple: sheep still white after the summer shearing. Louise didn't mention them. Her story lacked colour. Its tones were sombre: its characters dull: a lawyer's clerk, a quiet man in dark clothes who came to the Castle to make an inventory: someone to talk to after Mrs Maple died: someone to help in resolving the small uncertainties that had simply never arisen in Mrs Maple's time. The servants had noticed. "You could do worse, miss," the cook had said. Mrs Duncan had made enquiries into his background. It was modest but satisfactory: perfectly respectable. Louise hadn't thought of anything like that.

And then — it was a while before she went on — it happened in the kitchen, a huge, echoing place. (I supplied the echo and, gradually, the personality of Nicholas Vince.) There was an enormous grate and an iron crane for the big kettles. They were too heavy for Louise. Besides, she rarely went into the kitchen only she liked to starch her own petticoats. Nicholas happened to be there, warming himself by the fire. It was cold in the library where he worked. He had wanted to show her an engraving in one of the old books. Louise had knelt down by the fire to look at it though it wasn't interesting, really. She had looked out of politeness. A careless servant — it was all Kirsty's fault: she was always behindhand and clumsy; Louise had seen to it that she was dismissed instantly without a character — well, Kirsty had made up the fire too high and stood the kettle on the bar instead of hanging it back on the hook. It had come to the boil. A big piece of coal fell and the whole fire slid forward. The kettle was overturned. Nicholas's hands had been dreadfully scalded and burned too. The Duncans were away. He was two days without a doctor, then ill for weeks. They said he might have died.

"But he didn't," Louise said and paused. I had learned by this time not to supply the things she left unsaid but I was as sure that the remark was tinged with regret as I was sure of the response I ought to have made.

"But he did, Louise. He did die."

Not to say it or something like it was inexcusable.

Louise sighed. She had helped to nurse him. When he recovered they all said she should marry him. He wanted it so much. She must either marry or go back to Wickborough. Nicholas hadn't urged her. How could he? But it was all so different at Blairgouroch without Mrs Maple. Louise's own position was difficult. She belonged neither

159

above nor below stairs. While he was ill there were the bandages to hide the injuries. He was helpless but determined to get better. Afterwards he wore gloves, but it wasn't until they were married that she saw . . .

"Then when he had the gloves on, it was more frightening still to think of what it would be like when he took them off."

"Could you not have thought that he needed you."

That was what they had all said but no one could know what it was like to be married to those hands. She hadn't realised.

"I couldn't bear them to touch me. They were so ugly and unnatural."

Involuntarily I moved away to the water's edge. She had told the story prosaically without one tender word for him. Yet it must have been love for her that had brought him to Wickborough. Too humble to intrude, too loving to stay away, he had found out where we lived and had waited for her to come home, his purse empty of the money she had taken, his pockets heavy, no doubt, with mother's jewellery which he was keeping for Louise. I calculated that he had missed her by a few days.

Those words so tentatively spoken must actually have been "Miss Hester." Louise must have told him my name. "It's from Hester, my sister," she must have said, opening a letter. Why had I turned him away when he came to the door, nerving himself to speak to me? I thought of all this and of his cruel death as I stared down at the sunlit water, its innocence still unpolluted by the foulness of Sparrow Chare. Then I remembered how the moon had brightened the river and a spirit of calm had come to assuage the agony of his end.

"Let him rest in peace," I thought.

And truly it was reverence for him that kept me silent — at first, and the sheer impossibility of communicating to Louise the mystery and pain of the experience I had shared with him.

There were plenty of opportunities to tell.

"So you see how frightened I was when I saw the watch," Louise concluded. "I still don't know how father got it back. Oh, I know you said you hadn't seen Nicholas," she added hastily, remembering my anger, "and of course I believe you, especially now that you've given me your solemn word."

A few minutes had perjured me. The moment passed, taking with it the echo of my promise. "If ever I see him, I'll tell you, tell you . . ." He would never be seen again. Did that absolve me? "But father must have seen him. How else could the watch have got into the drawer? But then you said that father didn't know it was there. And I felt sure Nicholas would keep the jewellery safe for my sake. He liked me to have pretty things."

"Your dresses . . . did he . . .?"

"He paid for the lilac and the tarlatan, for my trousseau."

"The money you took," I interrupted, "was it all the money he had?"

"Oh, I don't think so. No, it can't have been because Julian said in his letter that Nicholas had settled the account at our lodgings. He wouldn't at all have minded my taking the money. He would have given me anything; and besides, he had the jewellery. At any rate," she added when she had puzzled over the matter a little longer, "I can never go back to Wickborough. He must have been at Wickborough, and oh, Hester, he may still be there."

As to where he was now, there was no certainty in water, earth or air. But he would never come near her again, not in the form in which she had known him. It was cruel not to tell her, as cruel as she had been to him. In so far as she deserved to be punished for her callous disregard of his deep and lasting love, events had fashioned for her a punishment as lasting; that is to say, it would last as long as I chose. Until she knew of his death she would live in fear.

But with every minute it became more difficult to tell. The secret, already kept too long, was as it had always been, unspeakable, more so than ever now that the telling would blight my own future. It was only when Louise said helplessly: "Where shall I go?" that I began to consider her altered position. She had changed from wife to widow as unexpectedly as she had changed from girl to wife. But no change of status could alter her. Nothing could. If I told her what had happened to Nicholas, she wouldn't really change.

"He's dead then," she would say, relieved, and presently take up her bead work.

"You made an unhappy marriage, Louise," I said with a deviousness that came all too readily. "If you had been free, would you have married Julian?"

"I wouldn't want to marry again but it seems the only way to have a home of one's own."

"But — Julian?"

"Yes, I would. At least he's someone we know."

Her indifference hardened my heart. Why should she have him to hold so cheaply when it lay in my power to prevent it? No action was needed. By doing nothing, I could keep them apart. It was so simple, so passive, as scarcely to seem wrong. But I knew very well that to withhold so vital a truth would be no better than lying. By keeping it to myself I would bring suffering upon others; upon Julian. He was unhappy and would remain so. But being Louise's husband had not made Nicholas happy. So I reasoned, not just then but continually. Endowed with a god-like power to influence the lives of those I loved, I shrank from using it and by doing nothing, used it to my own advantage.

"Now that I've told you everything, Hester, you must tell me what to do."

To the burden of guilty knowledge I must add the burden of Louise. Being unwilling to shed the one, I shouldered the other as well. Just for an instant, it was tempting to tell her that she was free and so pass on the burden to someone else: to Julian. How long would it be before in the closeness of marriage he felt the clogging weight of being tied for the rest of his life to Louise?

She was looking at me with the child-like appeal it was impossible to resist.

"One thing is certain. You can't stay at Mrs Hidkin's."

"But..."

There were plenty of good practical reasons. Even

Louise must see that it was impossible to run away, time and again, year in year out, from Nicholas Vince. She had already gone to the limits of common sense. Geographically she could go no further. Beyond lay a thousand acres of open moor. The goblin-haunted burial mounds on the purple sky-line were no place for Louise. It was useless to point this out: useless to reason with Louise at all. I saw a quicker way.

"Mrs Maple wouldn't have liked it," I said firmly.

17

WE TRUDGED BACK almost in silence. Having told her story, Louise had nothing more to say while all my thoughts were engaged in the conflict to which I had committed myself. We must go back to Wickborough. Shut up in the old house throughout the winter, I must watch Louise peeping from behind the curtain; and each time it would be I who saw again the tall figure by the print-seller's. She would look and I would see. Nicholas Vince would haunt us both. The solution was simple. I must tell her that he was dead. Then she could marry Julian. After all he was someone we knew. With every step my resentment grew. By the time we reached the Croft I wanted only to be rid of Louise, to wrestle with the problem alone.

Circumstances favoured me: not immediately but more swiftly than I deserved. Lettice had come back bringing news which was confirmed by a letter from Cousin Andrew. He had decided not to sell the Croft after all. He had happy memories of the place and might some day live there himself. Meanwhile he would let it to a Captain and Mrs Hawn. She was an old friend of the family, a wealthy brewer's daughter who had married rather late in life. Her husband had sold his commission and looked forward to a spell of leisure in the country after serving Her Majesty overseas for many years.

"Mr Amberley expressed the wish," Lettice said, "that one of the young ladies might stay on at the Croft to see Captain and Mrs Hawn settled, if so willing, Mrs Hawn being delicate in health. I ventured to say," she looked at me, "that if it was to be just one of the young ladies, it might suit Miss Mallow to stay, knowing Miss Hester has duties at Wickborough. I hope it wasn't forward of me."

"Oh, no, Lettice." She seemed overpowered by my warmth. "I believe my sister would like — Would you prefer to stay for a while, Louise? Or would you rather" — it was impossible to rid my voice of a certain grimness — "go back to Wickborough?"

Louise never wasted words. She went straight to the linen cupboard and counted the sheets.

Matters were clinched the next day by a letter from father. I was to go home at once whatever Louise chose to do. I replied by return of post, explaining the situation and promising to leave the day the Hawns arrived.

Household duties kept Louise busy for the next few days. She was luckier than I. Time lay heavy on my hands. Far too much of it I spent alone taking long walks and brooding on my secret. Almost every day I determined to tell Louise and hurried home to do it; but each time the painful prospect of blurting out, "He's dead," made me slow down at the gate or even turn back. Long before I knew who he was Nicholas Vince had made me aware of a new element in human suffering: he had entered a region of my mind and made it his own; but now he pervaded my whole life and was with me all the time.

One afternoon I took the path along the river's edge. The water was still and clear, bright as a mirror. Every tree rising from the bank stood rooted in its own image so that the water gave back a second scene more lovely and luminous than the actual one in which I walked. It brought an easing of anxiety, as if the river had power to restore all that it received, altered only in its quality and in that, improved and purified. Then, catching my breath, I saw in the water between the still trees a movement.

Above the branches in the inverted world, and inverted like them so that he seemed a creature of that element, walked the tall dark figure of a man. He came so aptly, almost as if my thoughts had summoned him that I gasped with fear and then I saw —

"Julian!"

"Hester!"

We came face to face. He was paler and thinner. I had opened my lips to tell him so when he said:

"You look tired, Hester." He touched my cheek. "Are you well?"

I nodded. He drew my arm in his. We walked under the trees in such comradely, loving closeness that I made up my mind there and then to tell him everything, if not for his own good then for conscience' sake.

"Julian —"

"I've been looking for you, Hester. There's so much to tell you. No, wait! My turn first." He had come from Wickborough, having returned from Scotland the night before. "At Blairgouroch they treated me like a bogle, the servants, I mean. The Duncans had a house-party there for the shooting. I didn't see them. I felt like the third son of the Wife of Usher's Well. I was the third man, you see, to have come asking about Louise: first Vince, then another fellow, Benjamin, a friend of Vince. He had worked with the same firm of lawyers. The Duncans' butler was a good sort. He told me a bit about Vince." Julian's manner puzzled me. He certainly looked glum but I sensed that he was also troubled and uncertain. "Do you know, Hester, I believe he's dead."

I stopped to pull my gown free of a bramble sucker. It took a little time with only one hand at my disposal. Julian stood absently holding my other arm. He had forgotten me — fortunately — except in my role as listener.

"Wouldn't that account for his not having turned up?" he went on. "The only explanation. He'd never have let her go. It could have happened in any one of a dozen ways. A fever, an accident, or more likely suicide."

"Oh, no."

165

"What could be more probable? He knew she didn't want him and never would. They told me at Blairgouroch he had been disfigured by burns, poor chap."

"Only his hands," I said quickly.

"Louise told you? It's a funny thing. I went there loathing the fellow, hoping for an excuse to give him a thrashing. But that's quite gone. I can't help sympathising with him. I can imagine his feelings because Louise doesn't want me either and never will."

I murmured some vague consolation.

"I've just seen her and told her what I've told you, putting it gently of course to avoid upsetting her. 'If we could have proof that he's dead', I said to her, 'would you ever think of me — in that way?'"

"What sort of proof did you mean?"

"Well, obviously, an entry in a parish register or a death certificate; or someone who was with him when he died. Except in the case of suicide it's very unusual surely for a man to die and no one at all to know."

A willow grew straight out over the water, its roots grasping the bank, its trunk making a low and level seat. I sat down.

"What did Louise say when you asked her?"

Julian turned his back, pretending to look for black-berries. I knew from the droop of his shoulders that he felt humiliated.

"You know how straightforward she is. It's wonderful to find such honesty as well as her — other qualities. 'I quite like the Croft now that I know where everything is,' she said, 'but what I would really like would be my own home. If I weren't married already, I would marry you because of the things you promised'."

He came and stood beside me.

"It frightened me, Hester. I had the eerie feeling of being an intruder, as if I didn't fit into the arrangement at all; and that's what it is, an intrusion, to speak to her about marriage when she belongs to another man. But it occurred to me that even as her husband one might have the same feeling of being there, not exactly on sufferance, but without being noticed, as if one were invisible."

The water was painfully bright. I closed my eyes, and for a bewildered second or two scarcely knew which of them stood over me, Julian or Nicholas, so similar seemed their plight. Was this the moment, when the existence of Louise's husband gave Julian an excuse to withdraw, to tell him that Nicholas was dead? Would it make things better? Whether it would or not, I should in honesty tell him.

Across the river the harvesters were at work. Through a gap in the low-hanging branches I saw the pale sun-bonnets of the women bonding the wheat as they followed the reapers. Stooping and stretching, they passed out of sight, followed in their turn by two men who lifted the sheaves upright and leaned them together, ten sheaves to each stook.

"When they've finished the next stook," I thought, "I'll tell him."

"It was a mistake to see her," Julian said. "I had forgotten how lovely she is. To tell you the truth, I wish I hadn't come back. Believe it or not, I was happier in Scotland."

I counted the sheaves as the men lifted them: two, four, six . . .

"When you love a person," I said, "you can be happy in that person's company without wanting more; and being parted doesn't make you forget."

"I suppose not." He spoke doubtfully. "There's only one consolation in the whole wretched business. So long as she doesn't know what's happened to Vince, she can't marry anyone else either. The one thing I couldn't bear would be to know for certain that she was free to marry again and preferred someone else to me."

The harvesters had moved on to the next stook.

"It would make things worse then, to know definitely?"

"It sounds ridiculous but to be honest, just at present, I almost prefer the uncertainty. If one can't do anything, at least there isn't the risk of doing the wrong thing."

He was as confused as I. The problem was beyond me. I gave up trying to do the best for him. It was from sheer selfishness that I decided to keep my secret a little longer, trusting to the remarkable ease with which one could forget Louise as long as she was out of sight. Stooping and lifting, the harvesters had moved out of my leaf-fringed picture. They could go on stooking corn till sunset for all I cared.

I should have been happier, then, with Julian at my side, closer to me in every sense than he was to Louise. The change in him was exactly what I had wanted. He was discovering for himself the hazards of being in love with Louise. Some day he would be himself again, as he had been before she came. It was what I had hoped and prayed for.

A passing cloud perhaps lowered my spirits. It took the golden look from the stubble field, leaving it flat and grey. The sheaves leaned hopelessly against one another as if the life had gone out of them. It was cool by the water. The best of the summer was over.

I exerted myself to help with the preparations for the Hawns and on my last day went into Bidewell to order groceries. The offer of a ride in her trap by a neighbouring farmer's wife made it possible for me to carry a pile of old periodicals to Ned: monthly parts of novels, ancient copies of Household Words, learned reviews once read by Aunt Tamar's husband and hoarded for his sake. Ned accepted them all with equal joy.

"These'll keep me busy for a bit. And I've news for you, miss. They're moving me into the house as a page from the first of next month."

"Does your friend know how well you've done, Mrs Tafferty's lodger, who encouraged you to learn to read?"

"I wish he did. But I haven't heard of him for a long time. He went away sudden at the beginning of April before I left Wickborough. Didn't tell me he was going. I went round to Mrs Tafferty's every night for a week and just hung about outside, but I didn't know his name and never plucked up courage to ask where he'd gone."

"What was he like?"

"To look at, miss? A tall, delicate-looking gentleman. The best friend I ever had, like yourself, miss. You're two of a kind." His face flushed. "Many a time I've wished he would walk into the Fleece one day. It was him being connected with the law that gave me the idea of going in for being a judge. If ever you were to see him in Wickborough, mebbe you'd give him my respects and thanks. He often walked down Silvergate. I wish he hadn't gone away."

"So do I," I said.

The house was in apple-pie order when the Hawns arrived. I had only an hour in which to make their acquaintance. Mrs Hawn was painfully thin and fragile: her husband red-faced and loud-voiced.

"So you're leaving us, Miss Hester." He addressed me as if the parlour were a parade ground and I on its utmost edge. "Got a shop in Wickborough, I understand."

"My father is a watchmaker," I said stiffly and was sufficiently nettled to add, "Mallows have been freemen of Wickborough for over two hundred years," then thought how vulgar it was to boast of such a thing.

"Capital," he roared, staring out of the window.

"Captain Hawn does not understand the distinctions of the business world," Mrs Hawn explained to me afterwards in a hasty whisper. "I have told him that there is all the difference between a craftsman such as Mr Mallow and those unfortunate enough to be engaged in retail trade."

Having given me her attention for a moment, she directed it once more, with unbroken concentration, towards Louise.

While the girls were sorrowfully putting my things in the cab, the Captain and I met again. He had prowled heavily round the house and was stamping uneasily about the hall. Louise's symmetrically arranged dahlias shook in their vase.

"Splendid thing!" he boomed. "Life in the country."

I saw in his rather prominent blue eyes a touch of bewilderment and liked him better.

"I hope Mrs Hawn will feel the benefit."

"Yes. She's been feeling pretty cheap." I understood

him to refer to her health. "Rest and fresh air. Good food. Honey, eggs and so on. The only thing."

He went out. Later as we drove along the lane, I caught glimpses of him savagely slashing at nettles with his stick.

"With other people in the house," I said to Louise when she offered her cheek for a farewell kiss, "you'll feel better. It will be more like the time when we first came, when Aunt Tamar was here."

I said it to reassure her. For me the atmosphere of the Croft was so cruelly changed that I was impatient to go.

"Yes," Louise said, "and there will be so much to do. There are four hampers of pears to be blanched and ever so many more on the trees."

Her husky voice died away, leaving an impression of inconsolable sadness. I recognised it as a matter of pitch and resonance. She was no more sad — I knew her now — than a fir tree is sad when the wind sets it sighing. It is the listener who feels the sadness.

She came to the gate. The overblown roses on the wall, the moss on the red roof, the green thorn hedge, all composed themselves into a picture with Louise as its centre piece in her grey striped gown and black satin apron. She wore her light-brown hair upswept except for two ringlets behind. Her eyes were as softly blue as a summer sky, her cheeks and lips innocently curved. Once again, in the pure lines of her faultless features I almost caught a glimpse of something else; a promise that to all the anxious questions of life there existed an answer, in some changeless realm where beauty could not fade.

Louise smiled and waved. Tears came to my eyes. She was so beautiful.

18

ONE SUMMER HAD made no difference to the house in Silvergate. It had survived so many summers. The change was in me; and perhaps in father. On the day of my return he actually took the afternoon off. At least he meant to. He came upstairs for five o'clock tea and changed his jacket.

"You've not picked up in health as much as you might have done. But then Tamar's death was a sad blow. These Hawns, Andrew tells me they're reliable people."

"Yes, indeed, father. Mrs Hawn is a most lady-like person."

"I wonder how long they will want to keep Louise. But that's a problem we can deal with later."

He ate absently, glancing at me thoughtfully from time to time as if on the point of broaching some new topic.

"You're a discreet little person, Hester," he said, feeling his way, "for your age. You used to be the chatterbox of the family. I don't know what has made you so — quiet." Dread of a direct question so stifled me that I would surely never speak again. "Unless it's something to do with Louise. Most of our troubles have something to do with Louise." He sighed and came to a decision. "She has told you about her marriage?"

I must have looked dismayed.

"You knew? Louise was afraid to tell you."

"Yes, of course I knew. When she came home I wrote to the Duncans, to find out under what circumstances she had left. There was the possibility she might have — Louise hasn't always been quite — Well, there's no need to discuss it. They were in London for the season. My letter didn't reach them at once. Their reply came after you had gone to Lullerbeck. They understood that Louise had left her husband. Naturally I wrote to Vince's firm. They had no news of him." He paused. "Does Louise know where he is?"

"No, father."

"To be candid, I suspect some tragedy. Naturally Louise has come out of it unscathed." His sardonic tone changed to one of concern. "Hester, you're as white as chalk. Why in heaven's name am I distressing you with this wretched affair." He jumped up, chafed my hands, fetched a foot stool and placed my unresisting feet on it.

"Thomas told me you weren't quite yourself. He was anxious about you. I guessed that Louise had involved you in this unhappy business. It was a mistake to let you go."

His kindness had caught me unawares. I turned my head away.

"It was ... You see ..." I made a weary effort to begin my story.

"No," father interrupted. "I absolutely forbid you to speak. We must put the whole thing away from us for the time being. Louise will come to no harm and now that she's married, she can do no harm to any other poor fellow, I hope. No lasting harm. I will not allow her to upset you."

He talked of other things; of Thomas, whose apprenticeship would end in two weeks' time. If he chose to stay on, father would take him into partnership some day. Listening, I composed myself, grateful for the safe drabness of old familiar things: Ceres and Minerva, the loving cup, the sagging floor boards, the wayward door, which in two hundred years had never come to terms with its doorway — and never has. Father — with the thought came an exquisite moment of peace — was glad to have me back. When Thomas came up to consult him and the two of them went downstairs, I slept a little in the comfortable firelight and woke refreshed.

"It's more like home," Mrs Wragge said, "having someone in the parlour."

The next afternoon I was at work in the window as if nothing had happened. Mrs Setterwort bowed and smiled from above her window boxes. She had taken out her geraniums and put in wallflowers. I must follow her example.

Julian called several times before taking up his appointment as tutor with a family in the country twenty miles north of Wickborough. Father was always with us. We scarcely spoke of Louise. She did not write. When Julian had gone, it was autumn. The evenings drew in. Wickborough grew murky, suspended between its river mists and chimney smoke. Once more we grumbled about the Setterworts when the wind was in the west.

Coming to the landing one morning, I found Thomas halfway up the stairs in a mysterious beckoning posture with his finger on his lips. I stole down after him and discovered the reason. The young man who had bought the butterfly brooch had brought his future wife to try on wedding rings. He had not changed his mind again. She was the same country girl. From the conversation I gathered that far from being dismissed for negligence, he had been promoted to a clerkship and was inclined to swagger.

"What do you think of that?" he asked the girl as Thomas enclosed a violet watch paper in the little parcel.

"It's pretty, isn't it?", she said, still breathless and blushing.

"That's what I thought you'd say," the young man said weightily. "You've got the sense to appreciate a thing like that, you have."

"What did he mean?" I whispered to Thomas when they had gone.

"I drew the conclusion," Thomas said, "that the other young woman had fallen short of his expectations."

"But they could hardly have quarrelled over a watch paper."

"Nothing would surprise me. If a woman's silly enough to want an insect for an adornment, she's silly enough for anything," Thomas said, ungratefully, since he was making a comfortable little addition to his income from that particular form of silliness.

After an absence in the country I felt more vividly than ever before the character of the town, a living body composed of widely differing members: the Abbey, solid as the rock on which it stood, the steep streets climbing to the market place, the mediaeval huddle of Sparrow Chare. I took to reading father's copy of *Annals of Wickborough* and trying to identify the relics shown in its engravings. One which especially interested me, I was unable to find: the Lady Audrey's window, called after the fourteenth century benefactress who had distributed bread there to homeless wayfarers.

"If you want to know anything about the history of Wickborough," father said when I appealed to him, "ask Thomas."

History, it appeared, was another of Thomas's hobbies.

"It's still there," he said. "One wall of the old building with the window in it. It's part of a second-hand clothes shop now. I wouldn't fancy anything they sell there. The place has gone down a bit since Lady Audrey's time. But never mind," he added cheerfully, "other things are going up." He may have been thinking of his own prospects. He was now working as father's paid assistant. "You can't miss it. A half-moon window, in Nidgate on the left going down from the market place."

It was easy to find. One afternoon late in October, on my way home from a visit to Mrs Windross, I turned into Nidgate chiefly to be able to tell Thomas that I had seen the window. Afterwards I regretted having gone. Coming within earshot of the cobbler's hammer, I almost turned back, but an array of old coats festooning a doorway just ahead drew me on; and there was the arch of Lady Audrey's window on the front wall. I glanced with some curiosity at the less venerable relics in the window below: a shabby assortment of worn clothes behind the written announcement: Ladies' and gentlemen's wardrobes bought and sold."

The shop was not the seediest of its kind. The ancient shawls, mantles and waistcoats would give plenty of wear to the decent poor before finding their way to the rag-and-bone merchants in the Chare; but they had a forlorn look dispiriting to dwell on.

As I stood listlessly looking into the window, a lean woman in a checked shawl and unlaced boots came flapping out of one of the alleys and swooped into the shop like a furtive vulture. The partition at the back of the window screened the inside but I could hear the voice of the woman behind the counter:

"This'll be the last then, is it? I wonder you didn't bring the whole lot at once. Well, I dare say you had your reasons."

"Any reasons I have are my own business, Mrs Sorby. It'll be the same, I suppose."

"Just the same. Sixpence and not a farthing more. Oh yes, Mrs Tafferty, you can trust me to keep my mouth shut."

The woman gave me a quick look as she came out, turned her head away and scuttled back into the alley. Almost at once the partition was slid to one side. The shop-keeper leaned out and pinned to the strip of green bunting at the left side of the window the article she had evidently just bought: or rather, the articles. There were two of them. She pinned them separately side by side: a pair of men's gloves of black cotton.

The sudden revival of buried memories was as shocking as if the gloves had been exhumed. There was an artless insistence in the way they hung there as if hat, jacket, ulster and wearer had all disappeared and only they remained, the last trace of Mrs Tafferty's tall, delicate-looking lodger to whom Ned had sent his respects and regards.

"Miss Mallow?"

The start I gave was violent enough to seem a start of guilt.

"You won't remember me."

I hadn't seen him coming.

"Yes, indeed I remember you." It was an effort to speak naturally. "And now I know your name, Mr Benjamin."

He had resumed his dark hat. It was not the season for a straw one. Otherwise he was dressed — I glanced down at his elastic-sided boots — as he had been at Codlin Croft. It was cool enough for an overcoat but he wore none.

"You have walked too far, Miss Mallow. Would you like to go into this shop and sit down?"

"Oh, no, really."

"I beg you'll allow me to take you home. Only there

is something I must see to first, if you can wait one moment."

To my astonishment he went into the shop, leaving the door open, and clapped a shilling on the counter.

"Yes, yes. As quickly as you can — and threepence change, if you please."

The shop-keeper slid open the partition, unpinned the gloves and handed them over the counter.

"That's the last, so she says, and I hope you're well fitted out with gloves by this time."

He made no reference to this extraordinary transaction but offered me his arm. I accepted it. The faintness had left me but I was most unwilling to offend him. My behaviour at Codlin Croft had been so distasteful to me and so much had happened to alter my first wild misjudgment of him that I wanted now to treat him quite differently. There was so much to think of that at first I didn't notice where he was leading me; not back to the market place but in the opposite direction past the cobbler's shop.

"This way is much shorter for you," he explained "Not so pleasant, perhaps, but we have only to go down one flight of steps, along the wharf and up to the pillar-box at the bottom of Silvergate. I don't suppose you've ever been here." We had reached the steps. I took my arm from his and grasped the iron railings. "I've got to know the byways of Wickborough pretty well in the past few months."

"Mr Benjamin," I said, "when you came to Codlin Croft . . ."

"You thought I was Nicholas. Until you spoke I thought you were his wife. He used to tell me how pretty she was." The compliment did not lower him in my esteem. "I never saw her. When Nick took her to Cairlie I had been moved to the other branch of the firm in Glasgow. I should have told you who I was but there was so much I was not sure of, as there still is."

I understood that he had been as suspicious and mistrustful as I had been. Here at last was an opportunity to speak openly. Frankness had become a luxury. All

176

the same it cost me an effort to confess that we had watched him from behind locked doors: that until then I had still believed him to be Nicholas Vince: that I had wrongly, I now felt, given in to Louise's dread of meeting her husband.

"I know that you are a friend. Julian Windross told me. He found it out at Blairgouroch."

It was soon told. We had come down to the wharf. The cold air from the river cleared my head, almost too successfully. With painful clarity I saw the irony of the situation. It would be here where he had died that I would tell how it had happened. Mr Benjamin of all people was entitled to know.

The last time he had seen Nicholas was just before his marriage. He had heard nothing from him since. Until then they had been close friends, two Englishmen working for a Scottish firm whose clients included gentry such as the Duncans with interests on both sides of the Border. Either of them could have been sent to Blairgouroch to make the inventory. It happened to be Nicholas. He was different after that, even before his accident: absent-minded, caught up by some idea, almost unable to speak of the young lady, as if it would be irreverent.

"We are neither of us young. Men in our position can't afford to marry young. It was a blow to me when he told me the young lady had accepted him but I wished him well. Oh, I wished him well."

But he had been lonely and glad to be transferred to the other branch. It was not until the spring that he took a short holiday in Cairlie. He had not been disturbed by Nicholas's failure to write. It was natural in a newly married man. But when he found that the Vinces had left their lodgings, leaving no address, he had gone at once to Blairgouroch. They were only too ready to tell him that Mrs Vince had left her husband. He had come there himself, six months before, asking for her father's address.

Absorbed in his story, I had come unconsciously to a halt. My companion must always have been serious-minded. Now his whole manner was one of deep sadness. The hardness I had seen in his eyes I now recognised as a look of sustained anxiety. He told his story tersely. By the time he had himself reached Wickborough, he realised that Nicholas must be short of money. How short, he could not know as well as I. His enquiries had taken him step by step down the scale of lodging houses until in one of the shabbiest in a dirty court off Sparrow Chare he had found his first clue. Mrs Tafferty had been surprised into admitting that a lodger, a tall, quiet man, had walked out of her house one evening in early April and had not come back. She hadn't wanted to tell because, though she denied it, she was selling the few possessions he had left behind.

"I couldn't blame the woman and it gave me an aim in life to watch out for them and buy them back." He took the gloves from his pocket. "These were Nick's. It's like being in touch with him again." He smoothed and folded them and put them back.

Of course he had gone to the police. What could they do? A man can disappear if he likes. Nicholas had done no wrong. He owed nothing. There was no evidence that any wrong had been done to him: no evidence at all, of anything. Still, he believed that the police had made certain enquiries and might still be doing so. But he had heard nothing. No, he had not mentioned Louise to the police. His face changed. I saw real hardness. He had no wish to bring her into the matter: no wish to meet her. It was easy enough in a little place like Wickborough to find out all about the Mallows. He knew that while Nick had waited here, penniless, she had been elsewhere, living no doubt in comfort.

"If you had known him, Miss Mallow, if you'd seen him after his accident, you would have wondered how anyone could leave him like that."

Nicholas had been full of courage, hardly able to believe his good fortune in winning Louise. Somehow he had taught himself to write again. The firm had kept his position for him. A man of his quality was not easy to replace.

In spite of the prejudice against Louise which Mr Benjamin could not conceal, he had attempted to see her.

178

That was when he found that we had gone into the country. But it had been as much a desire for country air and a cure for low spirits that had taken him to Bidewell. Once there he had vacillated and at last forced himself to call. It had been a relief on the second occasion to find that we had apparently gone away.

"I'm sure she could have told you nothing," I said.

I have often wondered if his feelings would have been different, his view of the affair less straightforward if he had ever seen Louise. As it was, he mourned the disappearance of his friend with simple heart-felt grief.

"I've walked the streets here, down Silvergate, up Nidgate, late at night and early in the morning as he must have done. I've asked here and I've asked there..."

He was standing at the edge of the wharf, looking down at the water.

"Oh, do come away from there, Mr Benjamin. It's such a dangerous river."

He paid no heed.

"On Wednesday, 5th April, that was the last day he was seen. It's surprising how much you can find out by just chatting to people. A little nursemaid for instance, used to talk to him when she was posting her letters at the pillar-box up there. She used to tell him about her home in the country. Nick had had a country boyhood himself. 'He was nearly like a relation,' she said to me only the other day. 'I wish I could see him again.' Then there's the matchseller in the market place. She remembers him. He was kind to her little girl. He gave her a doll. You'll think me sentimental, Miss Mallow, but I've got into the habit of buying my matches from the same woman on the same day as he did, a Thursday."

I waited. He had finished. It was my turn. Here, to the accompaniment of the water's thirsty lapping, I would hear my own voice telling how I had found Nicholas lying there against the crazy steps, his head horribly battered, his hand stretched out for help. I would tell — how could I tell of that awful moment of recoil? Had it been worse than that? For the hundredth time I tried to

179

remember whether or not I had pushed him away from me.

What comfort was there for his friend in my story? What ease of mind? — any more than in the black doorways of the decayed warehouses or the reek of rotting wood or the unfathomably menacing smell of water or in the whole comfortless world?

"There must have been foul play," Mr Benjamin said. "Why — I don't know. He wouldn't have hurt a living soul and his pockets must have been as near empty as mine are now. What could Nick have on him to tempt a thief?" He looked round at me so suddenly that I was almost startled into blurting out the answer but he went on, "I know, in my mind, that he's gone. But in my heart I don't feel it. For me, he's here in Wickborough, close to me. He was like a brother to me. Every time I turn a corner, there's the hope of meeting him. When I go into a shop, he may be there. Every morning I look for a letter from him. I'm a lonely man, Miss Mallow, by nature, and lonelier than ever now. If I hadn't this feeling, this certainty that Nick and I will meet again, there wouldn't be much to live for."

I listened, tormented by doubt.

"It's a strange thing," he said, "while we're standing here, I'm convinced of it."

"That he's alive?"

"That he's here."

He looked almost happy. We climbed the steps to the pillar-box.

"Will you stay on in Wickborough, Mr Benjamin?"

"Unfortunately I must go back."

I was distressed to hear that he had resigned his position and was now at the end of his resources.

"There's a chance the partners will take me back, since they've lost Nick as well. I'm familiar with the business of some of the clients. It will be a wrench for me to go. It's like leaving Nick on his own." He took off his hat. "But I'm happy to have had the privilege of your acquaintance, Miss Mallow. It's been the pleasantest experience I've had for a long time, to have this frank talk.

180

We shook hands.

"You'll come back?"

"Always supposing the firm takes me on again, I'll have a week's holiday every year."

"I'll look out for you, Mr Benjamin."

He went back, down the steps and along the wharf, presumably to just such another bare lodging as Nicholas had found.

It would soon be dark. On the other side of the bridge Fergus must have been coming down Southwell Street. Its lamps were going on, one by one. I looked at my watch. It was half past five.

These details occupied the surface of my mind. Deeper thoughts engrossed me. I had crossed a frontier into a territory as lonely as the twilight in which Mr Benjamin passed his days. By not telling him, I had committed myself to a lasting silence. If not to him, then to no one could I tell my story. To tell it at all would be to make it general knowledge and to take from him the pathetic illusion that he would meet his friend again. But if it was wrong to keep the secret — and I never doubted, despite every excuse, that it was wrong — silence brought its own punishment. Because I could not share the experience and so feel the burden lighten, I doomed myself to live it again and again in the solitude of my own mind, each time with a deeper remorse, a stronger conviction that somehow I could have saved him.

Since no living soul knew what had happened there on the wharf besides myself, no one could bring me the consolation of telling me that at least I had not made things worse; that it had been too late to save him. The anguish like the secret was mine alone. I must bear it for the rest of my life.

Caught up in this agony of spirit, I paid no heed to the tug at my skirt. It came again. A little girl was looking up at me anxiously.

"Please, miss, mother says can you come and help?"

19

"WHO ARE YOU?"

From the tattered bonnet that eclipsed her face to the
serge skirt reaching to her bare toes, her clothes were all
so much too big for her that I was almost obliged to take
her presence inside them for granted. She burst into some
sort of explanation, gabbling at such speed that only one
word reached me clearly: Windross.

"Mr Julian Windross?"

"Mother says you know him and if he was here he
would help us but he's gone away."

"Where do you live?"

"Down in the Chare. Weaver's Yard."

I supposed the child was from one of the families
whom St Aidan's had taken under its wing. The students
helped to administer the various charities vested in the
Abbey and did active rescue work among the poor. It
was work that had appealed to Julian before he broke
his connection with the College. I hesitated, but only for
a moment, before following the child down the steps,
along the wharf and into a narrow way leading to the
depths of the Chare. We soon passed the shabby little
houses where horse-keepers, porters and labourers lived,
and plunged into a labyrinth of dim yards and courts I
had never seen before. I was uneasily aware of men and
boys lounging in doorways but we walked so fast and
with such urgency that no one molested us. My chief
concern was to avoid the piles of slime and rotting
refuse in the evil-smelling gutters and ward off scavenging
dogs and curious children. With my skirt held high and
my handkerchief clapped to my nose, I hurried after the
girl until she turned abruptly down several steps into a
court. Here it was already night. We went down again
to the door of a basement and waited in pitch darkness.

"It's me and the lady, mother."

The door opened, showing a narrow chink of light
from a tallow dip. A woman put out her head.

"Come in, miss. I'm grateful to you, I'm sure."

I saw nothing clearly but the woman herself. There were children in the room but they sat still, huddled on a cot bed in the far corner. The grate was empty.

"I wouldn't have taken the liberty" — the woman spoke in the level, toneless voice of despair but she was neither uncouth nor degraded — "but there's nowhere else to turn. Mr Windross would have helped if he'd been here, or one of the other young gentlemen but Emmie Tafferty said she'd seen you outside Sorbys' shop. The young lady that walks out with Mr Windross, she said. So I sent Janey to look for you."

"You need money?"

"There's not a penny in the house, miss, and neither bread nor coals. I might have managed somehow. Emmie could have put me in the way of a bit of scrubbing. But to cap all, he's come home. The state he's in I can't leave him with the children."

Through the dismal yellow light I saw a man lying on the larger bed by the wall opposite the fireplace.

"Your husband?"

She nodded with a look of sick loathing.

"I thought he'd gone for good and prayed he'd stay away. But he's come back like a bad penny, more dead than alive and rotten with gin. My life's a torment, miss. I've done my best and can't do more." She came closer and whispered, "We've had two policemen here already asking questions. He'd hardly come home before there was this knocking at the door. Just enquiries, they said, but I don't know . . . Something that happened the night he went away. They've been waiting for him to come back. They'll be here again. He couldn't talk to them, the way he is."

"Is he ill?"

She told me his symptoms.

"I'll help you." I emptied my purse on the table. At the sight of the shillings and copper coins, she put her hands over her face and cried. "We must think what to do. Can Janey go for Dr Sidlow? She can tell him Miss Mallow sent her. And you must have a fire and something to eat."

She dried her eyes, marshalled the children and sent them off for coals, bread, cheese and tea. Three of the five had had their heads shaved for ringworm so that at first I did not recognise them as a brood of redheads; but Janey had taken off her bonnet and revealed even in that miserable light a wealth of red-gold hair. In sudden misgiving I went over to the bed and looked down into the eyes of Josh Blakey.

I knew at once that he was dangerous. He was desperately ill: his skin a peculiar bluish grey: his body in constant motion. One would have thought him not only incapable of harm but helpless. But he was sober enough to recognise me and his face expressed such an evil spirit of hostility that even under these circumstances, he frightened me.

I turned my back on him. In an unbelievably short time one of the children came back with coals bought from a more fortunate neighbour. I watched Mrs Blakey clear the grate and light a fire, and was conscious of a hopeful bustle in the room. Having rescued them, I could leave. Instead, I lingered, feeling a desperation not unlike Mrs Blakey's own. How was it that I had thought so little of the two wretches who had set upon Nicholas? Once having heard of Blakey's flight, I had forgotten all about them. The creature on the bed was a murderer. A series of chance incidents had placed him at my mercy. It was my duty to bring him to justice.

With a new, vivid insight, I understood that a crime does not end when it is committed, nor does it involve only the victim and the criminal. By not speaking out, I had condoned a murder. For this I must be ready, in my turn, to be judged.

The thought was awe-inspiring. Blinded by inner light, I almost forgot the squalid room, or was lifted for a second or two above its less noble demands. But so far I had thought only of a divine Judge, remote and even kindly, ultimately forgiving. I was to experience other moments of illumination.

To risk another glance at Josh Blakey was to come down to physical reality. There he lay, having drunk himself well-nigh to death (on his share of the proceeds from my poor mother's jewellery, I reminded myself, too much distraught to be shocked); and writhing in such wretched torment that to consign him to the further anguish of hanging was not only unthinkable but surely unnecessary. In my absolute ignorance of the law, I became once more abstracted, wondering, for instance, whether there could be a charge of murder if no body was found. In that case I might tell my story to the disadvantage of no one but myself.

Every kind of uncertainty assailed me; except on one point. I never doubted that the final decision lay with me. The choice was mine. Clumsy as I might be in manipulating the strings, I was the puppet-master, not one of the puppets.

So, in my, inexperience, I thought.

Feeling feverishly hot, I was undoing my jacket when he gave a strangled moan and seemed to be asking for a drink. He was certainly very ill. I half filled a cup from the jug of water on the table and took it to him. He drank. My watch dangled between us as I bent over him.

"You took it then, the watch," he said. "Oh, yes, miss, you saw me on the steps but I saw you too."

The cup jerked in my hand, slopping water on the ragged bed clothes. I put it down and looked round. Fortunately his voice was so feeble that it carried no further than the side of the bed. The tallow dip left most of the room in shadow. The effect was to divest him of a physical form. He was reduced to a voice, threatening me from a darkness that obscured not only the dreary bed but the whole gruesome episode in which he — and I — had been involved. Incredulously I realised that we were companions, conspirators in silence.

He lay shuddering and swallowing in an effort to gather strength to speak again. I waited, hypnotised. Indeed though I could not see their expression, he kept his eyes fixed on mine with what seemed a resentment so forceful that he was the stronger. The advantage lay with him. I had not foreseen how he would use it.

"And I saw you after that," he said, "down on the wharf, with him."

It was then that I knew how near I too stood to the perilous brink. He could ruin me almost as effectively as I could ruin him. An irrational dread of what he would say next so possessed me that I could have shuddered as violently as he; but I stayed still and said nothing.

"Yes, I saw you. I saw what you did."

I dared not ask what he had seen but waited, sick with despair. It was true then. That moment of revulsion had been fatal to Nicholas. To Josh Blakey it had seemed as if I pushed him into the water.

"I know why you never told on me." This time the voice was different, less certain. "Any way, I never touched him. It was Dan'l that set on him."

"No one will believe you," I said from the depths of my misery. "I don't."

: 'But it wasn't Dan'l that was with him at the end, nor me. It was you. He was alive when you found him," the dreadful voice said, "and when you left him he was dead. You daren't tell on me for fear I tell on you."

I dared not leave him either; dared not miss a word he said, but stood rooted there, considering my plight with a desperate concentration. A few words from Josh Blakey and all Wickborough — and father — would hear that there had been robbery and violence on the wharf and that I had been involved in it. Now that I knew father better, I marvelled at my stupidity in not having told him at once and realised how hurt he would be to learn that fear of him had kept me silent. How simple it would have been to make the facts known then! How difficult it would be now! No one would believe that I had not had some strong personal motive in covering up the affair. Like scenes in a ghostly magic lantern show, I conjured up hideous pictures in the style of Ned's *Illustrated Police News* with myself as the central figure under the head-line: 'She knew but would not tell. Murderer protected by woman's silence'.

Guided by such garbled notions of the law as I had formed on the slender basis of a chat with a shoe-black, I faced at last the possibility that I was not only morally guilty but criminally guilty too. I had never heard of misprision but I saw myself as an accessory: one of those women Ned had denounced if not for 'aiding and abetting and urging on' then certainly for 'covering up'.

How naïve seemed all my previous thoughts about Nicholas's death! My illusion of god-like power to shape the lives of others, including the creature in front of me, abruptly took flight, leaving me to quake with uncomplicated dread of the law. I was very far now from any wish to bring Josh Blakey to justice. Rather than breathe a word of accusation I would gladly have died.

But surely the same argument applied to him.

With a rush of relief I remembered that although Josh Blakey held me at his mercy to precisely the same degree as I held him, provided neither of us spoke, no one need know that poor Nicholas was even dead much less murdered. He was only missing. The police were making enquiries. Presumably Josh's sudden departure on the night when Nicholas had last been seen alive had directed their enquiries towards him. He must have been well known to them already. It was to our mutual advantage to say nothing. Scarcely had I reached this conclusion when it occurred to me that my case was worse than his. He had seen me with Nicholas. I had seen him running up the steps, no more.

Some lingering remnant of common sense came hesitantly to my rescue. No one would believe that I, little Hester Mallow, could be in any way connected with such wickedness. I had only been passing by. But the talk would be endless. I would never live it down.

"It's all come out," they would say. "Funny she never told."

Blinded by tears of self-pity, I groped my way to the door and up the steps, seeking to breathe the pure night air; but the air of Weaver's Yard was not pure and the first thing I saw beyond the broken-down wall was the unmistakable figure of a policeman, rocking to and fro on his boots like a man who had no plans for leaving. I retreated.

187

The fire was burning well. With admirable speed Mrs Blakey had set out tea and bread for the children. They were already finishing their meal. Three of them she dispatched to the woman next door, keeping only the baby. She did not come near the bed until Janey arrived with Dr Sidlow.

"What are you doing here, Miss Mallow?"

The answer was far more complicated than he could suspect. His question brought home to me more forcibly than ever a sense of my position in Wickborough. I said something about St Aidan's and the Windrosses and immediately regretted having mentioned the name. Blakey repeated it and growled some comment I didn't catch.

"Hold your tongue," Dr Sidlow said briefly, and examined him.

Mrs Blakey and I waited outside the door. Somewhere above the crazy roof-tops that shut us in, there must have been stars. They were invisible. Had they been there in their brightest legions I would not have seen them, seized as I was by a new preoccupation: the possibility that Josh Blakey had seen Julian too on the wharf that night. When the doctor came to speak to Mrs Blakey, I went back to the bed, lured there by the fear that Josh would say something loud enough for the others to hear. Was it likely that he would risk his own skin by forcing me to retaliate? To my alarm I now felt in him a loosening of restraint. He was forgetting even his own safety.

"Mister Windross," he muttered contemptuously, "swaggering about like a lord ... knocking people down, then handing out money." In the growing firelight I saw his face take on a look of detestable cunning. "You wouldn't be on the wharf all by yourself in the dark, not a pretty young lady like you."

Did that mean that he had or had not seen Julian? I could not ask for fear of putting the idea into his head if he had not, or goading him into shouting it out if he had. So long as he kept some command of his gin-soaked wits, he was unlikely to put himself at risk but there was no knowing what he might say when drunk or in the delirium of fever: nor any limit to the lies he might tell.

Julian's notion that he had knocked some sense of decency into Josh Blakey was of a piece with his other fantasies. Instead, he had knocked out what meagre allowance there had been, and made a bitter enemy.

"I'm done for," Josh Blakey said with a hopeless conviction that made all his former remarks seem trivial. "They can't do anything to me." He struggled to raise his head from the grimy pillow. "But there's plenty I can say before I go."

There was indeed. Mercifully he could have no idea who Nicholas was; but with new alarm I saw how unpleasantly certain facts could cohere if the whole truth were to come to light. The missing man was Louise's husband: Julian wanted to marry Louise. His blameless career at St Aidan's had come to an abrupt and inexplicable end when he had suffered what seemed a nervous collapse in the early summer and given up all thoughts of the Church. An impartial observer might see these changes in his conduct as symptoms of suppressed guilt. Even though he had in fact never seen Nicholas and at the time of his death Louise had not even come home, enquiries would lead to talk. Julian would lose his position as tutor...

These lightning associations brought before me more clearly than ever the pictures in Ned's *Police News*: drawings of fierce-faced criminals with long, wolfish teeth and vampire-like women, their hair streaming as they were torn from the arms of guilty lovers. Moreover I suddenly discovered an additional complication in the fact that the missing man had been in possession of my mother's jewellery. The Mallows were inextricably involved in the affair. A scandal of such complexity would enrich the unwritten annals of Wickborough for several generations.

"The doctor's gone." Mrs Blakey joined me. Josh had closed his eyes. She looked down at him with a new dispassionate calm. "Two days," she whispered. "That's as long as he can last, the doctor says." She leaned forward and wiped the grey face with a surprisingly clean handkerchief. "I took him for better or worse. There's been no better, only worse and worse. We both come of decent families and he's dragged us down to the very bottom. But I've stuck to him and done my best. When all's said and done he is my husband and he's come home. I'll be with him at the end."

She spoke for us both. My motives were different but my intention was as firm as hers.

"I'll stay with him too," I said.

I found a peg, hung up my hat and jacket and sat down at the bed-side, determined that he would leave before I did.

20

ON THIS SHAKY foundation I rose to a position of distinction in Sparrow Chare. Children in the court stopped playing when I went occasionally to the door, persuading myself that the air outside was less foul than the air within. Their mothers stared in amazement and respect. It was the least of my problems but embarrassing all the same.

We had sent Janey to Silvergate with a message for father, explaining that I was with 'one of Mr Windross's families' and asking for clean sheets, blankets and food. Thomas brought them in a laundry basket at about nine o'clock. The comfort of seeing him was indescribble.

"You've taken something on, Miss Hester. Are you sure you can manage?"

He observed the details of the room: the oozing walls, the wet floor, the sacking over the small window, the occupant of the bed and our primitive arrangements for nursing him. "Well, you can do it if anyone can." Mrs Wragge had sent a little meal for me, wrapped in a napkin. Thomas also produced a small flask of brandy. "Keep this for yourself and Mrs Blakey. He's had enough spirits to last him in this world if he never touches another drop. I'll be back first thing in the morning. If you need me before then, send the little girl."

I went with him to the door.

"You should be safe enough," he said, "with two policemen outside. What's he done?"

I shook my head.

"Well," Thomas said charitably, "it's not the time to be thinking of his crimes."

I thought of them with unbroken concentration while I watched by the bed and Mrs Blakey dozed in a chair. The harder and longer I thought, the more unassailable seemed Josh Blakey's position, the less secure my own. He was as reckless of his reputation on earth now that he faced the final reckoning elsewhere as I was jealous of mine. He had nothing to lose by telling colourful lies about Julian and me : I had everything to lose by telling the truth about him.

At about midnight my patient awoke and acknowledged me with a lowering of his sandy brows.

"There were two of you," I said at once. "Where is the other man?"

He may have been surprised into answering as promptly as his weakness allowed. On the other hand it may have been indifference. It no longer mattered how much he told, now that his own escape was certain. The thought was disagreeable.

"Dan'l Syne. He cleared out. He sold his share of the brooches and that and took ship for overseas. It was him that done it. I wouldn't have had the strength. And it was Dan'l that found out about the jewellery he had on him, from Emmie Tafferty ... There's only you and me left. Just the two of us."

He actually achieved a grotesque kind of grin. In some strange way our relationship had changed. Perhaps through the mists that were closing round him, he saw me as a figure already familiar, an acceptable shape in the pattern of his illness. Perhaps as the shadows darkened, he began to lose touch with his unsavoury world. As his grasp on reality grew weaker, mine grew stronger. I gave him a drink and rearranged his pillows.

191

"But the watch should've been mine." The words were only just audible.

"You went back for it?" I spoke in the same conspiratorial whisper.

"Never seen another like it."

"It would have been risky to sell it."

"There's always ways." The wan mouth twisted again. He could manage no more than the hint of a grin. "You're brazen, I'll say that. Wearing it, as cool as you please."

Having established this macabre comradeship, he slept again. His nose was white and sharp. Little as I knew him I could see that his face was changing. It was shadowed in a new way but with a fatal pallor round the mouth. The shuddering had ceased. Julian should never have given him the shilling, I thought, looking down at Josh with something like sympathy. It was the patronage that had humiliated him, and made him venomous. To have knocked him down once would have been enough. Julian should have left him with some vestige of self-respect.

Yawning in the murky stench of the room, I had little to do but open my watch from time to time and see how the gold hand crept from hour to hour. In the tallow light, the lady with the lyre had shrunk to the shape and size of a white bead. With bewildered astonishment, scarcely believing in her existence, I remembered Louise. It was just possible to imagine her in the mellow sunshine of Codlin Croft, moving about its leaf-shadowed rooms with angelic serenity, a creature so far removed from the reeking bed-side in Weaver's Yard that even with the detachment that time has brought, it is difficult to see her impartially as the cause of the whole disaster. At that time I could only feel confusedly that there was a connection, as if she had wound up a clockwork toy and set the figures in motion, then walked away without bothering to watch.

It must be impossible to supply a fellow-creature's humblest needs, to watch him relinquishing them one by one until only the need for water, air and a human presence remains, and not feel some primal sympathy.

Under these unpromising conditions my relationship with Josh ripened.

"It's that good of you, miss." Mrs Blakey's reverence put me to shame when she came to release me for a few minutes. "It's not fit — you shouldn't be doing such things."

"You look after the baby. I'll see to him."

It was not the time for delicacy. As he grew weaker, I felt no shrinking from his wasted and diseased body. As for his mind, somewhere in its depths there must have lingered traces of the respectable upbringing Mrs Blakey had spoken of.

"Wonder who he was," he murmured more than once, "and where he belonged. He wasn't a common chap."

Though he rambled a little, he never seemed to forget who I was but his voice was so weak and the connection between us so far beyond the limits of likelihood that Mrs Blakey could not have understood his references to the bond that united us.

"Seems to have taken to you, doesn't he?" was the nearest she came to perceiving it. "I never would have thought . . . There's no explaining it, life. It takes a bit of reckoning up."

It was still dark when Thomas came back. He filled the water buckets from the tap in the court and insisted on making coffee for Mrs Blakey and me. Heartening as it was, his presence caused me acute embarrassment. I tried to occupy his attention with a flood of meaningless remarks, pitched in an undertone.

"You've told me three times not to talk," he said as he quietly made up the fire," and you're chattering like a row of starlings."

"It's just that your voice is so deep, Thomas. You might disturb him."

To my dismay he went to the bed and gave Josh a long, steady look.

"Nothing is going to disturb him, the state he's in. He's lost touch."

Sure enough Josh opened his eyes and gave no sign of seeing Thomas. But the moment I appeared, hovering anxiously at the foot of the bed, a flicker of animation crossed his face.

"Watch . . . should have had it . . ."

"You see," Thomas said, "he doesn't know where he is. I had a word with the constable as I came in. If he's supposed to be stopping Blakey from slipping away, he's wasting his time. They were wanting him to answer questions it seems, about something that happened the night he went away, in April. A burglary, I suppose."

"They won't come in?"

"No. But you can never tell in a case like this. He might come to his senses and make a confession to clear his conscience, if he has one. You might hear things, Miss Hester, not suitable for you to hear. It would be a shock to you to know the sort of thing he must have been mixed up in. Wouldn't it be best for you to go home and let me stay?"

"How good you are to me, Thomas! No, I want to stay. Besides, Mrs Blakey likes to have another woman with her."

"She's lucky to have you."

The closing of the door as Thomas left, or the change in the room had roused Josh. He seemed to understand where he was and looked round anxiously. I thought he might have overheard Thomas's reference to the police but it was not the police he was looking for.

"Janey."

The child was asleep on the cot bed. I roused her and brought her stumbling to her father. He could only repeat her name. She knelt down, still only half awake, and soon drifted off to sleep again. Her head resting against the bed clothes was all he could see of her. He put out his hand and felt about until it rested on her red-gold hair.

"All like me," he said. "Redheads." A sudden painful distress altered his face. "All like me."

"She's a good little girl, Janey," I said soothingly, with no thought of irony or contradiction. But the remark did not help him.

"Nothing for them," he said — and looked at me with

the same yearning regret. It remained with him all day. He mentioned the children several times and gradually his distress began to take a different form. At first he had seemed to be thinking of the penniless state in which he would leave them. I tried to comfort him by saying that they would not go hungry: they would be given help. But he grew more and more uneasy. A continual movement of his right hand puzzled me. He kept on raising it an inch or two from the blanket and letting it fall again weakly. At last, when I lifted him up to give him a drink, he contrived to bring his trembling forefinger to his lips.

"Ssh!" His eyes were beseeching. He watched me in the same troubled way as I straightened the bed clothes. It was some time before it dawned on me that our wishes had become identical. My desperate need for secrecy was now matched by his. The other children were still being looked after by the neighbour but from his habit of looking at Janey and the baby, I knew that his distress was on their behalf; that they were not to be told. He cared nothing for the police but he was afraid of what the children might find out. In spite of Thomas's prediction, a confession seemed unlikely.

During the second night in the small hours there came over him the almost imperceptible changes which I knew instinctively foreshadowed the end. I raised him up and wiped his brow. He had passed by this time into a region so dark and lonely that to find me at his side must have brought some faint comfort.

"Fancy me seeing you there." He spoke faintly, from an immense distance.

His moment of extremity became mine. He was the only one, this pitiful remnant of a man, who could help me. He was the only one who had seen me on the wharf. When he was gone there would be no way, ever, in the whole span of time left to me, of settling whether I could have saved Nicholas. If I had grasped his maimed hand, if I had exerted all my strength, could I have dragged him out of the water and restored him to life?

A great terror of being left alone to re-live the experience endlessly in solitude and doubt made me say urgently:

"Tell me, Josh. What did you see?"

Weakly, with childlike obedience he said:

"You leaning out, trying to save him. No use. As good as dead when we left him. Thought he was dead."

Whatever I had done, no matter what anyone had done, it would have made no difference.

"Josh," I said, "I'll never tell about you. The children will never know. I'll never tell."

I laid him back on the pillow and took his hand. I was holding it when he died. I closed his eyes and breathed a prayer for forgiveness for us both.

The narrow passages of the Chare were still dark but when I came out on the wharf, the eastern sky was streaked with light. On the opposite bank the bare trees were just visible. A cool wind crept over the river, adding its faint sigh to the endless smooth rush of water in midstream and the insistent lapping on wood and stone here at the very edge by the submerged steps.

I had looked on death and felt for the second time the loneliness of the dying. But Nicholas at the end had been far more lonely. Whatever I had done, it would not have saved him; but surely I could have said something. He had lacked even the words of comfort I had whispered to his murderer. Moreover I had deprived him of earthly justice; of all mourners but myself.

The breeze strengthened and blew fresh on my face. Over the river a tree lifted its long branches in dark silhouette. The first jackdaws rose from their perches on the Abbey towers and sailed into a sky of scudding cloud.

"He's here."

Mr Benjamin might have spoken the words again in my ear, so vividly was I conscious of a living presence: of not being alone there. It lasted no more than an instant and was gone, as Nicholas was gone. And yet, to have become part of the water and the earth, the wind and the rain, was that after all such a sad thing to have happened to him? There was a kind of consummation in it.

Like Ned, I wished he had not gone away but he had not left Wickborough quite unchanged by his coming. He would have his own memorial. On the sombre monochrome of his death brighter pictures imposed themselves: of a boy reading in a sunny court-yard, all the splendours of his mind awakened: a girl blowing a kiss with the freely given affection of a warm heart to the quiet stranger who had been 'like a relation'. I envied her. Her tribute had reached him in time.

Perhaps it was not too late to breathe into the morning air the message I had been too frightened and ignorant to speak at the right time. As always the words when they came, fell far short of the feeling that inspired them.

"You mustn't mind," I said, to whatever else was there besides the river and trees and sky. "You mustn't mind too much." And although I guessed that he had not hoped for happiness any more than he would have demanded justice, I added: "Louise would never have made you happy, and you've been loved in other ways."

21

A COMPLETE SPRING cleaning of this old house in Silvergate would last the whole year through. Mrs Wragge and I never attempted it. The over-abundance of staircases, the absence of level floors, the failure of doors to stay shut or open unless held or propped, the remoteness of corners, none of them right-angles, the impenetrability of the countless cupboards — all foiled our efforts. But each year, usually in March, we did interrupt the daily routine and nibble at the edges of the problem.

It so happened that the March of 1877 found me in very good spirits, continually refreshed by small gusts, developing from time to time into positive gales of happiness. Among other revelations they convinced me of the need to dress my hair differently, clear out an extravagant quantity of old dresses and take all my gloves to be cleaned. The same mood roused me to spend my evenings in studying *The Young Lady's Treasury* and my mornings in shortening the tie-tapes of my underskirts to achieve the fashionable swan-like effect, doing it with such success that father remonstrated.

"You're not safe on these stairs, Hester. It makes me uncomfortable to see you waddling about like a duck."

That was enough. I lengthened the tapes again and ran up and down stairs in the old unfashionable way. But I felt rather sorry for father, who was too old to share the thrill of being poised on the brink of a new life. I could not have explained to him how the world had changed, or how, having been blind for years, I had been miraculously granted the gift of sight. Familiar things appeared in a new light. The house, as I said, was unaltered, but I now found in it all manner of interesting features: the graceful curve of the stairs: the finely moulded cornices: the smoke-dimmed but still elegant plaster work of the parlour ceiling. I saw these things, that is, when they were pointed out to me with loving admiration by a craftsman with a well-informed enthusiasm for the past.

My tastes changed. Theology was now no more to me than the recollection of stifled yawns. I became passionately interested in history, a study actively encouraged by the house itself. There were so many nooks and corners where one could be discovered innocently looking for traces of seventeenth century carving or oak dowel pins or bricked-up salt cupboards: places to linger in, when no longer alone, and surprisingly difficult to leave.

In this state of exhilaration it was possible to tackle even the spring cleaning with zest. I whisked into my room one morning, tossed the mattress, re-arranged the furniture and in emptying the pastille burner of a year's debris in the shape of keys, buttons, buckles and stay-laces, found the gold and black enamelled ring.

"Re : mem : ber : me," it said, but less mournfully than before and less reproachfully. Nicholas Vince had passed into my heart and mind with so gentle an insistence that no conscious effort was needed to remember him and when I put the ring experimentally on the third finger of my left hand, it was not of Nicholas I was thinking.

I took an armful of discarded dresses up to the attic, forced them into a trunk and sat down on the battered lid. It seemed a suitable time and place to re-read, undisturbed, a curious letter which had come on the morning post. I read it with my ears alert for the sound of certain longed-for footsteps on the stairs, hoping they would come soon.

The letter was from Codlin Croft but not from Louise. She had written briefly in December, giving me advice on how to candy peel and reporting accurately on the number of Christmas puddings she and Lettice had made. To my surprise Tilly and Edith had given notice. "Servants can always be replaced however," Louise reminded me. Since then she had not written. Plans for me to visit the Croft had fallen through from lack of enthusiasm on my part. I had such a very good reason for wanting to stay in Wickborough.

This letter was from Caroline Hawn. She told me

.... how very much we would enjoy a visit from you. It would be an opportunity for you to accompany your sister home. She has been with us now for more than six months. We must not presume indefinitely on her willingness to oblige us. Invaluable as her help has been, I cannot find it in my conscience to deprive Mr Mallow any longer of the assistance he must surely need in his own household.

My health continues uncertain. An invalid, you will readily understand, is soon discouraged by the trivial anxieties so easy to overlook in a state of health. My husband assures me that there is nothing to worry about. Gentlemen care so very much for their comfort and Miss Mallow is in every way competent. Indeed as a housekeeper she is quite admirable as I shall be only too happy to assure in the warmest terms any lady who might wish to employ her, should Miss Mallow seek another situation when in the near future she leaves us. In another household her position might perhaps be more clearly defined ... I venture to look

199

forward to hearing from you. Perhaps you would be so good as to write to your sister so that she can prepare for the journey . . .

Poor Mrs Hawn! Equally balanced between admiration for Louise and the longing to be rid of her, the letter also conveyed the atmosphere of unrest Louise contrived always to arouse. I pondered my reply. The small gusts of happiness had temporarily blown themselves out, leaving a breathless lull. My future had begun to take on an increasingly definite shape. Into that shape Louise did not fit. Knowing her talent for re-adjusting circumstances to a shape that fitted her, I was feeling the first familiar pangs of apprehension when footsteps on the stairs set my heart beating faster and diverted my thoughts from Louise. Their owner, having failed to find me in the parlour, came on and up.

"Hester."

"I'm here."

It was only Julian. Still, I was pleased to see him and laid my hand in my lap with the ring prominently displayed, hoping he would notice it.

"Good heavens!" He looked past me. "There's old Dash." He patted the proudly arched head with a look of tenderness I swear he never showed to me, and set the old war-horse rocking. "Wonderful times we had up here. Do you remember the Charge of the Light Brigade?"

Briefly I recaptured the thrill of it: the raking cannon fire, the hopeless gallantry, the bardic lines intoned by Julian from the saddle, 'Half a league, half a league . . .'! Only Julian could have been at one and the same time the Poet Laureate describing the charge and the Earl of Cardigan leading it. How he had burned, I remembered, to be Miss Nightingale as well! Only the fear of seeming effeminate had made him hand the lamp to me and drop in agony on the bed, writhing from ghastly wounds bravely borne.

"What was Louise?" I asked. "Wasn't she the Queen waiting to be told the news?"

Where had she been and what had she been doing while

she waited? Either the news of defeat had been too awful to impart or we had simply forgotten her. I felt her slipping away again as she had slipped away then.

Julian's expression was unfathomable. He sat down on a child's stool so that for once we were of the same height.

"I don't know. It's a strange thing. I can't remember her at all as a child. How is it," he looked guilty, "that one forgets her, like a view. There's nothing there, only what one sees."

He leaned over and stroked Dash's head. We both smiled, remembering how we had loved him.

"Have you seen her lately?"

"No." He was still puzzled. "I didn't go back to the Croft after all. There seemed a meanness in it."

"Mean to Louise?"

"Partly. But I was thinking of the other fellow, Vince. I'm not so sure now that he is dead. There's always the possibility that she had the same effect on him. For whole days together and longer, I've been able to forget her. Suppose when she left him, he gradually forgot her too."

"I don't believe he ever would."

"You speak almost as if you had known him. At any rate it just wasn't possible to go on telling Louise how I felt about her with him in the background, whether the poor fellow's alive or dead. He haunts me rather. Like a reproach."

"He haunts us all, I expect, even Louise. I mean, especially Louise."

"Yes." Julian had already discarded the topic. "And now, of course, it's all turning out for the best. That's what I came to tell you. The Vanscombes want me to take the boys and join them in Rome. From there we're to go to Florence. They've taken an apartment in the Via Montebello. Spring in Italy! I can scarcely believe it. I tell you I've soaked myself in Baedeker. Think of the galleries, Hester. One could spend a lifetime in the Uffizi alone among the greatest pictures in the world. So far I've only known them from prints." The attic resounded to his splendid roll-call: Fra Lippo Lippi, Botticelli,

Bellini, Giorgione ... Already they were his intimate companions. "And that's not all. We shall spend the summer in Switzerland, take in Dresden and Hamburg on the way home and then Paris. It's what I've always wanted but travel was out of the question when I was thinking of marriage. When I think that I might have missed this opportunity by tying myself down, it almost restores my faith." His voice trembled with earnestness. "That's what has been missing from my life." He gave Dash a push that set him galloping over wider and wider fields of the imagination. "The all-seeing detachment of art ... Beauty, not to be possessed, but experienced through the highest of all faculties ... neither heart nor mind nor spirit alone but all three together refined to the utmost excellence ... acting upon one another ... combining to create a new instrument of perception."

The words came surging forth. I watched and listened as I had watched him and listened to him all my life, expecting to see him lift up his hand in one of those supreme moments of vision: "I say unto you that it shall come to pass that ..." knowing that none of it had ever come to pass or ever would.

He had reached his peroration. Dash, still drawing fiery breaths, resumed the horizontal pose he would not forsake now for many a long year.

"You're going soon?"

"The day after tomorrow. I came to say goodbye, Hester."

He kissed me and I clung to him, my heart aching a little for the nursery days that were over now, quite over. None of the things he had prophesied, none of the dreams I had dreamed would ever be fulfilled; but he had been an incomparable playmate. Whenever memory uncovers the earliest days, compared to which all other days seem spiritless and dim, I find him there, and he perhaps finds me.

When he had gone, I stayed upstairs for a while with the sensation of putting away, besides my old dresses, a host of other things no longer needed. The little parsonage, the stone nymph and the kingfisher took their place

202

with all the beloved lumber of toys laid aside. It was a few minutes before the new kind of happiness came gushing back, but not more. Looking down at my left hand, I laughed. Julian hadn't noticed the ring. He had never noticed me in any more detail than an actor might notice an audience beyond the footlights. A warm, attentive presence had been enough. Once the discovery would have grieved me, but now any regret I felt was only regret for childhood outgrown. Secure in a new and happier love — soundly rooted as it was in mutual sympathy — I could acknowledge the hollowness at the heart of the old one, forget it and turn back to my own affairs, in which Julian had long ceased to have any part.

"So he's off on another tack," father said when I told him the news that afternoon. "One thing is sure: he would never have had the stability for a clergyman. Too high flown and burned up by his own ideas. He's got over his infatuation with Louise, I suppose."

"Not seeing her has made a difference."

I showed him Mrs Hawn's letter. He smiled and shook his head over it.

"We shall have to trust to time to put things right." He was looking younger, less haggard and serious. "I've been hard on Louise. No, not in deed, but in my opinion of her. The fact is, Hester, that finding the Upjohn watch after all those years gave me a change of heart. I was sure she had taken it. Oh yes, she took all your mother's rings and brooches and bracelets. It was no better than theft. But that didn't hurt me so much. She used to lay them out and play with them when your mother was alive. They mattered to her. But the watch was the most precious thing in the whole establishment. She was old enough at sixteen to understand how much I cherished it, for itself as well as for its associations. When I couldn't find it and thought she had taken that too, it convinced me that she was as I had always thought, heartless: cold to the very core of her nature. Finding it was a relief. In one respect at least I had misjudged her. But I've never felt able to speak to her about the other bits and pieces. You don't know, I suppose . . . ?"

"Where they are? No."

"I shall have to ask her." He sighed. "Mrs Maple understood Louise: that she has no moral sense, I mean, and must never be faced with a decision. She can't help it, poor child. She has always been treated with love and admiration and so she has never suffered the ill effects of her nature; never learned. She's been my despair from being a little girl. You mustn't think I don't love her, Hester. Not loving her might make things easier."

The street was quiet: the light was fading: the lamps were not yet lit. It was here and at this hour that the haunting had begun. Suppose, for Louise, it should never end. Suppose father had underestimated her ability to suffer. She could certainly suffer fear.

"There's something you haven't told me, Hester."

My heart contracted. I turned, panic-stricken. To my amazement he laughed. "You don't need to, my dear. Thomas told me himself. He has asked my permission."

"I was wanting to tell you, only . . ."

"You must know how pleased I am. You're a good little daughter and the best turn you could do me is to give me Thomas for a son." He put his arm round me and stroked my hair as he had not done since I was a child. "You'll both stay with me. It will be Mallow and Griff. More than I could have hoped for. There was a time when I feared it might be Julian. Let's have Thomas up this evening for a glass of wine. We'll make it a happy occasion." He took my hand and saw the ring. "That's a dreary-looking thing."

"Thomas didn't give me that." I snatched it off in confusion. "It's an old one."

"The trouble is that Thomas won't be able to find one good enough for you. So far as he is concerned, nothing is good enough for you, Hester. And I don't need to tell you that there isn't a man to touch him in Wickborough. He'll make the best mayor we shall ever have. Oh, it won't be for a good while yet but you'll see."

He went downstairs. I could have fancied he was humming a tune. Presently, hearing the step I had been longing for, I moved the kettle from the hob to the bar and set out tea-cups. Since Thomas had taken a step up in the world by becoming father's assistant, we had given up the muffins, feeling — so far as I recall — that even as an unofficial meal they lacked dignity. Over fingers of toast on the other hand there hovered the delicate frugality of Mrs Maple's room with all its enigmatic associations. Fortunately I had learned to make very good tea-cakes, a happy medium we have enjoyed ever since.

We beamed at each other across the table. Thomas was undoubtedly a fine-looking young man. Not that the discovery was new. I had made it one day quite early in the year when we were re-arranging the shop window and I handed him a jet ornament to hold: a souvenir in the shape of Wickborough Abbey. (I have it still.) Instead he grasped my hand and kissed it. It was then, with the sharp crenellations of the Abbey pressing into my palm that I saw how handsome he was.

"Oh Thomas!" I gasped, taken aback by both the sudden delight of the kiss and the wave of enlightenment it brought. "I never . . . You must have . . . I didn't know."

Overcome by happy astonishment, I gave up the attempt to express it while Thomas tenderly removed the Abbey from my tortured palm.

"I've always known," he said.

Though the happiness remained, the astonishment soon passed. What could be more natural than that we should love each other when every moment of our daily companionship had been harmonious; and in moments more eventful . . . ? I prudently avoided the memory of those distressing scenes in Sleedale and Weaver's Yard, thinking instead of Thomas's calm steadfastness, his sympathy and wisdom and the contentment I found in the very sight of him. Who could help loving Thomas?

When we had finished tea, Thomas lingered at the window to watch Mrs Setterwort as she leaned from the blue-green recesses of her parlour like a sea creature and put out slow tentacles to strip the yellowing leaves from her wallflowers.

"Did you know," he said, "that Mrs Setterwort married her father's apprentice?"

It was a shock. I cannot deny it. The similarity daunted me. I would not have chosen to model my life on that of the Setterworts. Faced with the threat of such domestic tedium as theirs, any young woman might flinch. I took a good look at Thomas. He was tall and well built. Mr Setterwort was short and chubby. Thomas's complexion was fair with no tinge of the coppersmith's ruddiness. But who knew what time could do to the complexion? Thomas's eyes, a greyish blue, were turned on me, seeing me as the centre of their world, alight with an active loving interest in me. No other interest, however enthusiastically followed — and Thomas had many — would ever lessen his enthusiasm for me. I was convinced of it. The conviction has been justified.

"They're so dull," I said, noting Mrs Setterwort's cap ribbons with renewed contempt.

"Yes, they're dull but who wouldn't be dull with Mrs Setterwort for a wife?"

"You don't think — we'll be like them?"

"How could we be? There isn't anyone like you." Thomas spoke with the serene confidence I have always respected and never more than at that moment. "There's something about you that sets you apart. I felt it the first day I saw you and every day of my life you charm me more."

This short speech appealed to me. I liked Thomas's description of my singular charm. He obviously meant it. There was even the possibility that he might be right. The gale of happiness blew more strongly than ever.

"There's no doubt in my mind," Thomas went on, and he smiled as I preened myself, "that when you are Mrs Setterwort's age, I'll still be the envy of every man in Wickborough."

To be forty! The prospect was so distant as to be beyond the range of vision. Besides, there could be more of Mrs Setterwort, in every sense, than could be seen from the street or gleaned from her oracular remarks. Had she secrets, for instance, that no one knew, not even Mr Setterwort?

She caught my eye. We bowed to each other across the window boxes.

22

IN THE SUMMER of that same year the Hawns left Codlin Croft and moved to Wickborough. A few weeks before the removal Captain Hawn and Louise came to town for a day to engage servants and make arrangements for decorating and furnishing the house, a comfortable residence on the leafy outskirts of the town, not far from Buckingham Street.

They called at Silvergate. Louise stayed for an hour while Captain Hawn drove on to eat luncheon at the Boar. But first father took him into his office where they talked in private. Afterwards father spoke to Louise. The outcome of these conversations was that Louise came back to Wickborough as Mrs Vince, her position with the Hawns being that of paid housekeeper. Young as she was for such a post, she had made herself indispensable. Mrs Hawn's attempt to disengage herself from Louise was doomed to failure. There had been no hope for the poor woman in so unequal a contest.

"I'm to have my own parlour," Louise said, "and my own piano."

The pathetic cadence of her voice could no longer mislead me into feeling sorry for her. She would have all she wanted.

If possible she was lovelier than ever; or so after almost a year's absence she seemed. It was hard to let her go when, punctually at the end of the hour, she rose. I put my arm round her as we went out on to the landing.

"You'll be able to come and see us often," I said, knowing that she would come rarely if at all.

"I always hated this house. It's so dark and inconvenient and all those clocks . . ."

Into the little silence came the sound of their ticking.

I remembered how as a child she had tried to match her power of counting against the relentless mechanism of the clocks and had given up in terror. If she had been afraid then, how would she fare in the immeasurable emptiness to which time was hurrying us on? Launched into eternity (the outlandish notion came to me) Louise's spirit would founder, unprepared. And for that matter, what of my own? I banished the sobering thought and asked:

"Was it only the clocks? Was there anything else you were afraid of?"

"Yes, lots of things." She glanced up one flight of stairs and beyond to the others above. "You and Julian." She seemed surprised to make the discovery. "When we were children I never understood what you were doing or what you wanted. 'Be this,' you used to say. 'Be that.' A princess or something. Then you rushed away. I never knew how to do it."

I laughed, imagining her bewilderment: her beautiful bewilderment.

"Poor little Louise!"

"It's always been like that." I remember how she looked and spoke in that rare moment of revelation. "People always seem to be expecting something else, something I can't give them. Father, you, Julian — and Nicholas."

It occurred to me, and I think the insight was a true one, that if his hands had been unmarred, she would have feared him just the same. It was the intensity of his love that had appalled her.

Her eyes rested not upon me but on some point in space behind me. They suggested, in their blue depths, a quality of feeling Louise was in fact incapable of. Yet once again I was deceived and waited to hear her say what anyone else in the world would surely have said:

"I wonder what became of him."

But she didn't say that at all.

"Only Mrs Maple was different." There was a desert of sadness in her voice: a genuine sorrow. "She was never like that. Mrs Maple knew ..."

"What did she know, Louise darling?"

208

"That there's nothing else inside me. It's no use expecting more. Perhaps it's different with other people."

She followed me downstairs and out into the sunlight. The street was thronged. She waited until one after another stepped aside, leaving her a small empty circle of pavement.

"It will be quieter in Villiers Street," she said and went away.

It was late in the summer before the house was ready for occupation. Louise was to come two days before the removal to have the rooms aired and instruct the servants in their duties. As she would have a good deal of luggage, I promised to meet her at the station and go with her in a cab to the new house.

I was eager to see her again. During the weeks of separation I had thought of her with quite a new kind of tenderness but as a different Louise, imagined rather than remembered, a quiet, frightened child in a narrow house full of ticking clocks and shadowy corners harbouring unknown threats. In my anxiety to be at the station to welcome her, I put on my things in haste and was almost ready to set off when an unexpected caller detained me and left me no time for the last-minute details of dressing. I ran down Silvergate, pinning on my hat as I went, and hurried all the way up the hill to the station, arriving in a flurry to find that Louise's train would be ten minutes late. I cannot recall whether it was a public holiday or whether it was the time of the Assizes, which always brought extra visitors to the town. At any rate the streets and the station forecourse were crowded. I sat down on a bench overlooking the wide cobbled verge where cabs drew up, with the intention of hailing one as soon as Louise appeared.

Absorbed as I was in watching travellers get down from an omnibus and go under the station arch, I might not have been aware of my companion on the bench, beyond noticing from the corner of my eye that she was a young woman; but she was one of those people whose physical presence makes itself felt, in her case by fidgeting movements of the feet, as if she were stamping, and little jerks of the head which gave the impression of anger or petulance and forced me to look. In fact, the irritable movements were unconscious, arising no doubt from an overflow of pent-up energy. She was as absorbed as I but in her own thoughts. Judging by the droop of her mouth and the discouraged slouch of her shoulders, they were unhappy thoughts.

As if noticing me for the first time, she shuffled along to make more room, turning her black eyes on me as she did so. I recognised her as the gipsy-like girl for whom the butterfly brooch had been bought: the girl who had been employed as a maid at St Aidan's. Instinctively I drew away from her. It was still difficult to forgive her for the bad turn she had served me more than a year ago. If she had delivered Julian's message punctually, I would have gone home decorously by the market place and remained in happy ignorance of the tragedy on the wharf which had cost me so much heart-ache. Immediately I was ashamed of the thought. It was callow — and disloyal to Nicholas; my brother-in-law; almost my brother. It pleased me now to recognise the bond and to acknowledge what I must long have known: that each of those strange encounters had enlarged my understanding. Sad as the experience had been, to have missed knowing so good a man would have been a loss more sad.

My companion could have no idea that she had influenced my life. She had not seen me either at the Windrosses' or in Silvergate. Times had changed for her too. She had lost the swagger which had given her a dubious sort of attractiveness. Her mantle was frayed. A strand of her lank black hair had got itself caught up in her crumpled bonnet strings. The bulging valise at her side suggested that she was leaving Wickborough. I peeped at the label and with a quickening of interest read the name: Cairlie.

Perhaps I made an involuntary movement: a start of dismay would have expressed my mood: a superstitious reluctance to find the smallest additional link connecting her life with mine. It would have been a simple matter to get up and walk away. I remained, transfixed. In any case it was too late. She had noticed me and roused herself to ask me the time.

I took out my watch and told her that it was twenty-five minutes past three. It surprised me that as a traveller she showed so little interest in the hour. She had evidently asked out of boredom and not from anxiety about her train. What did interest her was the watch. She changed her position so as to look at it more closely, then at me. I saw her scan my dress, hat and shoes appraisingly; but I never did discover whether she was concerned only with my possible resources or whether she made certain connections which her next remark might have led her to. I think not.

"You've got a lovely watch." She spoke with the touch of insolence I would have expected of her. "I've only once seen a watch like that before."

"It's uncommon, I believe."

I slipped the enamelled lady protectively inside my jacket. The girl had come quite strikingly to life and was looking me over with an air of calculation I very much disliked though I was not quite innocent of calculation myself.

"What time is your train?" I asked.

"Twenty minutes to four. The train I came for. But I won't be going on it." She flung herself back with a gesture of resignation. Like all her gestures it was dramatic. She still sat turned towards me with her arm along the back of the seat, her fingers almost touching me.

"You're waiting for a later train?"

It occurred to me that she might be waiting for a friend or relative who had not come in time.

"I'm waiting for the fare," she said. In the same flamboyant way she pulled out a woollen purse and emptied it into her lap. "Ten shillings and twopence. After all my scheming and working I'm three and tenpence short. This is all the money I have in the world."

I eyed her warily. She had all the plausibility of a practised charlatan and yet I thought she had been crying. She looked very tired.

"That's like my luck, to have planned and contrived for months, left my position and got as far as the ticket office and then to find myself short . . . That's the sort of luck I've had in Wickborough and now it looks as if I can't get free of the place."

"Why do you want to go to Cairlie?"

"Because there's nowhere else to go. I'm English," she said with a defiant glare, so that I murmured soothingly, "Oh yes, of course," without in the least knowing why. "But my mother came from Scotland and I've worked there. I've an old aunt at Cairlie that might take me in until I can find a position. She did once before when I lost my place."

"Wasn't it rather rash," I said, "to give up your place here before you had found another?"

"Yes. It was crazy. But I am half crazy. Things have gone badly with me, miss. I should have been comfortably married if another hadn't stepped into my place. It's on that account I'm leaving. You wouldn't like to see the one you love married to another, would you, miss?"

"No." For the first time I looked at her with sympathy. "I wouldn't."

She needed no prompting. The need to tell, expressed in those jerks and stamps, had reached boiling point. If she had intended to wheedle money out of me, I believe she forgot it; or it ceased to be her chief concern.

"He'd come into a bit of money and was free with it. He thought the world of me. Bought me this and that. It was over one of his presents we quarrelled. You say I'm rash and I am rash. I got into a wicked passion over it but I couldn't help myself."

"It surely wasn't because you didn't like the present."

"The brooch was pretty. A butterfly, better than real. It was what was wrapped up with it. As soon as I opened it, there it was, staring at me from a piece of purple paper. I took it and tore it into little bits and trampled on them."

I glanced at her rather long finger nails and thought how easily they could become talons. It was sad about the watch paper but matters might have been worse. With what relish she would tear and rend an enemy who fell into her clutches! Her lower lip protruded with a blood-thirsty thrust. I was more than ever convinced that the young man had had a narrow escape. But the watch paper with its quaint old design, father's pride! How on earth could it have aroused such resentment?

"The young man was disappointed?" I ventured, lost in amazement. She had not exaggerated in describing herself as half crazed.

"He turned as cold as stone — and what he called me I won't repeat. He took the brooch and left me. We've never spoken since. He's consoled himself. They're living opposite St Aidan's where I've been working. Every time I went out or in I saw him, or her, till I couldn't stand it no longer."

She relapsed into angry muttering, looking about her vindictively and curving her strong fingers so that they looked more than ever like talons. I saw all the advantages of moving away but to leave her with her story half told seemed like flying in the face of the providence that had, by so odd a chance, brought us together again.

"What was it about the piece of paper — that you disliked?"

"It was the name. Mallow." She spoke with such ferocity that I jumped and drew back. "Mallow, Mallow, Mallow ... The name of the one that ruined me. There it was staring from the paper like an evil eye."

"The one that ruined you?" The melodramatic phrase was distasteful to me but her venomous energy came from a passion of hatred hardly to be contained within the limits of conventional speech. She was not, at that moment at least, acting. As I spoke, she slid rapidly along the seat and pinned me in my corner so that I could not have moved without pushing her aside.

"Mallow," she repeated. "I tore it apart and trampled on it. That's what I did and that's what I'll do to her if ever I have the bad luck to see her again."

She had, to say the least, secured my attention; but with the small part of it that remained at my disposal I was aware of a train approaching on the line from Bidewell. It would come in on the platform over the bridge. I was conscious of the fact and of a peculiar anxiety arising from it. Otherwise all my interest was absorbed by the girl and her extraordinary story.

"You could say she came between me and him." There was a wild glitter in her eyes below the shabby bonnet brim. "When she'd ruined me once already."

"You could say it," I rejoined primly. Indeed any remark would have sounded prim in contrast to her weird manner of speaking. "But it wouldn't be true, would it? How could she have come between you and him if she wasn't even there when you quarrelled?" I paused. "Whoever she was."

"No." The girl's eyes filled with tears. "It was my own fault. It's always me that's blamed when anything goes wrong. It's always Kirsty's fault."

The words were arresting not only for a distressing sense of defeat in the way she said them but because they were familiar. I had heard them before.

" 'It's all Kirsty's fault'. That's what she said, that other time. Ice-cold she was, and I was crying my eyes out for the poor gentleman. That was at Blairgouroch Castle in Scotland. I had a good place there, miss, and would've been there still but for her. She had me dismissed without a character. What can a girl like me do when she's turned away without a line to say if she's honest and clean? I was starving when a minister of the kirk found a place for me at St Aidan's. They're Christian people there and don't sit in judgment on sinners. Anyway, I'd done nothing wrong. I was halfway across the kitchen when it happened."

She sat bolt upright with another crazy little jerk of her head and a defiant shrug that was defensive too.

"What was it?" I asked unwillingly. To be drawn once more into that ill-fated kitchen at Blairgouroch was an ordeal I would have been glad to avoid.

"A kettle tipped over. That's what happened and a man was scalded. A perfect gentleman he was. He'd never have had me turned away. It was her. And do you know why?" She fixed her eyes upon me with such a depth of brooding black solemnity that to this day I cannot tell whether she was mad or passionately sincere. "Because she isn't human. Not a tear did she shed for him. All she seemed to think of was how many coals I'd put on the fire. 'And you should have put the kettle back on the hook', she said. 'That may be,' I said, 'and you should be down on your knees giving thanks to Mr Vince,' I said. No, I didn't say 'to the Almighty' for it's my belief the Almighty intended something different."

She nodded significantly. I felt a chill of something like foreboding and did not urge her to go on. There was no need.

"There was only the three of us in the kitchen and I was the only one besides themselves that saw what happened. Smooth as marble she looked when she had me turned away. Standing there like an angel on a tombstone. She'd have been looking different if it hadn't been for him."

"What do you mean?"

"She was kneeling down by the fender with a book in her hand. He'd offered his chair but she wouldn't take it. A piece of coal fell and tilted the kettle — towards her. He saw what was going to happen. 'Louise,' he shouted. I'll never forget his voice. He leaned forward to push her away, never thinking of himself. But he needn't have troubled." Kirsty's lips parted, showing her strong teeth in a snarl rather than a smile. "She thought of herself too. In a flash she lifted the book — it was one of them big leather ones — and pushed the kettle away, towards him, deliberately. Then the whole fire slid forward and the kettle tipped right over. I never wish to see such a sight again. But things wouldn't have been so bad for him if she hadn't done what she did. That's what she didn't want me to tell. And if it hadn't been his hands, poor gentleman, it would have been her face."

I shivered, feeling all at once cold to the bone.

"Yes, it would have been her face. I'd like to get my fingers on it." Her claw-like nails were none too clean. They fascinated me. "She'd never look the same when I'd finished with her."

The Bidewell train had pulled in. Wisps of steam and smoke crept from under the roof and melted into the mild air. The first of the descending passengers were already on the bridge.

"I could have starved for all she cared," Kirsty said, "and I'll tell her so if ever I see her again and get my hands on her. The Lord Almighty meant it for a judgment on her when that kettle tipped over, to curb her pride, and Mr Vince got it instead. The Lord was defied. That's what I said to him when I saw him down there on South-well Bridge. "God is not mocked, Mr Vince, sir,' I said."

"You saw him? Here in Wickborough?"

"A bit of luck, wasn't it? He recognised me too. 'How are you, Kirsty?' he says. He must have come here thinking he might see her. I knew she had something to do with Wickborough because I'd seen the postmark on her letters but I didn't know she was related to the jeweller in Silvergate until I saw that piece of paper..." She dropped her voice confidentially. "He wants to marry her, I believe, but I suppose she won't have him or he wouldn't have been hanging about here in Wickborough."

I gathered that she had had no connection with Blair-gouroch since she had left, as she obviously knew nothing of the marriage.

" 'She's left the Castle then?' I said to him. 'She should be down on her knees giving thanks for what you did for her, sir,' I said, 'but it isn't in her nature to be grateful.' He was standing on the bridge looking at the swans. He gave a sad sort of smile. 'You'd best forget her, Mr Vince,' I said. 'How could anyone forget her, Kirsty?' he says. 'Just to see her again — there's nothing else I want in all the world.' For that matter" — her manner had been quieter as she spoke of Nicholas and her voice was still pitched low but I heard in it a relentless note that frightened me more than her previous wildness — "I haven't forgotten her either and never will. We're not all saints like him. There's nothing else for me in all the world either except to settle with her."

They were coming over the bridge thick and fast. Two or three gentlemen were already waiting for cabs.

"You must catch your train, Kirsty."

She looked at me vacantly. Desperate to get her away, I felt in my pocket for my purse, saw hope leap into her eyes and found that my purse was not there. In my haste I had left it on the dressing table with my handkerchief and other small possessions.

"I'm sorry I haven't . . ."

The new light in her eyes died away. For a few seconds she had seemed almost normal. Her brows lowered. She muttered something in a sullen undertone, then stared about her with fierce uncontrolled jerks of the head and irritable clawing movements of her strong fingers with their long dark-lined nails.

Most of the passengers from Bidewell had crossed from the far platform. Two porters were coming slowly down the steps to the cab rank, one with a trunk on his shoulders, the other carrying a familiar gladstone bag, portmanteau and hat-box. Panic seized me. If justice was to be done at last, I didn't want to be there. The fierce personality and physical strength of the girl were overpowering. She was breathing heavily, close to my face. I looked round for a policeman, saw none, pulled out my watch and opened the case. It was twenty-three minutes to four.

"She had a watch like that." Kirsty's fingers closed on it ravenously. She tugged at it so that the chain cut into my neck. "I wish I'd choked her with it when I had the chance."

I tried, in despair, to get up and go away. She held the watch tight. Dread of a scene kept me motionless, helpless. There would be a commotion just as Louise appeared. She would see me, would come to me; they would meet. With no recourse left to me but prayer, I prayed — hopelessly — that Kirsty would be removed, blasted by lightning, struck dead; a supplication so wicked as to blaspheme the name of prayer.

All the same, it was answered: not in the orthodox way of course but by Aunt Tamar. Wise, practical Aunt Tamar! My frantic hand closed on the long-forgotten sovereign. I turned the pocket inside out and unpinned

217

the chamois leather bag.

"Here — Run and buy your ticket. You'll just have time if you run, run."

She gazed, unbelieving. I jumped up and pulled her to her feet.

"It's a sovereign. You can keep the change. Go — now. It will change your luck, Kirsty."

Electrified, she took it and groped for her various bundles. Her relief was affecting. Never can a hard-luck story have been more brilliantly successful.

"God bless you, miss." She seemed distracted. I pushed her in the direction of the ticket office. "You won't be sorry. The idea of you having a watch like hers!" she found time to exclaim. "You're not like her in any other way, I can tell you that."

She was caught up, still bewildered, in a jostle of people, then appeared again at the ticket office, dragging her valise, her bonnet half off. Even at a distance she had a wild look. I could only hope that the old auntie at Cairlie was used to it. With my heart in my mouth I watched the bedraggled figure scurry across the platform and board the train, snatching in her skirt as a porter slammed the door. For once she had been in time. Her departure was punctual.

She would come back. So powerfully had she possessed my imagination (always more active than my common sense) that I thought of her disappearance as only temporary. She had flickered here and there in my life and would spurt up again, like a spiteful flame impossible to quench.

Tremulously I sat down on the bench, telling myself that Kirsty had been the cause of it all, the whole sad story. She was slatternly, irresponsible, untruthful. Her version of the incident was coloured by resentment at having been dismissed. Moreover Louise herself had said that Kirsty was unreliable. It was encouraging to be able to remember something Louise had definitely said. She had said on the whole so little.

It seemed to grow and swell, that vast kitchen, bigger than the railway station, booming with ominous echoes, charged with the sickening threat of what might have happened to Louise: of what, according to Kirsty, the Almighty intended. I had no confidence in Kirsty's fitness to interpret the Divine Will. The whole thing had been an accident.

And yet it had been a moment of decision. Louise, father said, must never be called on to make a decision. How fortunate for her that Nicholas had been there to make his decision too! How fortunate, in that avalanche of steam and fire, that it had been Nicholas and no ordinary man! To think of the other person at such a moment would need a rare selflessness, a unique power of loving. It would be, as Kirsty had said, almost saintly. In that terrible crisis at least, if never again, Nicholas and Louise had been at one. The instinct of each had been identical: to protect Louise. In that they had been united as in their marriage they could never have been.

With relief I remembered that Louise had taken her share of the nursing, then, picturing the spotless order and regularity of a sick-room presided over by Louise, found surprisingly little comfort in it. It occurred to me that she might have married him out of gratitude. The hope, the longing to believe that Louise could feel such an obligation was short-lived. It died in the harsh light of painful recollections. She had married him because Blairgouroch was no longer the haven it had been and because she couldn't bear to come home.

Then I saw her coming over the bridge, slim and erect in her simple grey travelling dress. She paused at the top of the steps with her hand on the rail, in the muted sunshine filtering through the glass roof. Heads turned upward to watch her as she came down to the level of the rest of us. There were only two cabs for hire at Wickborough station. One of them was straining up the hill as she came to the edge of the pavement. By the time it had drawn up, the three waiting gentlemen had unanimously stood aside. One of them removed his hat, opened the door and helped her up. She did glance round dutifully: I had promised to meet her; but the glance was perfunctory. She didn't need me.

The cabman took a wide turn before beginning on the descent to the town. I caught a glimpse of Louise between the two windows, sitting upright for fear of soiling her clothes; suspended, in the small dark rectangle, above the earth, not touching it. She was not looking up at the sky either; or at the people who stood aside to let the horses go by. Her level gaze was fixed on the windowless panel in front of her.

How long was it before, mysteriously, she and Nicholas exchanged roles? Gradually it came to be understood in the town that young Mrs Vince had been deserted by her husband and was waiting, faithful and uncomplaining, for him to come back. A piece of fiction so much less likely than even the unusual facts of the case could only be justified by the extreme difficulty of believing ill of Louise. It was impossible to see her and think harshly of her.

As time went by, Nicholas became a protection against unwelcome offers of marriage. In that effortless way she had of changing people, she transformed him from a ghost into an invisible escort. Without him she might have been pestered by offers. He saved her from the inconvenience of having to refuse.

"It's not as if I knew he was dead," she said once when the possiblity of marrying again loomed unpleasantly. "As it is, I can't marry."

Relieved, she took up the fine crochet which had replaced the beadwork, counted her loops and began a complicated series of double trebles.

Occasionally we exchanged visits and sometimes on summer evenings before we were married, Thomas and I used to walk along the tree-lined streets on the outskirts of the town: quiet streets undisturbed by any sound less pleasing than the notes of a piano carefully played. Heard in the twilight, through an open window, "Why do summer roses fade?" and "I shall not see the snowdrops" can have a plaintive sweetness, especially when rendered with absolute correctness of time and phrasing. They can take on too an eerie quality like signals in a void, as if the keys and pedals have gone on moving after everyone has left, even the player: as if, endlessly repeated, they have no human origin.

There is more life by the river. Every year, usually in September, I find Mr Benjamin sauntering by Southwell Bridge or coming up the steps from the wharf. We sit and talk on one of the seats on the wooded bank below the Abbey and watch the swans. He makes little excursions into the country and drinks tea with us in Silvergate once or twice before going back to Scotland at the end of the week.

Sparrow Chare holds no fears for me now. I am known there. Others besides the Blakeys have come to Thomas and me for help. Even in the dark I am not afraid to linger on the wharf. It is a long time since the tall shadow of a warehouse door or the ring of footsteps on the cobbles set my nerves tingling.

The fear has gone. But sometimes when the breeze is fresh, when moonlight moves on the water and the Abbey clock strikes the hour, that April night comes back to me in all its sad solemnity, with all its power to stir the heart to pity not only for Nicholas but for all lost and lonely creatures, even Louise: especially Louise.